'Something tells me you are truly wild at heart. Do you secretly prefer reck-lessly courting danger to pretending respectability, Miss Courland?'

'Don't presume to know me,' she snapped back, much tried and confused by her own reactions to the veiled threat in his husky voice.

'Then discovering your secrets will add spice to the game, my dear,' he mused.

Elizabeth Beacon lives in the beautiful English West Country, and is finally putting her insatiable curiosity about the past to good use. Over the years Elizabeth has worked in her family's horticultural business, become a mature student, qualified as an English teacher, worked as a secretary and, briefly, tried to be a civil servant. She is now happily ensconced behind her computer, when not trying to exhaust her bouncy rescue dog with as many walks as the Inexhaustible Lurcher can finagle. Elizabeth can't bring herself to call researching the wonderfully diverse, scandalous Regency period and creating charismatic heroes and feisty heroines *work*, and she is waiting for someone to find out how much fun she is having and tell her to stop it.

Previous novels by the same author:

AN INNOCENT COURTESAN
HOUSEMAID HEIRESS
A LESS THAN PERFECT LADY
CAPTAIN LANGTHORNE'S PROPOSAL
REBELLIOUS RAKE, INNOCENT GOVERNESS

THE RAKE OF HOLLOWHURST CASTLE

Elizabeth Beacon

First published in Great Britain 2011
by Mills & Boon, an imprint of Harlequin (UK) Limited.
Large Print edition 2011
Harlequin (UK) Limited, Eton House, 18-24 Paradise Road,
Richmond, Surrey TW9 1SR

© Elizabeth Beacon 2010

ISBN: 978 0 263 21879 4

Harlequin (UK) policy is to use papers that are natural, renewable and recyclable products and made from wood grown in sustainable forests. The logging and manufacturing process conform to the legal environmental regulations of the country of origin.

Printed and bound in Great Britain
by CPI Antony Rowe, Chippenham, Wiltshire

THE RAKE OF HOLLOWHURST CASTLE

To my cousin, Jude Taylor,
with love and thanks for your
encouragement and enthusiasm.
This one's for you so I hope you like it!

Chapter One

Roxanne Courland stood in the bay of delicately leaded windows that lit the drawing room of Hollowhurst Castle and watched darkness overtake the gloriously unimproved gardens. Soon the quaint old topiary would become a series of unearthly shapes and the holly grove the blackest of shadows. Rumours about the grove being planted by witches, whose terrible curses would fall on anyone unwary enough to visit it after dark, were rife in the surrounding villages. Roxanne thought such tall tales had been invented to frighten the maids away from temptation, though, and wondered if such cunning tactics still worked in the year of Our Lord eighteen hundred and eighteen. Not that it would make an ideal trysting place, of course, but once upon a time she'd have waited all night long for a lover among its spiky darkness, if he'd only asked her to.

Silly, impressionable Rosie Courland and her elder sisters had hidden in its shelter to catch their first glimpse of the guests their brother had invited for Christmas ten years ago, because it was close on midnight and even her elder sister Joanna should have been in bed hours before. How different that joyful season had been at the giddy age of fourteen, she thought now, her heart sore at the likelihood of spending another festive season in splendid isolation. Then she'd been so excited she could barely stop herself squeaking with anticipation as she shifted from one foot to the other in the snow, her boots gradually getting wetter and her feet colder, despite her restlessness.

'For pity's sake keep still, Rosie,' seventeen-year-old Joanna had hissed furiously at her. But keeping still was something elderly people like her sisters did, along with not running and never arguing with one's elders, even if they were wrong and needed to know it.

'It's prickly and dark in here, as well as freezing cold. Why can't we hide in the oaks by the Solar Tower, or up the Tower for that matter?' she complained half-heartedly.

'Because you can't see the drive, of course, and there's no leaves on the oak trees to hide us from anyone who heard a squeak from you and swung their lantern in our direction, you silly, infuriating child,' Maria told her scornfully, ever ready to trumpet her two years' superiority in age over her annoying little sister.

'Silly child yourself, maybe you can't see much from the ground over there, but we could have climbed the oaks, or even looked out from the roof with Grandpapa's telescope. Nobody would see us up there in the dark at any rate and we'd be a lot more comfortable.'

'Someone would have caught us sneaking up the stairs the way you rattle on, even if we could see anything up there in the dark with one telescope between three of us. Anyway, I'm not climbing trees in the pitch darkness and Uncle Granger threatened to send you to school the last time you borrowed his spyglass and broke it, so have some sense, do. Either go inside and wait quietly in the warm like a good little girl, or stay here and stop moaning,' Joanna had whispered impatiently, then gone back to staring fixedly at the avenue as if her life depended on seeing any sign of movement.

'You're both so stuffy since you started putting your hair up, I'm surprised you don't petrify like that silly statue of Virtue in the library. All either of you ever do nowadays is talk about clothes and novels that make no sense at all and you strike the most ridiculous attitudes so the boys will admire you, when they'd like you a whole lot more if you stopped being so stupid.'

'She's just a little girl who's scared of the witches, Joanna, ignore her,' Maria had urged.

It would have felt better if she'd bothered to whisper a few witchy cackles and invented a bloodcurdling curse or two to frighten her away, but instead Maria had turned her back and taken Joanna's arm, as if their annoying little sister was irrelevant. Roxanne had felt hurt and bewildered when her previously intrepid eldest sister became ever more remote and grown-up, then Joanna even began to agree with Maria's constant criticisms rather than taking Roxanne's part. If that was what growing up and falling in love did for you, she'd sworn to herself as she stood shivering in the shadows fighting off tears, she'd never commit such arrant folly.

Coming back to the here and now, she recalled that resolution with a wry smile. It must have been the worst-kept vow in the long and eventful history of the Courlands of Hollowhurst, for just then Maria's unusually sharp ears had detected the faintest jingle of a harness, and Roxanne had frozen into stillness as she heard how the sound of approaching voices carried uncannily across the deep snow. Not daring to move a muscle lest they be discovered and excluded from the Christmas feasts for standing in a snowdrift at twelve o'clock at night, all three sisters had stood like enchanted beings from some hoary legend and strained every sense toward the travellers.

Their brother David, riding his prized grey gelding, had shown up first through the darkness and they had strained their eyes to see who was with him. Roxanne had heard her eldest sister's involuntary gasp of pleasure and relief as she glimpsed Tom Varleigh's chestnut hunter when the lodge-keeper Fulton's lamp swung towards him; then Fulton turned back to guiding the young gentlemen up the drive, and Rosie had felt her heart thud in fear for the changes some instinct warned her were surely coming. Telling herself she was exasperated because Joanna had made far more noise than she, Rosie nudged her sister sharply to remind her where they were and what they were risking, and peered through the darkness to see if Davy had brought anyone else back from Cambridge with him. Then she forgot her apprehension, trying to make out the third rider when it became obvious not even two young gentlemen could make such a merry outcry on sighting journey's end.

Suddenly there was a blaze of light as the household within finally heard the sounds of horses' hooves, and the ringing calls of young men at the end of a long and gruelling ride were carrying on the still air. Then a huge horse, as fell and powerful as the darkness itself, reared up at the unexpected bloom of lights and Rosie held her breath, expecting to see his rider plunge heavily into the nearest snowdrift. Instead, that remarkable young man controlled the great brute with an ease the fiery animal must have found near to insulting and only laughed at his antics.

'Get down with you, Brutus, you confounded commoner,' a voice as dark and distinctive as his mount rang out joyfully, as if his rider had enjoyed the tussle for supremacy that Brutus already seemed to know he'd lost from the half-hearted nature of his last trial of strength with his conqueror—until the next time.

Rosie had watched with spellbound awe as the stranger mastered the curvetting horse with ease, then leapt out of the saddle as soon as the fiery beast was quiet and produced a carrot from the depths of his greatcoat pocket, which he bestowed on the huge black stallion with an affectionate pat.

'He's certainly not changed for the better since I was last in England,' the young man had shouted cheerfully at Tom Varleigh, who was watching the show with an appreciative grin on his face.

'Why d'you think I chose the chestnut when my father offered us the pick of his stable?' Tom replied.

'Because you have an unfriendly wish to see me summarily unshipped into the snow, dear cousin?' the stranger said as part of his identity became clear to the girls, who strained to see and hear all.

A cousin of well-connected Tom Varleigh, and he'd been overseas, probably with the military if the cut of that greatcoat was anything to go by. Rosie could practically hear Maria calculating his eligibility or otherwise to become her husband as soon as she could arrange it, and she had felt a primitive scream of denial rise just in time to hold it back and briefly wonder at herself, before her attention was once more fixed on the young man in front of them.

'I've a far stronger one not to take a tumble myself,' Tom had admitted.

The tall stranger responded by laughing and picking up a handful of snow to throw at Tom. They had a fine snowball battle going and all three young men looked as if they really had fallen off their horses into the heavy drifts after all when Sir Granger Courland appeared in the wide doorway and laughed even more loudly than his youthful visitors at their boisterous antics.

A smile lifted Roxanne's wistfully curved lips now at that poignant memory of her great-uncle, enjoying his duties as master and host of Hollowhurst Castle to the full, even as she blinked back a tear that he was no longer here to do so. Uncle Granger had been born to welcome guests and throw open his generous hall to them, she decided, picturing his still tall figure that had grown a little stout over the years. Sir Granger's hair had still been dark at sixty-five, even if his side-whiskers were grey, and his great voice could often be heard from one end of the hunting field to the other. He'd seemed so undimmed by the march of time while she was growing up that she'd made the mistake of thinking him indestructible.

'Welcome, one and all, and the compliments of the season to you,' he'd bellowed at the suddenly still group, she remembered, finding the past more attractive than the present again. 'Whoever have you brought me, Davy? It's not that Varleigh fellow we kept falling over at every turn last summer, is it?'

David had laughed and pulled Tom into the light, where he smiled sheepishly and earnestly said he hoped he hadn't worn out his welcome.

'Never, you'll always find one by my fireside, lad—but who else do we have here? A circus rider, perhaps, or some damn-your-eyes cavalry officer?'

'Neither, sir, I'm Tom Varleigh's cousin, and only a humble sailor. Your grand-nephew invited me here for the season out of the goodness of his heart.'

'Goodness of his heart? He hasn't got any,' Uncle Granger teased his heir, who was nearly as soft-hearted and hospitable as he was himself. 'If he had, he'd have managed to get himself sent down weeks ago, for we all miss him sorely. Come on in, boy,' he bellowed and the stranger obeyed, laughing at some unheard comment from his cousin Tom as he went.

Once in front of the great doorway and almost

within sight of a warm fire and a good meal after his long day, the stranger had taken off his sailor's bi-corn and the flaring light lovingly picked up the brightness of his curly blond hair that reflected gold back at them. From her hiding place, Roxanne had strained to see every detail of his lithe figure; a totally novel admiration she didn't truly understand making her drink in this splendid young man, from the wide grin on his tanned face to his travel-stained boots. He bowed elegantly to his host and presented himself to be duly inspected. The lamplight twinkled on the highly polished brass buttons and the single epaulette on his dark blue coat that indicated he was a lieutenant in his Majesty's Navy, once he'd stripped off his wet greatcoat and presented it to the waiting footman.

'Lieutenant Charles Afforde of the *Trojan* at your service, Sir Granger,' he had said in that deep husky-toned voice that sent shivers down Rosie's spine as she peered out of the darkness, as enthralled as if she truly was under the spell of some ancient sorceress.

Little Rosie Courland had stood in her chilly hiding place and forgotten the cold and the spiny darkness, awed by every detail of this young demi-god as she fell youthfully and completely in love after all. She'd felt the deep, unknown thrill of it shiver right through her at the very thought of actually meeting such a splendid specimen of manhood instead of worshipping from afar. Miss Roxanne Courland recalled with a cynical grimace how underwhelmed he'd been by that meeting when it came and tried not to squirm for her youthful, deluded self, even as her memory insisted on drawing her back to that snowy night so long ago, as if intent on reminding her what folly extreme youth was capable of.

'Didn't know Samphire had a boy in the navy,' her uncle had roared on, oblivious to the fact that his youngest great-niece had just had her world rebuilt by one careless smile into the snow-laden night from his unexpected guest.

Roxanne remembered wondering how her great-uncle could be oblivious to such a momentous moment and smiled wryly at her childish self-importance. It had certainly *felt* unforgettable to the silly schoolroom miss who had stood and watched Lieutenant Charles Afforde hungrily that night, as if recalling every detail of his handsome face might one day save her life or change the orbit of the spheres.

'He doesn't, sir,' the blond Adonis had admitted cheerfully. 'The last earl was my grandfather and took me in as a scrubby brat, but I'm just a mere nephew to the new earl.'

'Well, any relative of old Pickle is welcome under my roof.'

'Thank you, sir, although my grandfather didn't care to be reminded of that nickname in his latter years.'

'Grown too full of his own importance, had he?' Sir Granger had roared gleefully. 'I must tell you how richly he deserved it when you're not frozen and tired half to death.'

'And I warrant that's a tale that'll make good listening,' Charles Afforde had remarked laughingly.

'That it will, m'boy,' Uncle Granger had replied, 'but come on inside, all three of you, so we can shut the doors. I prefer what warmth there is from the fires we light to try and keep this great barn warm kept inside instead of taking the chill off the park, my lads.'

With a quick glance of concern for his mount, Lieutenant Afforde had obviously decided he was as well, and as bad tempered, as ever, and left the animal to his host's head groom so that he could enter the welcoming portals of Hollowhurst Castle with a light heart. For one moment he'd paused on the threshold and it seemed to Rosie Courland in her cold and prickly hiding place as if he had somehow seen all three of them, bunched together spellbound in the darkness as they watched the new arrivals play like boys, then be welcomed as men.

That younger Roxanne had held her breath as if he might hear such a soft sound over the yards that separated them and decided that, one day, she was going to marry Charles Afforde, when she was properly grown up and beautiful and he'd become a great admiral, easily as famous as the great, much-mourned, Viscount Nelson. For that minute at least, she'd known that he had seen her and acknowledged their meeting was deeply significant to both of them. Even when he largely ignored her during that Christmas season in favour of Joanna, Maria and the vicar's Junoesque eighteen-year-old daughter, she'd still been convinced he was amusing himself while he waited for her to be ready for marriage. She would wait for him, she'd decided with all the fervent passion of her headlong nature, but instead she'd grown up and discovered fairytales were just that.

Roxanne's lips twisted into a grimace of distaste and impatience at her young and over-romantic self. Sir Charles Afforde was indeed a lion nowadays; successful, courageous and independently wealthy from prize money and the family trust he'd finally taken control of, according to David's sporadic letters. Then there was that baronetcy he'd won by his own efforts, bestowed on him by a grateful country for gallant service in the late wars. His elevated naval rank of commodore might revert to a mere captaincy when he was on land and no longer in command of his squadron, but no doubt at all he'd have been made admiral if he had stayed in the navy when Bonaparte was finally defeated, even if the Admiralty had had to promote a dozen senior officers to flag rank ashore on half-pay to give such a capable and proven captain his admiral's flag.

On the other hand, Miss Roxanne Courland had fulfilled her early promise by growing up to be as dark as the fashion was fair, and far too decided a character for the ridiculous mode that demanded a lady should pretend extreme sensibility and embrace idleness. Little wonder few gentlemen had the nerve to so much as dance with her, let alone lay their hands and hearts at her impatiently tapping feet.

Just as well she'd long ago given up her secret

dream of capturing Charles Afforde's fickle heart then, for no doubt he'd choose a sophisticated beauty when he finally took a wife and not a countrified beanpole of four and twenty but, considering she doubted he possessed a heart to lose, wasn't that just as well?

She was happy enough as Aunt Roxanne now Joanna and her Tom Varleigh had made her so three times over; and she was just good old Rosie to her brother, the spinster sister who held the reins of Hollowhurst in her capable hands while he travelled to the furthest corners of the earth. So the real question was what on earth could that dashing hero Sir Charles Afforde want with her humble self? His letter lay on the delicate rosewood desk that she used for her correspondence and she cautiously considered it through the gathering darkness, as if to get closer might somehow conjure him up out of the dusky shadows.

The wretched thing had done nothing but disturb her since it arrived two days ago, its terse content worrying away at her customary serenity until she was tempted to throw it in the fire and have done with him, even if she couldn't bring herself to actually do it. Maybe something remained from the old days, then—not the illusion that she could tame the wild rover under all that rakish charm, but a dream dead and done with that was reminding her a much younger, ridiculously romantic Roxanne would probably hate the person she'd become.

Chapter Two

With an impatient sigh, Roxanne decided to put Sir Charles Afforde out of her mind until he called and told her what he actually wanted with her after so many years. There was plenty to divert her, after all, for times were hard since the end of the war and it was proving a struggle to keep Hollowhurst untouched by it all, and then there was Davy's latest letter. She shivered, sensing something new and worrying behind her brother's evasive reception of her ingenious solution to some vexing estate business.

Instead of carelessly agreeing to anything she proposed as usual, Sir David Courland wrote instead of the many charms offered by his latest landfall. Despite the late war between Great Britain and the American States, he seemed very welcome in New England and wrote enthusiastically of its many beauties, particularly those of a certain Miss Philomena Harbury, whose virtues apparently knew no bounds. Her brother was obviously fathoms deep in love, and Roxanne hoped her family would not stand in their way.

David might be a baronet and wealthy land-owner, but his constant racketing about the world would make him a challenging husband, even without the fact of him owning Hollow-hurst to ensure they would be parted from her kin by a vast ocean sooner or later, if he and his Philomena married. Given that the girl would have to give up so much to marry him, how could Roxanne expect the new Lady Courland to share her strange new home with a sister-in-law accustomed to ruling it unopposed?

She'd learn to love Mulberry House, Roxanne reassured herself, picturing the neat and airy dwelling in Hollowhurst village that her uncle had purchased lest his nieces were unwed and now left to her because she was going to need it. The mistress of such a fine house would command respect in the area, as long as she learned to behave more like a lady and less like the lord of the manor. Yet she watched the quaint old gardens fade into darkness and sighed as she tried to visualise herself occupied with planning rosebeds, visiting her neighbours and good works. She'd have time to stay with her favourite aunts in Bath at last and at Varleigh with the ever-expanding Varleigh family, maybe even a duty visit at Balsover Granta with Maria, now Countess of Balsover, followed perhaps by the heady delights of London for the Season. Roxanne shook her head and wondered how she'd endure a life of idle uselessness.

'You're very lucky, my girl,' she chided herself out loud. 'You should be counting your blessings.'

'Should you indeed, Miss Courland?' a deep voice spoke out of the darkness and nearly made her jump out of her skin. 'I always considered that a sadly futile exercise when ordered to do so by my tutors.'

'Who the deuce are you?' she snapped back, although she would have known his deep voice anywhere.

'What a very good question,' he replied, the devil-may-care grin she remembered so well becoming visible as well as audible when he stepped out of the shadows and into the dying light from the bay windows. 'I remember you very well, ma'am, but no doubt I've faded into the mists of your memory by now. Charles

Afforde, very much at your service, Miss Courland.'

'Sir Charles,' she acknowledged absently, still struggling to settle the errant heartbeat the mere sound of his voice provoked.

'Perhaps you remember me, after all, considering you take such a flattering interest in my humble career, Miss Courland?'

'My brother writes of you in his letters, and reports of your daring deeds reach us even in a backwater like Hollowhurst, Commodore Afforde.'

'The navy and I have parted company, so I don't use my rank, and I was only ever a commodore when in command of my squadron, you know.'

'Do you miss it?' she asked absently, then told herself crossly not to ask such personal questions on the strength of the merest acquaintance. 'I beg your pardon, that was impertinent of me.'

'Not at all, our families have been friendly since before the Flood and your eldest sister is my cousin's wife, so I think we may presume on both connections and friendship, don't you? And the answer is, yes, I miss the limitless possibilities of the sea, but a battle is as grim a business at sea as on land and I'd been fighting them for far too long. They do say a true sailor only retires when he's safely underground, or underwater, so life on shore might pall one day, I suppose.'

'So you're giving shore life a try out, then?' she replied sharply, for his easy assumption that he could spring up out of the shadows in her own home and be offered a warm welcome was annoying now the shock had abated.

'You think me presumptuous perhaps, Miss Courland?' he asked, apparently unmoved by her sarcasm.

'I think you're likely to be bored and disillusioned when the novelty wears off, Sir Charles.'

'You have become very frank in your opinions,' he replied solemnly, but she could see enough of his expression through the gloom to know he was laughing at her. 'And what a paltry fellow you do think me.'

'How could I when your deeds are trumpeted throughout the land? That would be presumptuous and ungracious, Captain.'

'Then why do I think you don't care if I consider you a perfect lady or a hoyden, Miss Courland?'

'I really don't know, why do you think so, sir? Could it be that you just walked into my home unannounced and strolled about as if you owned it? It would never do for me to be so lost to the claims of simple hospitality as to point out such a vast presumption on your part, now would it?'

'No, particularly now that I can't stay here, as I planned, with you living alone in this scrambling fashion,' he replied, the humour fading from his deep voice as he looked surprisingly stern in the shadowed light.

'My mode of life is none of your concern.'

'Ah, but it is, Miss Courland. It's of very material concern to me, since it currently stands between me and my new life.'

'Don't be ridiculous. Nothing I do has an effect on the way you live your life, Sir Charles, and I think you're fit for Bedlam if you believe it does.'

'Again, you are very frank,' he said, such genial amusement in his deep voice that she wished she could forget she was a lady long enough to slap him.

Then he sobered again and she saw he was eyeing her shadowy figure in the fading light. Her dark gown must be adding to the gathering gloom and her face probably appeared almost ghostly in the twilight, but that was no reason for him to stare at her as if trying to resolve a vexing riddle.

'You haven't heard from your brother lately, I take it?' he asked softly at last and there was something in his voice that sounded almost like pity. She shivered in sudden fear as she tried to reassure herself all was well.

'Not for several weeks,' she finally admitted as if the words had been racked out of her.

He was silent for a while as if pondering his next move and she refused to fill it with idle chatter when she hadn't even invited him to walk into her brother's drawing room and make himself at home. Anyway, she hated discussing her family with a man who was now a stranger, and the fact that she'd once heaped so many ridiculous hopes on his broad shoulders just made it worse. He was standing closer now and she'd be a fool not to notice he was more ridiculously handsome than ever. The careless glow of youth had left his face, along with any lingering innocence, and his features had hardened in maturity until he looked like a formidable Greek god—powerful Zeus instead of careless Apollo, perhaps.

Yet he seemed almost impatient of his looks, although he probably made little enough effort to fight off the women who flirted with him whenever he ventured into society or the *demimonde,* if rumour was true. No doubt the idiotic females lined up to be seduced by the smiling devil he was now, and they were welcome to him. Roxanne infinitely preferred the younger, less jaded Charles Afforde of a decade ago to this cynical rake.

Colours were beginning to fade from the world along with the daylight, so she couldn't tell if his eyes were as breathtakingly blue as ever, but they were certainly sharper and more disillusioned as he looked down at her as if trying to read her thoughts, which was one more good reason to keep him at arm's length. The last thing she wanted was to become an open book to him, so he could amuse himself with a list of her peculiarities whenever he had an idle hour to spare.

'I think you'll find Davy's life has changed more than usual during that time,' he said carefully at last, as if he was weighing every word, then tempering them to avoid a hysterical feminine reaction.

Luckily she'd given up the vapours at a very early age, as Maria was far too good at them to stand competition. 'Tell me,' she demanded flatly, suddenly knowing this was going to be one of those painful revelations no words could soften.

'He's wed, Miss Courland. In fact, I was his groomsman, so there can be no doubting the truth of it, and a very fine wife he's won himself, as well.'

'I'm not in the least surprised,' she returned calmly enough, for hadn't she been thinking of that eventuality ever since that last letter from her brother was so full of his lovely Philomena? Even if she did feel shocked by the stark fact of David marrying without taking trouble to inform his family of it himself.

'He also assured me he has no intention of returning to England for more than a visit. I'm sorry to break such news to you so abruptly, but either Davy couldn't put his soul on paper, after all, or his letter has gone astray.'

Sir Charles Afforde looked distinctly uncomfortable about being the one to tell her. She could imagine him as sternly self-composed when having to go in front of his admiral with ill news, although Davy's happiness wasn't bad news, of course, yet she was torn between joy for him and terrible anxiety for all she held dear here.

'Not coming back?' she said at last and couldn't hold back the most important question, 'But what about Hollowhurst?'

Roxanne had no idea why she asked him the fate of her home with an absentee master committed to another country. Maybe her reign would continue, but apprehension set flocks of butterflies aflutter in her stomach and confirmed it was unlikely. At least she hoped it was apprehension, for Charles Afforde was very close now, and she was human, even if she was also a superannuated old maid.

'That's where I come in, I fear,' he admitted gruffly.

'You fear? When did you ever do that, Sir Charles?' she asked stiffly, wondering just why he hadn't said all this in a letter.

'You'd probably be surprised, but my flawed personality isn't pertinent to the facts. The truth with no frills and furbelows on it, Miss Courland, is that your brother has sold me the castle and estate so he can invest in his wife's estates and other ventures in the country he's adopted as his own.'

Roxanne gasped and let herself feel the momentous weight of change on her slim shoulders for a long, terrible moment. Then she braced them and forced her chaotic feelings to the back of her mind as she met his eyes steadily. The appalling reality of Davy's betrayal could wait until she was alone; she refused to let her shock and grief show in front of Charles.

'But what of legal formalities and viewing the farm accounts?' she heard herself protest, feeling as if she was listening to a stranger producing caveats as to why the truth couldn't be true.

'No need of that between us, he named a fair price and I paid it. Your brother was ever an honest man.'

'You call him so, but took advantage of his honesty, I dare say. He's newly in love and that's never time to take a hard look at the future,' she shot at him, fury surging through her in an invigorating tide as she looked for someone to blame and found him very handy indeed.

'You know better, Miss Courland. I always took you for the most intelligent of your family, so you must know your brother found his inheritance a burden rather than a joy. Davy has no love of the land and takes little pleasure in being lord of the manor. It's my belief that America will suit him very well, and he already insists on being known as plain Mr Courland and is impatient with the old order for holding back the new.'

'You don't share his Jacobin notions, Sir Charles?' she snapped scornfully, as lashing out at him staved off the painful thought that Charles Afforde knew her brother better than she did herself.

'No, I'm quite content to command, but I was raised to it, Miss Courland, and learned early that it was my duty as an officer to lead. The life that never suited Davy will do me very well.'

Roxanne shivered again and hugged her arms about her body as if hoping to ward off the chill of the autumnal evening and this appalling news. She was having her childish dreams come true in the most twisted and cheerless fashion imaginable. Once she'd yearned for this man, striven to become a correct young lady in order to deserve him, until she finally realised he wasn't worth it. She'd wasted the painful intensity of the very young on a handsome face and now felt betrayed again. Except he meant nothing to her, so retiring to Mulberry House sooner than she'd dreaded wasn't the catastrophe it currently felt. What a relief to be spared the sight of him striding along in Uncle Granger's shoes and lording it over her beloved home.

'My brother was raised to take command here one day,' she heard herself protest weakly and wondered why she bothered.

'Of course he always knew he'd inherit,' Sir Charles Afforde told her carefully and Roxanne wondered if shock made his voice echo in her ears like the voice of doom.

He'd be horrified if she gave in to the painful thudding of her heartbeat in her ears and fainted, but at least the mere sound of his voice no longer made her tingle down to her toes and at too many points in between.

'You must know he never really took to the life, though, Miss Courland,' he continued. 'Indeed, Davy always claimed you were more suited to the role of landowner than he, but Hollowhurst would be too great a burden for a woman to bear alone, given the nature of the society we live in.'

'Thank you for knowing my capabilities better than I do myself, Sir Charles, and on such a short acquaintance, as well.'

'Ten years is no trifling term, ma'am.'

'It *is* when we barely knew each other even then and have not seen each other to speak to since my eldest sister's wedding to your cousin nine years ago.'

'Then we can look forward to improving our friendship, can we not? Especially as we're to be such close neighbours.'

'I hope you don't expect me to be overcome with delight at the prospect,' she muttered just loudly enough for him to hear her, then fixed a false, social smile and hoped he knew how much she'd love to slap him. 'So we are,' she said aloud with a forced lightness he'd be a fool to mistake for cordiality. 'Pray, how long do I have to remove myself from here, sir, or do you wish me to decamp tonight?'

'I would never be so hardhearted, Miss Courland, despite the fact you obviously think me capable of any crime short of murder.' He gazed at her through the increasing gloom and she saw his eyebrows rise in apparent amusement, the infuriating devil! 'Ah,' he went on, the laughter she'd once listened for so eagerly running through his deep voice in a warm invitation to share his amusement, 'so you don't set even that limit on my villainy.'

'Of course I do,' she spluttered as the good manners everyone had tried so hard to drum into her made a weak attempt to control her temper and, she had to admit it to herself, her pain. 'I can tell you're not a monster.'

'Can you, my dear Miss Courland? I doubt it, but take as long as you like to gather your new household about you, and take what you want with you, so long as you leave me some furniture and a bed to sleep in.'

'I'll take no more than is mine,' she informed him haughtily, seething at his apparent belief that she'd strip the house to its bare bones in some vulgar attempt at revenge.

'And have the neighbourhood accuse me of turning you out with not much more than the clothes on your back? That really wouldn't do my credit any good in the district, now would it? I claim the privilege of changing my mind and will return tomorrow to make sure you don't distort my good intentions into infamy, Miss Courland, and leave with little more than the clothes you stand up in. I'd be a scandal and a hissing in the area if I turned you out with such apparent cruelty.'

'I doubt it,' she said impatiently, imagining the effect his looks and wealth would have on the local ladies. 'Do as you please, sir, and, as this is your house, I certainly can't stop you coming and going as you please.'

'You can so long as you persist in not employing a chaperone.'

'Whatever follies I choose to commit are mine, Sir Charles, and have nothing to do with you.'

'They do when you make yourself extraordinary by them. You're the sister of one of my oldest and dearest friends, Miss Courland, and while you might have run rings round him however early he got up in the morning, I'm no easygoing David Courland in search of a quiet life.'

'That's self-evident,' she told him darkly, those good manners she'd congratulated herself on threatening to slip away if she yielded to temptation and punched him on his patrician nose as she longed to do.

'Good, then, as we've established I'm certainly not your brother, hadn't we better consider how we're to remedy your chaperone-less state?'

'No, *we* had not. If I'm to be saddled with one, I'll select her myself. Indeed, it would be highly improper for a man like you to select a duenna for a single lady.'

'True,' he said without noticeable shame, 'but I do have the odd female relative, you know. And one or two respectable friends who've yet to cast me off, who have ladies to lend their aid if I explain your situation.'

'You do surprise me, sir.'

'I always endeavour to confound expectations, ma'am, especially when they're so very low.'

'I'm quite sure you do, but pray don't put yourself to the trouble of disproving mine. I look forward to us seeing very little of one another once I've packed up and left Hollowhurst for good. You'll be far too busy managing such a large estate to worry about socialising with your neighbours for a while, and I intend to travel, so I dare say we'll hardly ever meet. My brother isn't the only member of our family possessed of itchy feet,' she lied.

Chapter Three

In fact, Roxanne would have been content to continue at Hollowhurst for the rest of her life if fate had only allowed it, but she needed an excuse to avoid the new owner of her beloved home in the months to come. Travelling would do as well as any other plan, and was far better than staying and risking being charmed out of her fury by the very man who'd just deprived her of useful occupation.

'But I hope you don't plan to set out just yet, and certainly not alone?'

'That, sir, is my business.'

'In so far as you are of age I suppose that's true, but David asked me to look to your welfare and happiness in his absence and I warn you that I fully intend to do so. I suspect we're both about to discover that there's no stricter mentor for a lady of quality than a reformed rake, Miss Courland.'

'Then you're reformed, are you, Sir Charles? I can't claim to have seen any indication of it so far.'

'You may not think so, ma'am, but you've enjoyed the fruits of my good intention ever since I walked in and found you communing with the twilight.'

'I have? How fortunate for me.'

'Fortunate indeed,' he returned blandly and even through the gloom she'd be an idiot to mistake the wolfish glint in his eyes for anything but what it was and feel unease, despite her determination not to let him fluster or intimidate her.

'Then perhaps you'd take yourself back to wherever you came from for the night, Sir Charles, since it would be such a shame to spoil it all now.'

'Yet something tells me you're truly wild at heart. Do you secretly prefer recklessly courting danger to pretending respectability, Miss Courland?'

'Don't presume to know me,' she snapped back, much tried and confused by her own reactions to the veiled threat in his husky voice.

She'd got over the idea that Charles Afforde was put on this earth to be her destined mate many years ago. He was a dangerous rake and, despite his undoubted heroism in battle, she doubted he made a single move on land without calculating its effect. Why, then, was her silly heart racing with excitement like some mad moth sighting a brilliant light and speeding towards it, eager for its own destruction? She was woman enough to know he'd just introduced his sensual appetites and experience into this shadowy encounter, but she was old and wise enough not to call his bluff now, wasn't she?

'Then discovering your secrets will add spice to the game, my dear,' he mused, almost as if he was talking to himself; suddenly he was very close.

It was so dark now she could only gauge his intentions by the tension in his silence and a hint of something new and unsettling in the outline of his powerful body. Then he lowered his head and captured her lips with his and only that contact sparked between them like lightning, but such a contact that she felt half-scorched and half-terrified. She was free, she told herself with little effect; she could disengage from the searing touch of mouth on mouth and be in sight of sanity in a mere breath. Yet the clamour of emotions and curiosity that took over her reeling senses wouldn't let her move.

His mouth was surprisingly soft on hers; deliberately unthreatening, a cynical voice informed her sternly, but she blocked her inner ear to it. The sensual reality of Charles Afforde's kiss on her eager lips at last overcame her defences with no effort at all and she felt him deepen the pressure of his kiss with such a warm welcome, she bitterly decided when she reviewed events later, that she might as well have offered him everything he hadn't already taken from her and let joy be totally unconfined. Not that joy made much of an effort to restrict itself as her mouth opened under his in a wanton response to his more insistent caress. She felt such a lift of her silly heart that he might be excused for thinking her an experienced flirt, if not a full-blown sensualist.

But wouldn't he know the feel of one of those abandoned women when he met one, for it would only be the sort of welcome he was used to? That hated, warning voice was at it again, even as the sound of his breath hitched just a second or two quicker than usual. She struggled between the heady notion that he wasn't used to such fire flaring between him and his lovers and the cold voice of common sense. Then he opened his sinfully tempting mouth on hers and silently asked for something even more intimate. Gasping in breath they could only share, so close as they were, she succumbed to heat and pleasure and curiosity and opened for him as he silently demanded.

Now she was done for, even at the moment when he'd proved himself a rake, after all. His tongue first probed the swollen wetness of lips that finally knew what they'd been made for, then delved within, as if exploring the most exquisitely delicious sensation he'd ever encountered. He gave an unconscious hum of satisfaction in his throat that woke her sensual self from its silly daydreams and showed her just how potent a kiss could be. A flush of heat threatened to melt her as he openly revelled in the chaos he'd wrought, the feel of him seducing and plundering with her absolute consent warming her primly covered bosom and suddenly rosy cheeks in a sharp flush of need that warned what untold, forbidden pleasures he still had left to teach her.

Breathing fast and shallow, she forced herself to jump back from him as if he'd scalded her.

He might well have done just that, she decided, and she wouldn't know the full extent of the damage until she had privacy and calm enough to assess it. Yet her mouth felt bereft as his kiss cooled on the chill evening air, and suddenly she felt the cold of the October night and noted the diamond wink of stars emerging in an almost frosty sky.

'Oh, what have you done now?' she heard herself gasp out, as if protesting something crucially important, but also impossible.

'I hardly know,' he replied and his deep voice was hoarse with something that sounded like bemusement and regret, as if he had felt the wonder and novelty of that kiss as deeply as she. Which was a self-deceiving lie, of course; he'd kissed so many women he probably couldn't provide a full list of them even under torture!

'Liar,' she accused softly and stepped back again so that the scent and heat and reality of him couldn't trip her senses again.

With distance came the full slap of sanity, and she was tempted to sink on to the cushioned window seat and cradle her silly head in her hands and weep. What had she done, for goodness' sake? Only actively encouraged a rake to believe her a great deal more willing to be seduced than she was and rekindled all those silly girlish fantasies of being kissed by her pirate prince. No, she wouldn't permit them to haunt her, and she resolved to avoid his company whenever possible, as they'd be living too close until she went on her travels.

'I think you should leave now, Captain,' she heard herself say in a stiff voice that should tell him what a proper and starchy spinster she really was.

'I believe you're right, Miss Courland,' he replied softly and the thread of something she couldn't quite read in his deep voice tantalised her with ifs and maybe's, but she stalwartly shrugged them aside.

'The Feathers does an excellent ordinary,' she went on blithely, as if she had no idea he could make her forget her own name with an idle kiss.

'My thanks, but I have good friends living not ten miles away.' For some reason he sounded as if he didn't relish being dismissed as a lightweight who'd forget what had just happened on the promise of a hot meal and a soft bed for the night.

'Indeed?' she replied with a haughty look that was probably wasted in the gloom. 'Then I'll call for a groom to light you to your destination.'

'No need, it's a fine starlit night and I have my private servant and a groom with me. It's more than time we were on the road if we're to reach my friends' house before they retire for the night, so I'll wish you a good night, Miss Courland,' he replied, and she could just discern his quick bow of farewell before she could ring for a lantern to guide his way. 'Rushmore will have acquired a light by now,' he assured her shortly.

'Goodbye then, Sir Charles,' she said, wishing there was the slightest hope he wouldn't return to haunt her.

'Until tomorrow,' he confirmed, and she listened to his assured steps as he found his way down the hall and into the early darkness, seemingly without the slightest hesitation.

She waited until she heard three sets of hoof-beats retreat down the drive before she rang the bell for candles and all the help she could muster. There was a great deal to do before she could sleep tonight if she was to be all but gone when Sir Charles arrived in the morning. Another encounter like that and she might do something even more ridiculous, and suddenly there were worse things than being evicted from her beloved home, after all.

* * *

While Hollowhurst Castle was jolted out of its accustomed calm by a mistress who'd become a whirlwind of frenetic energy, a dozen or so miles away Westmeade Manor was serenely comfortable. Charles tried not to envy his old friend Rob Besford, the younger son of the Earl of Foxwell, his contented domesticity with his lovely wife and smiled as he contemplated what Miss Courland would think of such a disgrace to the rakehell fraternity as he was proving to be. Not a great deal, he suspected, and absently contemplated the intriguing task of changing her mind.

'So will you do it, Charles?' Caroline Besford asked him.

Charles wondered cautiously what he was being asked to do, but luckily Rob took pity on him and explained.

'My wife is asking you to be godparent to our next offspring in her own unique manner, Charles. On the principle that you've already committed most of the follies he or she will need to steer clear of if they're to grow into an honest and sober citizen, I suppose,' Rob Besford told him, looking lazily content as he lounged beside his very pregnant wife.

'Couldn't you ask Will Wrovillton instead? After all, you plan to give this one his name,' Charles argued half-heartedly.

'Only if it turns out to be a boy,' Caro said with a wicked sparkle in her eyes as she encouraged him to imagine the fate of a girl called William. 'If it does, we want to name him after Rob's brother and James insists it must be a second name as it would cause too much confusion if there were two James Besfords, even though James is Viscount Littleworth as well, and I can't see it myself. We thought Charles James unkind, since Charles James Fox has only been dead for a decade or so. So we couldn't name this one after you *and* Rob's brother, Charles. Maybe next time,' she ended with a teasing look at Rob that he carefully ignored.

'With Fox having been so fiery a Whig and notoriously profligate with it, it'd be a back-handed turn to serve any brat to name him so, I suppose, but did Will turn down your offer to make him the child's godfather after landing him with William James as a name instead?' Charles asked suspiciously.

'He couldn't turn us down because we can't find him. No doubt he's knee-deep in some daft venture,' Rob replied with exasperated resignation.

'With his wife at his side,' Charles agreed with a reminiscent smile, for if ever he'd come across a fine pair of madcaps they were Lord Wrovillton and his highly unconventional lady.

'That's a certainty, I should say,' Caro confirmed.

'She's as bad as he is,' Charles pointed out.

'Worse,' she agreed placidly, considering Alice, Lady Wrovillton, was her best friend, 'and it's my belief you never forgave Alice for marrying Will instead of you, Charles.'

'No, it's Rob I'm furious with for wedding the one woman I'd gladly sacrifice my single status for,' he argued solemnly and for a moment Caroline looked horrified, until she noticed the wicked glint in his brilliantly blue eyes and threw a cushion at him.

'Boy or girl, your coming child has no more chance of growing up a sober citizen with you two as parents than its big sister has, and she has my sympathy, by the way,' Charles informed her with mock severity. 'It's clearly my duty to set a better example to your children and, as little Sophia is halfway to being as big a minx as her mama, I might as well start earlier with the next one.'

'More than halfway, if you ask me—so you'll do it, Charles?' Rob asked, as if the answer really mattered to him, despite Charles's rake-hell reputation and apparent unsuitability as a spiritual guide.

'Gladly,' Charles agreed at last, touched to be asked, watching the besotted look on Rob's face as he smiled at his wife and feeling the lure of seeing a wife of his own great with his child.

First of all he'd need to marry one, of course, and that might prove more of a challenge than he'd expected. Rosie Courland with her ardent dark eyes and wild midnight curls had become a strong woman with guarded dark eyes and tightly restrained midnight curls, so what of his promise to win and wed her that he'd made Davy Courland now? An idea born of guilty conscience on Davy's side and convenience on his, perhaps, but he needed a capable wife to help him run his new house and estates, even if tonight it had all felt much less convenient and more urgent. Memory of their kiss in the twilight threatened to spin him into a world of his own again, so he forced himself to concentrate on the matter in hand.

'If she's a girl, you might run off with her yourself one day, of course, so we'd best find you a wife to save Rob killing you,' Caro teased roguishly.

'You, my girl, haven't improved at all with marriage and motherhood,' he replied sternly, hoping pregnancy would stop Caro from introducing him to half the neighbourhood when he'd just met the woman he was going to marry.

'Never mind that,' Rob told his wife impatiently, obviously sharing Charles's fears. 'Here's your maid come to cluck over you and quite right for once. It's high time you were in bed, Caro.'

'Only if you'll take me there,' she said with a wicked smile and a shameless lack of hospitality Charles could only applaud.

To watch them now, who'd think the Besfords' marriage had got off to an appalling start? Charles suppressed a shudder at the memory of that stiff and chilly ceremony, with bride and groom as loving towards each other as the Regent and his unfortunate princess must have been at theirs. Luckily they came to a better understanding once Caro had grown bored with being Rob's despised and neglected wife and pretended to be Cleo Tournier, courtesan to one very particular, stubborn aristocrat, who looked as if he loved being stuck fast in his devious wife's toils nowadays.

'I'd like nothing better, my Cleo.' Rob answered her brazen encouragement to take her to bed forthwith with a scorching look that made Caro blush like a peony, Charles was amused to see.

All the same, he felt a sneaking envy of their delight in one another. He'd never love Miss Courland as Rob undoubtedly loved his Caroline and she loved him, yet he'd seen enough of the closeness and fire between them to wonder what such absolute intimacy would be like. He'd always taken life more lightly than Rob he mused as he accepted his candle and obligingly took himself off to his comfortable bed. A marriage of convenience would suit him, especially when it promised passionate nights of mutual satisfaction. He couldn't embrace the married state with the enthusiasm Rob demonstrated, but he'd be an attentive and faithful husband to Miss Roxanne Courland until death did them part, whether she liked it or not!

Roxanne had gone to bed very late after packing the first of her belongings and got up early to begin the task of despatching them to Mulberry House and starting on the rest. She supposed she should be grateful to Sir Charles for provoking her into moving house so quickly, for if she'd been left to linger over each old letter and beloved childhood book it might have taken weeks, if not months. As it was, she'd set herself a mere day of frantic activity to remove all she held most dear, and already the farm dray was setting off, laden with a quantity of trunks and boxes of books that astonished her. Her lips tightened as she contemplated what the arrogant baronet would say about the half-empty shelves in Uncle Granger's personal library, but she wasn't having a stranger selling or disregarding what it had taken him a lifetime to collect.

Having seen the lord-of-the-feast side of her great-uncle, she wondered if Charles Afforde knew about Uncle Granger's quieter interests: his love of fine music and his patronage of poets and artists once thought obscure and outlandish. She must make sure someone packed the fine collection of watercolours from her own room as she shuddered at the thought of coming back to beg for anything left behind. Among them was an exquisite painting of Hollowhurst Castle by Mr Turner that she'd no intention of leaving for the Castle's new owner. Considering he was rich enough to buy Davy's heritage, he'd just have to commission one for himself if he wanted one.

Like an automaton that had wound down in mid-dance, she suddenly sank into a chair and let the truth sink in. Hollowhurst and all it meant to her had a new owner, and what had once seemed set in stone was now as fugitive as a house of cards. How could Davy do such a thing? she raged silently. Surely he trusted her to run the estate and keep the castle in good order? And one day his son might feel very different about the impressive heritage he should have had. She felt angry tears threaten the rigid composure she'd imposed on herself since she realised just why Charles Afforde had returned and barely managed to fight them back.

'It was never meant to be like this, you know.' Charles Afforde's deep voice interrupted from the doorway, and she was so startled she looked up with fury and grief naked in her dark gaze.

'I can't see how you expected me to feel otherwise,' she said and tried to freeze her sorrow until later, when he wasn't by to watch.

'I expected Davy to prepare you for this, if nothing else,' he said rather cryptically, and she wondered what on earth he meant.

What other disaster could there be, given her home was now his and her whole world was rocking on its axis? She shivered at the very thought of more unwelcome revelations and dismissed the idea; nothing could be worse than the bombshell he'd already dropped, after all.

'Well, he didn't,' she replied flatly.

Surely the end result was the same? Possession, she decided furiously and once more wished futilely that she'd been born a man. Not that it would have done her any good since Davy was older and the heir, but he might have reconsidered if he'd a brother devoted to the estate he found a burden. Yet a mere woman must stand by and watch the lords of the earth dispossess her of all she held dear, she railed silently.

'Obviously not, and I suppose the mail boats between here and America are unreliable at this time of year,' he replied with a hint of impatience at her truism, 'but I never intended driving you from your home at a moment's notice, Miss Courland. Take as long as you like over the business, I have time since I left the sea and can spare as long as you need and more.'

'I'll be ready today; I always knew I'd have to leave when Davy married. I can't see how two women could rule the same roost and stay friends.'

'Such is the unfairness of English law, is it not? The eldest male heir gets the best plums and the others scrabble for what's left.'

Chapter Four

Roxanne wondered fleetingly if Sir Charles resented not being Lord Samphire's heir, then dismissed it as a silly idea. If ever she'd met a man capable of forging his own destiny, it was Sir Charles Afforde. No doubt he'd been able to buy Hollowhurst by his own efforts after such a successful career, even without that very substantial trust fund from his mother that Davy had told her of long ago, when she was still eager for every snippet of information she could garner about this stranger.

Naval captains with a reputation like his must have been turning crew away instead of having to press-gang them, eager as they'd be for a share of his prizes. None of which meant she had to like him, she reassured herself stalwartly and managed to recover her barely suppressed fury at him. If she didn't, she'd break down in front of him, and such weakness was intolerable.

'I've no need to "scrabble", sir,' she assured him stiffly. 'My uncle left me a fine house in Hollowhurst village and his personal property. Didn't my brother inform you of the terms of his will when he sold you Hollowhurst?'

'He said there was a fine line to tread between his great-uncle's personal property and the goods and chattels that came with the castle. One you must have expected to walk if he brought a bride home.'

'I might feel more generous towards my brother,' she snapped, because she saw pity in his blue eyes and she'd prefer anything to that, even a cold fury she sensed would freeze her to the marrow if he ever unleashed it.

'Yet I've no intention of arguing about a few court cupboards and worm-eaten refectory tables, Miss Courland, so pray take what you like,' he countered coolly.

'And *I* won't ransack the place in search of my inheritance, Sir Charles. My house is already furnished and all I require will fit on the farm dray when it returns. You'll find your book-shelves a little empty and one or two walls bare, but I'm no magpie to be going about the place gathering everything I can.'

'I suspect you'd rather leave much of what's yours behind out of sheer pride, lest you be thought grasping. I give you fair warning I'll send it after you if you're foolish enough to do that.'

'Then I'll send it back. I already told you I've no room.'

'Perhaps we should place the excess in a field halfway between our houses and fight a duel for it one morning?' he said as if their argument was mildly amusing, but in danger of becoming tedious.

Well, it didn't amuse her; she set her teeth and wondered why she'd got into this unproductive dispute in the first place. Of course she'd intended to be gone before he arrived, but he'd outmanoeuvred her and she suddenly knew how all those French captains felt when the famous, or infamous, *Condottiere's* sails appeared on the horizon.

'Do you intend to fill the castle with daybeds in the Egyptian style and chairs and tables with alligator feet, then?' she asked sweetly.

'No,' he replied shortly. 'I prefer comfort to fashion.'

'Then you'll just have to accept that most of the furniture was built to fit a castle and would look ridiculous in a house less than fifty years old.'

'And you'll have to accept I'm here to stay and have no intention of being cut by half the neighbourhood for throwing you out of your home at half a day's notice with little more than your clothes and a few trifles.'

'Even if you have,' she replied with glee, feeling almost happy she was leaving for the first time since he announced his purchase last night.

'Not a bit of it; I've just told your local vicar that I'm away to stay with my family for at least a sennight in order to give you time to find a suitable chaperone and remove from the Castle. He and his wife thought it a noble act of consideration on my part.'

'But they occupy a living bestowed at your discretion, do they not? And know you not at all, Sir Charles.'

'Only by repute,' he said with a significant look she interpreted as a reproach to her for judging him on that basis herself. He'd no idea how bitterly he'd disappointed her young girl's dreams in making that rakehell reputation, and it was up to her to make sure he never found out.

'Then I'm sure you have nothing to worry about,' she said stiffly. 'A returning hero takes precedence over a wronged woman any day of the week. Witness Odysseus's triumphant return from ten years of chasing about the Aegean after assorted goddesses and nymphs, in contrast to poor Penelope's slaughtered maids and all that interminable weaving she had to do as well as fighting off her importunate suitors.'

'Oh, I hardly think you fall into that category, Miss Courland. Indeed, I doubt any man would be brave enough to try to make you do anything you didn't wish to. Anyway, I can hardly throw you out into the snow with nothing but the clothes on your back when you're known to be a considerable heiress, and one who's very fastidious indeed about *her* suitors.'

She hadn't thought local society took much notice of her or her potential marriage, except to criticise her for acting as her uncle's steward and refusing to employ a duenna to look down her nose at such a poor example of a lady. She had much to learn about her new occupation of doing very little in a suitably ladylike fashion.

'You'll be much sought after now that you're

free to be entertained by your neighbours,' he went on as if attempting to reassure her. Roxanne could tell from the glint in his apparently guileless blue eyes that he was secretly enjoying the notion of her struggling to adapt to her new role, and tried not to give him the satisfaction of glowering furiously back. 'You'll have time on your hands enough to visit all of them now, Miss Courland,' he went on smoothly, as if he was trying to be gallant and not utterly infuriating, 'and they certainly wish to visit you if the vicar, his wife and their promising son just down from Oxford are anything to do by.'

'I'm glad my uncle taught me to discern a false friend from a true one then,' she replied stalwartly, trying not to let a shiver of apprehension slide down her spine at the very thought of such an existence. 'I've no desire whatsoever to be wed for my money.'

'Nor I—perhaps we should wed one another to avert such a travesty,' he joked, and she felt a dart of the old pain, more intense if anything, and cursed that old infatuation for haunting her still.

'Since that's about as likely as black becoming white, I suggest you look elsewhere for a bride, Sir Charles,' she said scornfully.

'I'll settle into my new life before looking about me for a lady brave enough to take me on,' he parried lightly.

Roxanne tried not to be disappointed as he reverted to type and took on the shallow social manners common among the *haut ton,* at least if her memory of her one uncomfortable Season was anything to go by. She'd felt out of place and bored for most of her three months in the capital, and as glad to come home again as Uncle Granger was to see her. Her sister Maria had delighted in that milieu and had worked her way up the social ladder from noble young matron to society hostess, but Roxanne hadn't felt the slightest urge to join her, let alone rival her in any way.

'Indeed?' she replied repressively.

'I'll need to feel my way among local society after usurping a long-established family,' he replied with apparent sincerity, then looked spuriously anxious as he watched her struggle to remain distantly polite. 'But first I insist you find a congenial companion, Miss Courland. No lady of your years and birth can live alone without being taken advantage of or bringing scandal on herself and her family. If you don't look about you for a chaperone, I'll do it for you.

The local matrons will consider a respectable duenna essential now I've come amongst you, and no lone damsel can be considered beyond my villainy, and I've my own reputation to think about, after all.'

'You don't have one, at least not one any lady dares discuss and be received in polite society. As for employing a duenna for me, I have already told you it would be highly improper. I'd be ostracised if I took one of *your* choosing,' she said haughtily, her gaze clashing with his.

'I promised your brother I'd look after you in his stead,' he told her with a glint in his eyes that looked very unbrotherly indeed.

'Exactly how old do you think I am, sir?' she asked defensively.

'Hardly out of the schoolroom,' he replied, with a wolfish smile that gave his words the lie.

'I'm four and twenty and on the shelf. I dare say I could take up residence at Mulberry House without any chaperone but my maid and nobody would raise an eyebrow except you.'

'There you're very much mistaken, my dear, but if you choose not to be visited or invited out, I dare say you'll grow used to the life of a recluse,' he replied ruthlessly, but at least she'd wiped that annoying, indulgent-of-female-folly grin off his face.

Impatient of the petty rules of society she might be, reclusive she wasn't, and hated to admit he was right. She *could* live so, but it'd be a very limited existence and she was too young to embark on a hermit's career.

'I'm not your dear, Sir Charles, and will thank you to address me in proper form.'

'You have no idea what you are just yet, Miss Courland, and I suggest you take a few weeks to find out before you launch yourself into local society as their most scandalous exhibit,' he retorted brusquely.

'You could be right, but this subject is becoming tedious, or do you want me to put that admission in writing and have it published?'

'No, I want you to behave yourself,' he informed her as sternly as if she was fourteen again and he her legal and moral guardian, not the biggest rogue to break a score of susceptible hearts every time he came ashore.

'Really? And I just want you to go away so that I can start my new life,' she snapped back, smarting at the idea of all those unfortunate, abandoned females and how nearly she'd become one of them.

'Then want must be your master,' he said laconically and lounged against the intricately carved fireplace, since she'd omitted to invite him to sit.

She was about to spark back at him, regardless of the fact she must get on with her neighbours in future and he'd be the most important of them, but a rustle of silk petticoats announced a new arrival and stopped her.

'Good morning. I believe you must be Miss Courland?' a lady very obviously with child greeted her from the open doorway.

Roxanne sprang to her feet and offered the stranger a seat, trying to feel as overjoyed at so timely an interruption as she ought to be.

'I couldn't make anyone hear so I'm afraid I invited myself in,' her visitor told her with an engaging smile.

Roxanne could see no resemblance whatsoever to Sir Charles Afforde about the lady's warm golden eyes and heart-shaped face and searched her mind for any possible clues as to her identity. She doubted the lady was related to him and was obviously far too respectable to be a left-handed connection. Not that he'd sink so low as to install his pregnant mistress at the

Castle before Roxanne had quit it, she decided with weary resignation.

'Pray forgive me, Miss Courland, I'm Mrs Robert Besford of Westmeade Manor, but please call me Caro. My husband and Sir Charles have been friends since they were unappealing brats in short coats, so I barged in, since I couldn't wait any longer to make your acquaintance.'

Roxanne could see no reason why a boyhood friendship between this lady's husband and Charles Afforde should make her and Mrs Besford friends, too, but found it impossible to snub the vivacious young woman or refuse the warm understanding in Caro's golden-brown gaze.

'I'm very pleased to meet you, Mrs Besford,' she said, holding out her hand in greeting and having it firmly shaken by one that looked too small and slender to contain such strength and resolution.

'Caro,' her new friend insisted and Roxanne smiled back.

'Then I must be Roxanne, Caro, for I gave up being Rosie when my brother insisted on calling me Rosie-Posie long after I grew up.'

'Gentlemen can be so effortlessly maddening, can't they?' Caro replied.

'My apologies, Caro,' Sir Charles said, looking uncomfortable, 'I'd no idea you'd arrive so close on my heels. I'll make sure my groom has seen to your horses, as Miss Courland's men are busy, if you'll excuse me?'

'Gladly. Pray go and soothe Rob's anxiety about me by discussing where you're going to acquire the bloodstock you intend on breeding,' Mrs Besford said with an airy wave and, to Roxanne's surprise, he meekly did as he was bid.

'He thinks he has to humour me,' Caroline told her with a conspiratorial smile. 'Especially since he woke my household last night by shouting something incomprehensible at the top of his voice in his sleep. According to my husband, many men have nightmares after taking part in battles or skirmishes, but goodness knows what set Charles off in the midst of the Kent countryside in peacetime. His manservant managed to calm him down without waking him and the rest of us went back to sleep, but Charles is mortified this morning and I'm taking shameless advantage. I'll soon be kept busy at home with this new baby and my little daughter, so I exploited his guilty conscience when he tried to leave me behind this morning. I think Rob's still fighting off the vapours after dreading every bump and bend we travelled over on my behalf,' Caro confided. 'I dare say he almost wishes himself back at Waterloo, the poor man, but I'm bored with being treated like spun glass and thought you might welcome some support, even if I'm of precious little use.'

'I was beginning to wonder if I'd get out of here without turning into a watering pot, or throwing something fragile and irreplaceable at Sir Charles, so you're very welcome, I assure you.'

'You seem too strong to give way to your emotions like that, Roxanne, but I know how hard it is to stay serene in such trying circumstances,' Caro said, and Roxanne saw a fleeting shadow of some remembered sadness cloud her guest's unusual eyes.

It was scouted the instant Robert Besford appeared, a worried look on his handsome face. Roxanne thought Caro was blooming, but since he evidently cared a great deal for his wife, Mr Besford's anxiety was rather touching.

'Good morning,' he said with a graceful bow, while his startlingly green eyes ran over his wife as if taking an inventory.

Caro rolled her eyes and tried to look stern, before laughing and shaking her head at him, 'This is Miss Courland, Rob,' she admonished.

'I know. We've met before, haven't we, Miss Courland?' he replied with a rueful smile of apology for his distracted state.

'Good morning, Colonel Besford,' she replied with a smile, for who could resist the Besfords' evident delight in each other?

'I'm colonel no longer, not even in my brevet rank as staff officer, now I've sold out,' he told her cheerfully enough.

'Or so he says,' Caro added darkly and Roxanne laughed at the look the Honourable Robert turned on his wife.

'And no order of mine was ever knowingly obeyed by my wife,' he told Roxanne ruefully and ducked dextrously as a cushion flew past his left ear and thudded harmlessly against the oak panelling.

'Oh, I'm so sorry,' Caro said, hand over her mouth and her eyes dancing. 'It's become a habit,' she admitted, and Roxanne decided she'd enjoy local society if it offered such lively company, after all.

'I'll make sure I take a suit of armour with me to Mulberry House,' she replied solemnly, and they were all laughing when Charles entered the room.

* * *

He was enchanted by this light-hearted and laughing Roxanne Courland. He'd turned her world upside down and behaved like a bad-tempered bear this morning, so no wonder he'd not seen her so until now, but suddenly he knew she'd break his heart if he let her and felt the breath stall in his chest as he saw her as she ought to be, if her family had cherished and adored her, instead of leaving her alone to brave the world. He acquitted Sir Granger of deliberate cruelty, but to raise her as mistress here, when she could only be second-in-command at her brother's whim, was unthinkingly callous.

Roxanne must at least taste the life of a single young woman of birth and fortune before he wed her, but it'd have to be a mere bite, as this need dragging at him insistently wouldn't be ignored for long. He imagined her beautifully gowned and coiffured and decided he was about to let himself in for the most tortuous few weeks of his life. Stepping forwards, he watched the mischief leave her darkest brown eyes and her merry smile die. There was time to alter that state of affairs, he reassured himself. Perhaps she'd look favourably on his suit if he made her mistress here again. Highly unlikely she'd wed ever him for himself, now, and wasn't that just as well?

'I asked for refreshments to be served here, if you don't object, Miss Courland?' he said.

'I've no right to object, Sir Charles,' she replied.

'A lady always has rights,' he argued. She had rights, and obligations—common politeness being one of them.

'How nice for us,' she replied stubbornly.

'It must be,' he replied, and she glared at him before embarking on a discussion about babies with Caro designed to exclude sane gentlemen, except that his friend Rob seemed to find it as fascinating as they did.

He'd never be that much of a fool about his wife and children, Charles assured himself. He'd be an interested and even a fond father, especially as his own sire had consigned him to his formidable grandmother's care without a backward look at an early age. Charles's lips twisted in a sardonic smile as he recalled a day when the father he had yearned for came home at last. Louis Afforde had fainted at the sight of him, coming round to murmur artistically, 'The boy is too like her—my one, my only, my dear departed love. He offends my eyes and grieves my suffering heart.'

Louis, an aspiring poet, promptly went straight back to London and his current 'only' love and left his son with an aversion to romantic love and a gap in his young life where his remaining parent should have been. Packed off to live with his grandparents at the age of six, Charles swore he'd never fall in love, whatever love might be. Eyeing Rob now doting over the wife he'd once professed to hate, he decided he still didn't know what it was and was quite content with his ignorance. He'd respect and admire his wife—if he desired her as well that was a handsome bonus—but he'd never love her.

Nor would he make a cake of himself over being a husband and father as Rob appeared happy to. His children would have fond but sensible parents, which was just as well considering his grandmother was too old to take on a pack of brats now. He thought the Dowager Countess of Samphire would like Miss Courland as a granddaughter-in-law and he doubted Roxanne would quail at meeting such a brusque and ruthless old lady, and then caught himself out in a dreamy smile with horrified shock.

Roxanne would make a good wife and mother

and he'd be faithful and respect her, but he'd not live in her pocket. Something told him it wouldn't be that simple, but he ignored it because he'd promised her brother he'd marry her if she'd have him, and he wanted her. Having his child would settle her into her new role as his wife, and the thought of it made him march to the window and gaze out at the view while he got himself back under control. The idea of seeing Roxanne sensually awake and fully aware of herself as a woman for the first time sent him into such a stew of urgency that he was unfit for company. It boded ill for his detachment, he admitted to himself as he fought primitive passions, but very well for begetting his brats!

'Fascinating view, is it?' Rob asked with a satirical smile as he came to stand by his old friend, too much understanding of Charles's response to Roxanne Courland in his steady green gaze for comfort.

'All the more so for being mine,' he replied softly.

'Possessiveness, it's the curse of our sex,' Rob taunted, and Charles wondered if he wasn't yet truly forgiven for trying to win Rob's lady off him, although he'd been as blithely ignorant of who she really was as her husband had been at the time.

He had admired Caro's refusal to sit back and meekly accept that their arranged marriage was an abomination to her husband, and her ingenious campaign to win him to her bed by foul means when fair ones must fail, since Rob had vowed never to share any room with his wife after their wedding. Rob had danced to the seductive and scandalous new courtesan Cleo Tournier's tune without a clue that she was his unwanted and despised wife, and Charles decided vengefully that he was glad he'd helped her tame the one-time rake now watching him as if he was a specimen on a pin.

'You could be right,' he replied calmly enough.

'Be careful what you're at,' Rob warned him silkily. 'Miss Courland isn't up to the games you play and she's far from unprotected.'

'She needs no protection from me,' Charles replied shortly.

'Have you undergone a sea change then, Charles?'

'A permanent one,' he replied, gaze steady on Rob's challenging one.

'Good God, I think you really mean it.'

'I do.'

'It'll provide me with an interesting diversion to watch you try to achieve that aim then,' Rob said with a grin that almost made Charles wish them both twenty years younger, so he could treat him to the appropriate punch on the nose. 'I don't think Miss Courland will be easily persuaded you're not a wild sea-rover any more,' he warned with unholy delight.

'I'm beginning to agree with you,' Charles muttered darkly and stared broodingly at the quirky old garden he'd acquired with his new property.

'Sometimes the chase is all the more worth winning when it seems nigh impossible,' Rob said, softening his challenge as he sent a significant glance at his lady, who'd led him a fine dance before letting her husband catch her just as she'd planned all along.

'I'm planning a change of lifestyle, not abject surrender,' Charles protested uneasily.

'And sometimes there's victory in defeat, although that's not a concept I expect a grizzled old sea dog to understand.'

'Since you talk in riddles, no wonder I can't make head or tail of them.'

'You'll see,' Rob said with an irritatingly superior smile and turned back to the fascinating spectacle of his wife like a compass to the north.

Chapter Five

Taking tea and cake in a lady's sitting room like some tame *cicisbeo,* Charles fought an unaccustomed urge to snap and snarl at all and sundry and reminded himself he had a reputation as a dangerous charmer to uphold. He didn't feel very charming when Roxanne Courland refused to look at him and made certain their fingers didn't touch when she passed him his teacup. If his one-time crew could see him now, they'd laugh themselves into a collective apoplexy and save the hangman a job, he reflected bitterly.

Instead of dwelling on his current woes, he decided to set about solving one or two of them. First he must find a suitable lady to chaperone his prospective bride. Not easy when only he and Davy Courland knew he was to wed. He sipped his tea with a creditable attempt at looking as if he enjoyed it and took a mental inventory. His formidable grandmother would put in an appearance when Caro's whelp was due since she doted on her, so he must have someone in place before she decided to take the role herself.

There was Great-Aunt Laetetia Varleigh, his grandmother's spinster sister. Yet Aunt Letty lacked the inner core of loving softness Lady Samphire hid behind a formidable manner. No, she wouldn't do, even if she'd leave Varleigh village to lapse into the hotbed of scandal it might become without her constant vigilance. He was reluctantly contemplating advertising when his latest conversation with Tom Varleigh slotted into his mind and made the solution seem so obvious he felt a fool for missing it.

'Stella refuses to come and live with myself and Joanna now poor Marcus Lavender's dead,' Tom had told him. 'She claims Joanna doesn't need another female cluttering up Varleigh Manor, so she's living at the Dower House with Mama and Great-Aunt Letty. She's stubborn and headstrong, but even my big sister doesn't deserve that, Charles. Before six months are up, she'll murder one of them or be fit for Bedlam herself.'

It would be ideal, he told himself, wondering fleetingly if he was as interfering and arrogant as Miss Courland believed him to be. Cousin Stella was in her early thirties and the respectable widow of a fine man who'd died at the ill-starred Battle of Toulouse when, if only they'd known it, the Great War was over and a peace treaty already signed. Stella would be glad of an alternative to living at Varleigh Dower House even if she was too stubborn to admit it, and her chaperonage would be more theory than fact if he knew Stella. Yes, that would suit all three of them very well. Now all he need do was get Stella here without Roxanne realising it was his doing.

A carefully worded plea to Roxanne's sister to send her word of any suitable duennas might serve, as long as Roxanne never discovered he'd sent it. Eyeing Caro speculatively, he wondered if she numbered the sociable younger Varleighs among her recent acquaintance. He shuddered at the thought of her entrée to the *demi-monde,* even if it was gained in pursuit of her renegade husband, and hoped it never became common knowledge.

Such a scandal would certainly not enhance the standing of his bride-to-be, if her chaperone had come recommended by even a pretend courtesan and, unlike Rob Besford, he intended to make sure his wife never had the slightest excuse to cause a scandal in pursuit of his closest sensual attention. He reassured himself it was perfectly natural to want to watch his Roxanne blossom in her proper sphere and that he was in no danger of falling in love with her. His wife must be a socially assured and adept hostess and serenely self-possessed under pressure, and if she became his passionate lover in the bargain, that would just be a wonderful bonus.

Yet did he want her to change? She was rather magnificent as she was, and he admired her stubborn determination to go her own way—except it would ultimately prove disastrous. If he let her, she'd dwindle into a maiden aunt, neither happy nor unhappy and criminally wasted. Or she'd marry some weak-kneed idiot who'd let her govern both their lives. The very idea of her chancing instead upon some tyrant who'd try to break her glorious spirit made him shudder and drink his tea after all, only realising he'd drained his cup when he looked into it with offended disdain.

'It's all right, Charles, some of us drink it all the time and so far have come to no harm at all,' Caro teased.

'But you don't know what it might do to me if I drink enough of it.'

'I admit I'm not a man and have absolutely no desire to be one, but it's a risk I'm quite prepared to take as a mere female, even if you're too much of a coward to take it on,' she parried effortlessly, and he saw Roxanne shoot her a doubtful look, as if Caro might not know she was supping with the devil and therefore needed a very long spoon.

He smiled into his surprisingly empty teacup and wondered if he ought to inform her that his friend's wife was perfectly safe from any wiles he had stored up for the unwary. Best not, perhaps, it might be useful to keep her in ignorance of the fact that, unlike Caro, she was very unsafe indeed.

'You mustn't do that, Miss Roxanne, it's no job for a lady,' Cobbins, formerly head gardener of Hollowhurst Castle, informed Roxanne a week after she moved into Mulberry House. Even Sir Charles hadn't been able to protest her managing for the time being with the chaperonage of her personal maid, the Castle housekeeper and far too many members of her former household to fit comfortably into Mulberry House.

'Why not?' she challenged grumpily, since every time she found a promising occupation to while away the tedious hours, somebody would raise their head from doing nothing in particular and tell her it wasn't ladylike.

''Cause you'll get scratched,' he explained with the patience of a responsible adult addressing a child who'd stolen her mama's best scissors to deadhead the few late-blooming roses Mulberry House rejoiced in. 'You could even get muddy,' he added with every sign of horror.

As if he hadn't seen her muddy and exhausted many a time after a long day spent in the saddle going about Uncle Granger's business, Roxanne thought with disgust. 'Right, that's it!' she informed him sharply, reaching the end of a tether she'd clung to with exemplary patience. 'I've had enough of this ridiculous situation. In a quarter of an hour I expect you and your many underlings to assemble in the kitchen, where Cook will undoubtedly curse you all for getting in her way, but I plan to address my household and it's the only place you can all fit without being tight packed as sprats in a barrel. Pray inform Whistler that I expect the stablemen to attend as well, and woe betide them if their boots aren't clean.'

'But why, Miss Roxanne?' Cobbins protested with the familiarity of a man who'd known her since she was born.

'Do as I say and you'll find out soon enough,' she informed him smartly and swept back into the house to issue an edict to the indoor staff.

'Whatever's going on, Miss Rosie?' asked Tabby, her personal maid and suddenly the strictest chaperone the most finicky duchess could require for her precious offspring, whether Roxanne wanted her to be or not, which she definitely didn't, she decided rebelliously.

'In ten minutes you'll find out along with everyone else, and you might as well occupy five of them by setting my hair to rights and give us both something to do.'

Tabby sniffed regally. 'Some of us can work and talk at the same time, ma'am,' she claimed but took down the rough chignon Roxanne had scrabbled together when she managed to rise, dress and steal out of the house without encountering any of her entourage for once, only because she did so before anyone but the boot boy and the scullery maid were stirring. Never mind *their* aghast expressions on discovering the lady of the house was stealing through the side door even before the sun reluctantly rose on a misty autumn morning, she'd managed her wild ride over the autumn landscape at last, and it'd been worth every exhilarating moment.

'But we undoubtedly work faster in silence,' Roxanne told her newly dragonlike maid in a tone she hoped was commanding enough to brook no argument and refused to elaborate, even in the face of extreme provocation. Despite her impatience with such finicky and ladylike occupations as fine grooming and pernickety dressing, Roxanne felt better once her hair was neat and she was dressed in a slightly more fashionable gown, so maybe Tabby was right about ordering some new ones next time she went to Rye.

Such frippery notions went clean out of her head when she reached the kitchens and met the eyes of her assembled staff. Just as she'd predicted, Cook looked as if she'd like to beat the stable-boys with her formidable-looking ladle, and the gardeners' feet were shuffling as if they had a mind of their own and might carry them back to their proper domain of their own accord if something wasn't done or said very soon.

'What's afoot, Miss Rosie?' Cook asked her

with a terrifying frown that would reduce most ladies to a heap of fine clothes and incoherence.

Luckily Roxanne knew a heart of gold beat under that formidable exterior, and it only needed the long line of giggling maids who lined up to be abused by the paper tiger as soon as they were old enough to work to confirm that Cook inspired love and loyalty in all those who served her, which brought Roxanne neatly back to her sheep.

'I asked you all to assemble here this morning in order that I might tell you how deeply I'm honoured and moved by your steadfast loyalty to dear Uncle Granger and myself and to thank you for following me to Mulberry House in such large numbers. Which brings me neatly to the other reason I wanted to speak to you: by now I think we all realise this house is too small to accommodate a household large enough to run a castle, and I suggest…no,' Roxanne corrected herself as she saw the stubborn set to Cook's, Cobbins's, Whistler's and the butler's collective mouths, 'I *insist* that most of you return to Hollowhurst and take up your accustomed roles.'

An incoming wave of muttered protests threatened to become a tidal roar, but she held up her hand and it subsided to a few harrumphs of disagreement from the ringleaders.

'I want you to consider how you all intend to occupy yourselves serving a mistress who doesn't entertain or visit much and has no need of the exceptional skills required to run a castle or to progress in your chosen spheres.'

The maids and gardeners, grooms and stable boys eyed each other doubtfully, and Roxanne tried to tailor her speech to make the tougher part of her audience return to their proper domains and quit hers.

'Sir Charles needs skilled staff to guide him in his new life. Command at sea must be very different to life as a country gentleman with a huge old house and a large estate to administer. I was wrong to encourage any of you to leave, but you know my hasty temper and no real damage has been done yet. Stay here much longer and Sir Charles will hire a pack of strangers to run Hollowhurst, and I doubt that's what any of us want.'

'Maybe you're correct, Miss Courland,' Mereson, the stately butler, acknowledged with a bland look that led the assembled audience to doubt it, 'but Sir Granger's first concern was always for your welfare, so Cook, Cobbins,

Whistler and myself will remain in your service.' He eyed the other three sternly, but received only fervent nods and ayes and managed to look pleased with himself without spoiling the impassive façade of a superior butler, trained from birth to run Hollowhurst below-stairs as Sir Granger had been raised to rule above them.

'I thank you, but my uncle would be the first to tell you not to be an awkward pack of idiots and get back to where you're needed.' Mulish expressions turned to doubtful frowns as they silently admitted she was right. Sensing victory, Roxanne pressed ruthlessly on. 'You trained your deputies, so how can you doubt they're capable of bothering me with unsolicited advice at all turns while running my house, stables and gardens almost as efficiently as you would? Meanwhile, you can help Sir Charles in his new life as the master of Hollowhurst Castle, knowing that I'm in safe hands.'

'Bravo, Miss Courland, I couldn't have put it better myself, and I must add a personal plea for as many of you as Miss Courland can spare to take pity on me and come and help me run the castle before I'm properly in the basket for lack of your skills.'

Sir Charles Afforde then strolled further into

the overcrowded room to stand by her side, and Roxanne wasn't sure if she was more furious with him for looking as if they'd hatched this argument between them or with her staff for silently ghosting out of his way as if he'd every right to barge into her house and interfere without the least encouragement. Holding on to her temper while trying to look as if she concurred with his every word, although she'd like to kick him sharply in the shins, took every ounce of self-control Roxanne possessed.

'Good morning, Sir Charles,' she managed to greet him civilly.

'Good morning, Miss Courland, and good morning to you all,' he responded cheerfully, as if he was calling on her in her drawing room and not lounging about the commodious kitchen as if he owned that as well.

A general murmur greeted him, ranging from stately politeness to a flutter of delight from the flightier maids, and again Roxanne had to choke back fury. Just because he was ridiculously handsome and a hero of the late wars, everyone forgot he was also a rake and a rogue. Wishing she hadn't encouraged any of the female staff to return to the castle, she frowned repressively at them and won nervous, excited giggles for her pains. Hoping he was too gentlemanly to take advantage, Roxanne scowled fiercely at him, but he seemed unimpressed and just gave one of his piratical grins.

'I suggest you take the rest of the day to consider what I've said,' she suggested to her assembled staff, having little hope of the female section of it hearing her, as their attention was centred on Sir Charles lounging beside her as if he was as welcome as the flowers in spring.

'Indeed we will, Miss Courland,' Mereson intoned on behalf of all his minions. After giving the chief among them a few significant looks, he made sure they dispersed to their supposed places in her household, and Roxanne wondered, not for the first time, how on earth they managed to fit into it without constant collisions.

At last only the kitchen staff were left, and the last giggling housemaid had been towed away by more sensible friends. Roxanne looked on Sir Charles with even less favour as he refused to notice she wanted him gone.

'There's scones and fresh blackberry jelly if you'd like me to send them through to the drawing room, Miss Rosie,' Cook prompted, and Roxanne decided her light-as-air touch with such pastries was no compensation for an interfering nature, and Sir Charles was welcome to her.

'Then will you join me, Sir Charles?' she managed to say graciously enough. 'Such a treat is not to be lightly missed, I can assure you.'

'My thanks, Miss Courland, but it defeats me how you managed to find room for so many in this rather compact house and still omitted to engage a companion to make my visit respectable,' he carped as she led the way to her not-yet-formal drawing room.

'If my companion and my reputation were any concern of yours, Sir Charles, I might explain myself. As they're not, I feel no need to do so.'

'They soon will be if you get yourself ruined in the eyes of the world because you're too stubborn to engage a duenna. I feel compelled to see you set right, Miss Courland, as I'm the most likely cause of our neighbours whispering scandal about you living alone so close to the Castle if you don't see sense and employ a duenna.'

When she would have burst out into an indignant denial that he had any rights or obligations toward her, he held up his hand and Roxanne could see just how this supposedly light-hearted rogue had commanded his own ship and several others with ease.

'It's not because I possess a managing nature that I plague you about this, although I admit that's part of it, but I promised your brother I'd make sure you were well settled and happy. Setting the gossips tattling about you before you've hardly got your boxes unpacked and your furniture arranged doesn't augur well, Miss Courland. But if you cherish some bizarre plan to get yourself ostracised by polite society so you may become a recluse and ignore all your neighbours, then tell me now and I'll leave you to get on with it.'

Oh, how she'd like to snap some smart retort back at him, to claim her position in local society was too secure to need his approval or interference. Inwardly seething, she managed to give him a sickly smile in recognition that he was a guest under her roof, and her uncle had taught her that obliged her to at least try to be hospitable. Somehow she managed to contain the flood of protest longing for release into what she hoped were a few pithy sentences he wouldn't be able to argue with.

'You're not my brother and I'm not obliged to explain myself to you, Sir Charles. I absolve you from any promise you made him and beg you won't give me another thought. I have many plans for the future, but none of them are any concern of yours. You'll have most of your staff back by nightfall, so I suggest you put your own house in order and leave me to manage mine.'

'You're the sister of a good friend as well as my cousin Tom Varleigh's sister-in-law, so do you honestly think I'll stand by and watch you ruin yourself in the eyes of your own kind when I've any power to stop you, ma'am?'

She'd been wavering until he added that 'ma'am'—such a world of impatience and frustration as it contained, and such an awful promise of what she might become: a mere ma'am, a superannuated spinster with too much money and too little sense to find herself a husband. Now she was no longer the mistress of Hollowhurst, would she be seen by local society as another annoying female with no male to guide and centre her, a dangerous woman contained by their disapproval and then, when the years passed and she'd become a quiz, maybe their laughter? Roxanne shuddered and did her best to hide her misgivings from the abominable man.

'I'm very pleased to say you possess no power over me, Sir Charles,' she informed him haughtily and enjoyed the frustration in his eyes.

'Mrs Lavender has arrived, Miss Roxanne,'

Mereson intoned from the doorway, which called an abrupt halt to their argument and made it annoyingly plain she'd already listened to him and found herself a chaperone.

'Stella!' Roxanne gasped and ran out into the hall to welcome her visitor, genuinely pleased to see her, but also glad Stella's arrival gave her the excuse to ignore the wretched man for a few precious moments. Her letter asking Tom Varleigh's sister to lend her countenance, if she could tolerate the task, had met with a very ready response, considering it must have got to Varleigh only hours before Stella set out.

'Oh, Roxanne, how lovely to see you again, and if you're quite sure I won't be in the way, I'd really love to stay,' Mrs Stella Lavender greeted her.

'I think you're the only female I could endure having here to lend me countenance, if you're prepared to take on such an onerous task.'

'It'll be my pleasure, especially since this rogue's nearby to make sure you need a chaperone rather badly,' Stella replied, with a delighted chuckle as she sighted Sir Charles lounging in the drawing-room doorway. 'How d'you do, Don Carlos?' she greeted her cousin and hugged him as impulsively and affectionately as she just had Roxanne.

Standing back to watch them exchange cousinly and not particularly respectful greetings, Roxanne wondered about this new Charles Afforde. With his cousin he was affable and charming; there was none of that knife-edge of rakish impudence or insufferable superiority she disliked so much marring his manner with this woman he evidently loved and respected.

This Sir Charles seemed infinitely more dangerous than the one who'd been inciting her to fury so very recently, and she wondered wistfully what it would be like to be at the heart of his family rather than reluctantly hovering on the edge of it, doing her best not to long for a loving friendship between them. Well, perhaps a little bit more than friendship, if the truth be known—a dash of danger, perhaps a spark of the fire he'd lit in her with that incendiary kiss the first day he came back to Hollowhurst?

Transformed by such caring, his potent caress of mouth on startled mouth in that romantic autumn twilight might easily have seduced her into falling in love with him all over again, at the very moment he'd taken her once-safe world and blown it apart as efficiently as if he'd landed a broadside on it from his old flagship. It was just as well that he showed no sign of either loving or respecting her as he plainly did Stella then, wasn't it? If her heart was to stay safe and well armoured against him, she could do with all the help she could get from his arrogant determination to get his own way and the memory of just what disillusion awaited any female stupid enough to dream impossible dreams about Captain Charles Afforde, R.N., of course.

'And you, Mrs Star?' he asked his cousin now, with a frown of gentle concern as he saw and probably felt the loss of weight from an already slender frame and pushed Stella a little further away to note her shadowed eyes. 'You're not as well as you'd like us all to think, are you, my dear one?' he quizzed her gently, and Roxanne blinked back a tear in sympathy with the one Stella surreptitiously wiped away, then did her best to turn into a smile.

'I shall be now I'm away from Mama's attempts to marry me off to every unattached gentleman she knows under the age of seventy and Great-Aunt Letty's perpetual gossip,' she said with heartfelt relief.

Chapter Six

At last Roxanne felt the promise of easing into her new life and her new home, as seeing how much Stella wanted to be useful made her feel better about needing her help. Used to coping alone, Roxanne finally admitted to herself that she needed Stella's lively company and good advice on making her new place in the world. Perhaps being needed would help Stella adjust to life as a widow of limited means if she felt she had a place and a purpose.

She'd dreaded engaging a duenna until Joanna's last letter told her how unhappy her sister-in-law seemed. If Stella agreed to join her, much about her current situation that seemed out of kilter would be tolerable after all, she'd decided, as she made the invitation to join her at Mulberry House. She might even enjoy socialising with her neighbours and attending assemblies in the local towns with such lively company. She took a second look at Stella's fine-drawn features and too-slender frame and decided even such mild dissipation must wait until they were both a little better prepared to enjoy it.

'I hardly dared hope you'd come so soon,' she informed her new chaperone as she ushered her into the drawing room and urged her closer to the fire.

'Wild horses wouldn't have kept me away, but I really ought to change,' Stella demurred, with a doubtful glance at immaculate black skirts.

'Don't be ridiculous, Cousin,' Sir Charles argued impatiently as he strolled into the room in her wake, for all the world as if he owned Mulberry House as well as Hollowhurst Castle, Roxanne thought rebelliously. 'If you want to catch a chill, I doubt if Miss Courland wants to nurse you through it.'

'I'd happily do so if necessary, but I'd prefer you to stay hale and hearty for your own sake, Stella, dear,' Roxanne assured her friend and wished he'd go away. Instead he gave her that annoying, bland smile and sat in a gilded and brocaded chair she immediately disliked for not collapsing under him as he crossed one long, elegantly booted leg over the other.

'How reassuring,' Stella joked rather lamely and began to look better as the warmth from the fire reached her chilled limbs and pinched-looking fingers.

'And here are the promised scones and jam at long last,' Sir Charles murmured; if Roxanne hadn't been so relieved to see the tea tray on Stella's behalf, she might have risked a hostile glare and violated all the Courland traditions of hospitality.

'Ah, this is wonderful,' Stella informed them with a sigh of satisfaction as she sipped fragrant China tea and stretched her sensibly shod feet towards the warmth.

'And I thank you for encouraging Cook to return to the Castle if this is an example of her handiwork, Miss Courland. It was an act of supreme self-sacrifice,' Sir Charles said as he took another scone and added jam and cream as eagerly as a hungry boy.

Roxanne had to fight against the appeal of so masculine and powerful a man allowing boyish delight to eclipse his usual rakish persona. He's an unscrupulous rogue, she reminded herself sternly. The occasional glimpse of the younger, less cynical Charles Afforde she remembered only proved what a hardened rascal he was now. Forced into the role of gracious hostess, Roxanne rang for more scones and innocently informed Mereson that Sir Charles was so partial to Mulberry House tea he'd surely need another cup, so he should send in a pot especially for him.

'Vixen,' she heard Sir Charles murmur with a sleepy suggestion of intimacy that made Roxanne shiver with a feeling she assured herself was just a goose walking over her grave.

'The master of Hollowhurst must learn to appreciate the finer things in life,' she assured him solemnly, only to see a gleam of devilment light his azure eyes.

'I assure you, Miss Courland, that I enjoy them already,' he informed her even more softly, and she was intensely annoyed to feel herself flush as she avoided the open challenge in his brilliant, taunting gaze.

Only just restraining a flounce of disdain even she'd only half-believe in, Roxanne was puzzled at catching a distinct glow of satisfaction in Stella's warm brown eyes over their ludicrous exchange. What was there to be pleased about in his empty attempts at flirtation, and what could Stella be thinking of? Surely she didn't imagine there was anything more between her and Charles Afforde than exasperation on both sides?

Nothing could be less likely to re-ignite the sweet schoolgirl fantasies she'd once woven about Lieutenant Charles Afforde than current reality, and she was glad to have made such a recovery from those silly daydreams. Somehow or another, Roxanne resolved, she'd make her companion realise she was immune to his charm. He was Stella's cousin when all was said and done, so she supposed she must go about the task gently and not come straight out and tell her she found Sir Charles Afforde the most annoying gentleman she'd ever met.

'Now that my presence here is as respectable as a bishop's,' he went on now, certain he was right in his own eyes at least, 'at least I'll be able to call and pay my respects to you both without sneaking in through the kitchen door to avoid the curiosity and censure of our neighbours, Miss Courland.'

'You'll certainly arouse it now if they see you leave by the front door when it must be obvious you sneaked in the back,' she replied disdainfully.

'We'll have to hope they're not in the habit of watching the comings and goings at Mulberry House very closely then, or risk my leaving by the back door and causing wild speculation if anyone sees me,' he countered effortlessly, and she found herself hating him all over again.

'I dislike dishonest dealings above anything, Sir Charles. Of course you must leave openly, with no excuses needed to call and see how your cousin did after her journey, even if you had no idea she was coming.'

For a moment Roxanne thought she caught a hint of chagrin in Sir Charles's cerulean gaze, but told herself she was mistaken. She thought he'd probably bend the truth so someone he loved could hear a lesser version, but at heart he wasn't a liar and she wondered how she knew that so surely.

'Of course you do,' he responded lightly, so she decided she must have been mistaken in thinking he'd something to hide, 'and what a useful addition to Miss Courland's household you're proving already, Stella, love.'

'Yes, it quite gives me a glow of virtuous self-satisfaction,' Mrs Lavender told her cousin lightly, and Roxanne was glad to see the ghost of her friend's mischievous smile light her pale face, reminding them she'd once been a very happily married woman and not the shadow of herself grief and the blundering attempts of her mama and great-aunt to 'take Stella out of herself' had made her.

If Stella could find another man who'd love and appreciate her as her major had done, she'd be so much happier creating a comfortable home for her own family than enduring her mother and great-aunt's company, or hiring herself out as companion or chaperone to ageing maidens such as herself. Roxanne resolved to go against all her previous resolutions to avoid local society as often as she could, now Sir Charles must be a part of it, and accept as many invitations as Stella's currently precarious health allowed. The thought that where a cousin he cared for went, Sir Charles Afforde would almost certainly follow, Roxanne dismissed as something to be endured in the cause of friendship and fell to plotting how to get Stella out of mourning and into something more cheerful.

'Ah, here's your tea, Sir Charles,' she rewarded herself by gloating as Mereson led the usual procession into the room.

'No, no, ladies, I'd hate to deprive you of a

drink you all seem to love so well,' he protested lamely, and Roxanne almost let her heart soften.

'But there's plenty for all of us,' Stella put in with a sly wink in her direction that made Roxanne realise she liked her new companion even more than she remembered, especially as she seemed to have even fewer illusions about this handsome rogue than she did herself.

'True, but alas I can't linger here enjoying myself all day. It's high time I returned to my echoing hall and readied it for the return of those who know how to make it a bit more homely,' Sir Charles said with what sounded like a weary sigh, and Roxanne wondered if she was supposed to feel sorry for him. She didn't, of course, she reassured herself fiercely; if he didn't like being master of a huge and ancient pile he shouldn't have bought it in the first place.

'I hope the staff I'm doing my best to send back will be welcome, Sir Charles?' she asked loftily as she rose to bid him adieu.

'With wide-open arms, Miss Courland,' he replied with a bland look and a careless bow that settled one of her internal arguments about him.

She definitely didn't pity such an arrogantly devilish gentleman his lone state. There'd be be-

sotted young ladies lining up to do that as soon
as they could decently persuade their parents
to call on him, and she'd just made that more
possible by restoring his senior servants to their
accustomed place and making sure his household ran almost as smoothly as if he possessed
a chatelaine to keep a sharp eye on it all. Good,
she told herself with approval, as pitying the
wretch in any way would stretch her compassion
to its limits.

'Hurry up, Roxanne, we'll be dreadfully late!'
Stella called from outside the door and Roxanne
fidgeted on the dressing stool once again.

'No, you don't, Miss Rosie,' Tabby counter-
manded and took the irons from their stand by
the fire and applied them to Roxanne's glossy
ebony locks with fierce concentration.

'Don't you hear Mrs Lavender, Tabby? She
says we'll be late and the last thing my hair
needs is more curls,' she protested weakly, wondering where the self-confident chatelaine of
Hollowhurst had gone.

'Who cares if you're late? When you get
there, at least you'll be worth looking at—
and I'm not adding curls, I'm putting the ones
you've already got into some sort of order for

once. You're going to be the belle of the ball if I have anything to do with it, Miss Roxanne, like it or not.'

'You and half the tradesmen in Kent,' Roxanne muttered like a rebellious child and thought vengefully of all the mercers, dressmakers, milliners, glovers and shoemakers Stella had dragged her to over the course of the last week. No doubt the whole lot were dining out on the vast amounts of money they'd made out of her for the first time in years.

'And it's high time you sent some trade their way,' her maid scolded back, 'they've made little enough out of you these last few years, and I've had no chance to practise my skills as a proper lady's maid, either. So hold still, Miss Rosie, or else I might burn your ear.'

'Had I known you longed to work for a fashion plate, I'd have given you a reference so you could do so, you know,' Roxanne said half-seriously and surprised a look of horror on her maid's face that was swiftly hidden.

'You're well enough when you remember to act like a lady, Miss Roxanne,' Tabby informed her sternly and then stood back to examine her handiwork critically. 'And you certainly look like one tonight, so we're halfway there,' she ventured, a smile softening her tight-lipped expression.

'Yes,' Roxanne agreed without vanity, 'I do look very neat and well groomed, don't I?'

'Neat and well groomed?' Tabby echoed incredulously, raising her eyes to the heavens as if seeking divine inspiration. 'You look lovely, Miss Rosie, and there's a good many gentlemen bound to agree with me tonight.'

'They won't pay me any extraordinary attention; most of them have known me since I was a babe and are quite used to me.'

'Oh, but I think they will, and even if some don't, not all of them are blind or daft,' Tabby replied with an infuriating, I-know-better-than-you smile.

'We'll see,' Roxanne said, rising to her feet and enjoying the unaccustomed luxury of dusky rose silk flowing about her as her skirts settled and whispered with her every movement.

In truth, she was rather in awe of the immaculate lady of fashion looking back at her from her pier-glass tonight. For so long she'd taken little note of her hair, except to see that it was neatly confined to a net or the severe chignon she adopted when the management of Hollowhurst began to devolve on to her shoulders and she had little time for anything more elaborate. Then there was her figure, which she now realised hadn't been so obvious to all and sundry since she came out and was much less womanly. She'd battled with Stella and the dressmaker about the low neckline of her fashionable gown when it was being made, and only the lure Stella finally offered of putting off her blacks if she did as they said had persuaded her to do as they wanted and not order a fichu or another half an ell of fabric inserted into this ridiculously low neckline.

Yet, as she smoothed the already immaculate silk over her flat belly and softly curved hips, Roxanne felt a secret lick of pleasure at the radical transformation in her appearance since Stella and Tabby decided it was high time they took her in hand. Nobody could call her a quiz tonight, or overlook her as she gossiped with the older ladies who were inclined to annex her and tell her how they'd all been desperately in love with her great-uncle once upon a time and tried all the tricks under the sun to attract his attention to no avail. One of them had hinted that Uncle Granger had been in love with her grandmother and, once she arrived at Hollowhurst wed to his brother, had never looked at another woman.

That comment had sent her home feeling so sad that it was days before he'd been convinced she wasn't sickening for something and they could enjoy their usual easy banter. All that was lost to her now, she remembered and had to blink back a tear he would have scolded her for.

'Sir Granger would be so proud of you tonight,' Tabby murmured, showing her mind was running on similar lines, but luckily Stella finally lost patience and bustled into the room just then and ended what was in danger of becoming a welter of sentiment.

'Oh, just look at you, Roxanne!' Stella said with a very satisfied smile as she took in the new gown, the stylish hairstyle and the soft sheen of a fine set of pearls about Roxanne's slender neck. 'You look lovely, just as you always should have done.' Roxanne must have looked puzzled, for Stella went on, 'Don't try to tell me Maria Balsover didn't choose all those limp and totally unflattering gowns you wore when you made your come out under her and her mama-in-law's supposed wing, for I won't believe you, Roxanne. She was determined you'd not outshine her—how shocking to her pride if you had made a marriage equal in status to her own.'

Stella sounded as if she'd been bottling up

her feelings on the matter for a very long time and could no longer contain them and Roxanne could hardly take umbrage on her sister's behalf when it was probably true. She'd been too young and then too indifferent during that long-ago and disastrous Season to see what Maria was about. At first she'd fooled herself that she was waiting for a certain dashing naval officer to come home from the sea and to realise she was the only wife he could ever dream of taking. Then she had realised what a rake and a rogue he'd become and didn't care what she looked like because she knew she'd never marry.

Little fool, she chided herself now, yes, he was too busy stealing other men's wives to look at her twice when she was seventeen, but there were better men she could have wed. Yet she couldn't regret coming back to Hollowhurst and spending those precious years with her uncle, even if all she'd learnt about managing the estate and the castle was wasted now she was a mere country gentlewoman.

'Mrs Lavender's right, Miss Rosie,' Tabby seconded with a wise nod. 'Miss Maria refused to listen to a word I said about what suited you.'

Roxanne shrugged, for she hadn't met any man in London she'd the least qualm about leaving behind, so it didn't matter now. 'Well, tonight Maria isn't here and we are, and you, Mrs Lavender, are looking particularly splendid in that pretty silvery lilac, especially considering I very nearly had to knock you unconscious and have you carried into the dressmaker's with it, you were so wedded to that interminable black.'

Stella's mouth set in a stubborn line for a moment, then she caught a glimpse of herself in the pier-glass and couldn't hold to her resolution never to be happy again once she lost her dashing major.

'I do like it,' she admitted, looking so shocked that Roxanne and Tabby laughed, and it set the evening off on a light-hearted note that lasted all the way to the mellow old hall the Longboroughs had lived in as far back as anyone could recall.

'By Jove, you look so very fine tonight I hardly dare speak to either of you,' Squire Longborough assured them in his gruff voice. 'You'll have our local bucks falling over themselves to dance with you as soon as you show your faces, so just see you save me a dance each, eh? Got to do the pretty until Lavinia says I've poured enough oil on all comers to choke a duchess, but save me a good old country dance apiece, there's good girls.'

Seeing Stella half-confounded and half-delighted to be called a girl and gruffly ordered to dance with their host when she fully expected to get away with her usual excuse that widows didn't dance, Roxanne was about to twit her about it when she turned a little too far and met the intense, intent blue gaze of Sir Charles Afforde instead. Arrested in mid-laugh, she felt as if someone had just launched a hot spear straight at her most intimate core and altered everything. Everyone else faded into a murmur of faintly heard babble, a bright veil of dream figures no more real than ghosts. Suddenly she was a girl again, as sure that he must love her as strongly as she knew one day she would be mature enough, deep enough, to love him.

Missing a step, she felt her breath stall, her heartbeat race and her skin flush with some unknown, unthought-of heat she certainly shouldn't be feeling for someone who tormented and infuriated her as severely as Sir Charles Afforde did. Held still and bound to him for a long moment by his bright, compelling gaze, she stood on the edge of something even she never quite anticipated in her wildest dreams. Her lips were a little apart, her breath a little hurried and her eyes a touch feverish as they darkened to pure velvet black in the candlelight.

'Ah, Miss Courland,' the son of the house interrupted their discovery of each other.

Young Joe Longborough shot a glare at the man he obviously regarded as an interloper and gave Roxanne a reproachful look she didn't care for at all. She didn't relish being so violently awakened from her daydream, she decided with an exasperated glare for both gentlemen that should have put them firmly in their places.

'Ah, Mr Longborough,' she parodied crossly.

'I came to claim a waltz,' he informed her pompously.

'Then I suggest you go away again,' Roxanne told him crossly, 'and don't come back until you've learnt some lessons in gentlemanly conduct from your papa, Joseph Longborough,' she ordered and turned back to Stella with a condemning glare for both gentlemen.

Joseph's ears reddened visibly and his rather heavy features contorted with temper. He shot out a hand to pull her back and force his mastery on a mere woman who dared find his manners boorish and his personality lacking in charm, but he felt his arm locked in a grip of honed steel instead.

'You won't lay so much as a finger on Miss Courland without her express permission,' Charles told him in a low, menacing murmur even sharp-eared Roxanne failed to pick out of the general hubbub in the splendid old room. 'Try it,' he warned his host's son with a look intended to freeze the dolt to his very bones, 'and I'll break your arm and make you wail like a baby in front of everyone here tonight.'

'How dare you threaten me in my own home? I'll see you thrown out on your misbegotten ear,' Joseph blustered, but he wasn't fool enough to raise his voice above a whisper and let their dispute become public property.

Sensing extreme masculine tension, although she hadn't heard any of their actual words, Stella intervened. 'Have you met my famous cousin, Mr Longborough? Commodore Sir Charles Afforde, lately of the Mediterranean Fleet and now of Hollowhurst Castle. And, Charles, this is Mr Longborough, elder son of the Squire and his charming lady,' she said genially, even if her eyes warned Charles that he must contain the temper, which only his close friends and those unfortunate enough to rouse it were aware he

possessed, while under his hospitable neighbours' roof. Joseph gulped and backed swiftly
away, just as she'd intended.

'Longborough,' Charles responded with a per-
functory bow.

'An honour, Sir Charles,' Joseph managed
almost convincingly. Apparently even he didn't
want to carry on behaving like a boor in front
of a hero of the late wars, a seasoned warrior
who could outdo him on every field of arms he
could think of. 'I must greet my father's other
guests,' he mumbled and stumped off to do what
he'd vowed not to when his mother had asked
for his support.

Chapter Seven

'Well, Charles?' Stella asked ironically.

'Not nearly as well as yourself and Miss Courland, that's very plain to see,' he replied as smoothly as if he hadn't just offered both an outright and an implicit challenge to his host's son.

'Why, thank you, how flattering,' she returned and shifted her attention to Roxanne, who was strangely silent at her side.

'How do you do, Sir Charles?' finally Roxanne managed in a distant voice, still reeling from that odd moment of recognition between them, the eerie feeling of being isolated with him outside reality. Something she didn't quite catch or understand had just passed between him and Joe as well, and normally she didn't like not knowing everything that was going on about her.

'Better now,' he told her with a smile that mocked himself for once instead of her and threatened to rock her back into the strange world they'd almost stepped into just now.

'Good, but it's a little warm in here tonight, is it not?' she asked him, in the face of Stella's incredulous expression that told her that, while it was a noble and impressive venue for a country ball, Squire Longborough's ancestral hall was definitely *not* warm, despite the fires burning at each end.

'I dare say it will be as soon as the dancing begins,' he replied with a look suspiciously like that a man might give when overlooking an eccentricity in a woman he respected or maybe even loved.

What a mistake it would be to sink into his subtle enchantment and believe he'd ever passionately love her. Better to remember that foolish illusion had once lit up her life with a false, glittering promise only ever alive in her imagination. He hadn't lifted a finger to draw such a silly little idiot in as she'd been then; perhaps she deserved the pain her infatuation had caused her all those years ago. Nothing was to be trusted about tonight then, least of all her senses, and Roxanne wished she'd worn her old brown velvet evening gown and not ventured into the dangerous world of fashion.

'So may I have your dance cards, ladies?' he enquired, as if they'd been deliberately withholding them.

'You can have Roxanne's, but I don't intend to dance,' Stella said.

'Then I shall not, either,' Roxanne declared, deciding that would suit her very well.

'Shall I declare my resolution to do likewise and stand out every measure with you both, like a third wallflower?' Sir Charles teased his cousin, but if Stella didn't know he was determined to see her dance despite herself, Roxanne rather thought she didn't know him, after all.

'You can if you like, I still don't dance,' Stella countered mulishly, and Roxanne realised she'd underestimated her. Her companion knew her cousin very well, and was determined to go her own way despite him. Admiring such stern resolution, she lifted her chin in silent support.

'I will if you will,' he taunted softly, and Roxanne was certain something more than just the surface banter, half-serious and half in jest, was at issue between them.

'But I've already loved and lost,' Stella argued,

confirming Roxanne's conclusion that she didn't fully understand what they were arguing about.

'Which makes you a very lucky woman. So are we three going to dance tonight or not?' he asked, with a sly, almost beseeching sidelong glance at Roxanne that seemed to hold more meaning for him and his cousin than it did for her. She held her breath while the silent debate went on, feeling excluded, wondering if she would ever know either well enough to make out what they were arguing about.

'If you really must,' Stella finally conceded, sighing long-sufferingly as she handed over her dance card and watched him initial it.

'Miss Courland?' he asked expectantly, once he'd handed Stella's card back to her and held out his hand expectantly for hers.

Feeling as if she was committing herself to something far more than a mere dance, she finally gave it to him, feeling disconcertingly as if a spark had leapt from his fingertips to hers as they touched fleetingly during the transfer.

'Two waltzes?' she protested as she received her card back so cautiously she only touched it at the opposite side to him and even then with the very tips of her fingers.

'More would render us conspicuous,' he told

her flippantly, and suddenly her palm itched for a very different reason, since she'd very much like to box his ears with it.

'I barely know you, Sir Charles.'

'Something two waltzes might fairly be expected to remedy, don't you agree, Miss Courland?'

'Not in the least. I intend to save my breath for my dancing and shall use my eyes to guide my steps, this being the first time I've danced a waltz in company. It was considered scandalous hereabouts until recently, you know.'

'And yet you still know how to dance it? How very shocking of you, Miss Courland, to have acquired such a *risqué* skill in secret.'

Wretched, wretched man, Roxanne decided, clenching her teeth determinedly to stop herself telling him exactly what she thought of him with almost half the county within earshot.

'There is little anyone could call secret about being taught the steps by my sister's husband Tom Varleigh and their eldest daughter while my sister played for us all, especially considering my niece is but eight years of age, or have you quite forgotten her, Sir Charles?'

'Nobody could forget little Julia Varleigh, and I certainly shouldn't dare to,' he asserted with a reminiscent smile at the thought of the Varleighs' precocious eldest daughter; Roxanne saw it with a sinking heart.

If only he'd carried on being careless and even a little callous, distaste for such a flinty-hearted man might have built up some sort of armour about her much-tried senses. Instead, he looked like a doting uncle when he spoke of her adored niece, and she began to see that he was as capable of feeling strong affection and maybe even love as the next man—indeed, probably *more* capable than a good many careless gentlemen. How very unfair of him, she decided huffily and frowned at the monster for his failure to be one.

'No,' Stella intervened with a significant glance at one of the local gossips who was straining every nerve to overhear as much as she could of the new owner of Hollowhurst and its dispossessed chatelaine's conversation. 'Nobody would dare overlook my niece, and nor should they, but she's not here and you are. So are you both intent on setting the tabbies in a flutter by arguing over Roxanne's dance-card all night, or can the rest of us please get on with enjoying ourselves?'

'Very well, but why do I have to waltz twice with Captain Afforde when there are perfectly good sets of country dances planned?' Roxanne protested querulously, much as eight-year-old Miss Julia Varleigh might at being sent off to bed on such a night and not allowed to join in, so a part of her wasn't at all surprised when the cousins exchanged rueful glances over her head.

'Because Captain Afforde doesn't enjoy seeing his partner flirt with her host for the night in the middle of what was supposed to be their dance,' Charles informed her with a heat in his gaze that told Roxanne he was only half-joking about her easy, joking flirtation with their host for tonight.

'Mr Longborough was a boyhood friend of my uncle's. Indeed, he's more of an honorary uncle to me than what you vulgarly classify as a "flirt", and his wife knows it and thinks it's as funny as the rest of us do. To imply otherwise is just stupid and crass, Sir Charles,' she accused, trying to tell herself he'd no right to unnerve her with heated looks that promised more than that swift, disturbing, overheating kiss he'd pressed on her lips the first night they met again, even if it would only be to maze her senses into getting her to do whatever he wanted.

The too-brief caress of his firm mouth on her surprised one had caused her more than enough trouble over the last few weeks, thank you very much, without adding more sleepless nights and silly daydreams to it and make her wonder even more if she'd really changed from the deluded girl who'd once thought herself so in love with him. It had all been an illusion, after all, and she had to remember that in the face of any temptation he could offer.

'Then consider me stupid,' he replied with a wry twist of his intriguing mouth as he admitted to what she could only interpret as jealousy—but surely to be jealous he'd need to care about her in the first place? 'Now here's your partner for the first dance come to claim you, Miss Courland, so pray recall how much you hate to be conspicuous and go and dance with the poor man, will you?' he teased.

Roxanne wondered if she'd ever understand the infuriating, intriguing man, even as she guiltily realised she didn't want to leave his side to dance with another.

'Gladly,' she said and went to do so with a decided flounce of the whispering old-rose skirts that had given her such satisfaction when she put them on tonight. She wouldn't let his rakish tendencies spoil a special night, and she smiled and danced to such effect that Sir Charles had to fight his way through a crowd of her admirers before he could claim her for the first of those waltzes.

'Young puppies,' he muttered under his breath when she finally tore herself away from her court, with a dazzling smile of farewell for a boy she'd known since he was in his cradle.

'I beg your pardon?' she replied innocently enough.

'You heard, and be very careful whom you encourage to chase after you to prove to me that I'm one of many.'

'One of many what?'

'You know very well, but in case you feel the need to flirt with any more schoolboys or roués to prove your point, I'll gratify your vanity by admitting to be a member of your court tonight, Miss Courland. Satisfied?'

As if she ever could be, Roxanne silently despaired, wondering if he'd known where she was during every instant they were apart as acutely as she'd been aware of *his* every move. Nothing she could find to berate herself with about feeble-minded females, who'd yearned after the impossible once and should never do so again, could cure her of being acutely conscious of Sir Charles Afforde and all that he said and did—

always and, she suspected, for ever. However, she *could* conceal her besotted state from him until he grew bored with his games and amused himself elsewhere.

'Was I doing that?' she asked innocently, even as she felt his strength envelop her with warmth and power as he swept her on to the dance floor, and couldn't quite suppress a gasp as her body threatened to betray her.

'Oh, yes, you definitely were,' he murmured and went some way to chilling the wildfire that threatened to eat her up as he controlled their physical reaction to each other and led her smoothly into the dance.

'How silly of me,' she muttered darkly and risked an upward glance at his face as their bodies managed the waltz without much input from her. He looked blandly charmed by her company, on the surface. So why did she think he was less than charmed by this whole business than he pretended?

'I don't think you silly at all,' he told her rather absently. 'Life might be very much simpler if only I could,' he ended, as if he couldn't help himself, and then watched her with guarded, even sombre eyes.

'Then pray feel free to do so,' she invited in

a rather hollow attempt to pretend there was nothing very significant between them. 'I'm all for simplicity, Sir Charles.'

'Hah! If only that were true, Miss Courland, how easy this whole business would be for us to conclude.'

For some reason a shiver chilled its way down her spine, despite the warmth generated by their movements and the shockingly real feeling of his guiding hand upon her waist, his body next to hers. Such a wild mix of excitement, turmoil and apprehension he sparked in her that Roxanne almost longed to be dancing with someone less disturbing, less masculine, less in every way than Captain, lately Commodore, Sir Charles Afforde.

'What business?' she finally recalled her wandering wits enough to ask.

Was that a conscious, almost guilty expression that flitted so fast across his handsome face she wondered if she'd imagined it? It must be, for the next moment he assumed his familiar, cynical mask of the genial and not-often-denied rake, and she seemed a fool to herself for ever imagining he was other than as he seemed.

'Becoming lord and master of so much history and tradition, of course, Miss Courland—your great-uncle left very large boots for a man to try to fill.'

'That he did,' she agreed loyally, wondering if that was why Davy never seemed to feel much joy at the prospect of inheriting them.

'And of course you have your own dubious reputation to live up to,' she half-teased and half-taunted him, then regretted wanting to do either as a flicker of what might be pain lit his suddenly expressive face, as he left himself unguarded long enough to let her see something of his innermost thoughts.

'Of course,' he echoed with all his defences firmly back in place while he obligingly leered at her to prove it.

'Pray try not to be any more annoying than you can help, Sir Charles.'

'Why not? You expect so little it seems a shame to disappoint you.'

'I could respect you,' she offered, half-seriously.

'Don't do that, never do that,' he said so fervently that she stared full into his extraordinary eyes; she saw there such turmoil and slumbering passion that she'd have faltered to a halt if not for his strong, steady arm guiding her so ruthlessly efficient in figures he could obviously dance in his sleep.

'Ah...' Momentarily silenced by something glimpsed and then just as swiftly hidden again, she gathered her wits and reminded herself he was right.

By profession, he was a defender of his country, a fearless warrior with the wits and training as well as the strength to beat a cunning and determined enemy time after time. By reputation, he was a seducer of beautiful women, a cuckolder of careless husbands and a cynical manipulator of society's skewed rules that dictated a single gentleman could sow wild oats with delighted abandon, whilst single ladies must keep themselves chaste and pure and ignorant of what their potential husbands were up to. A small voice in the back of her head told her that a man about to put his life at risk so often during a distinguished but lonely command was entitled to seek comfort in a willing woman's arms, but she suppressed it ruthlessly.

'Very well, I promise to please us both in future by regarding you with unyielding contempt, and I think our dance is at an end, Sir Charles, so you may now let me go.'

'Always happy to oblige a lady,' he drawled

and carelessly renounced all the warmth and intimacy her body had been cunningly enjoying while her mind was busy elsewhere, at least most of the time.

Roxanne shivered as he bowed as elegantly to her as if she were a duchess. She gave a disdainful, too-deep curtsy in return, then rose from it lithely before he could offer his hand to help her rise.

'So I have heard, Sir Charles, so I have heard,' she drawled back and maintained an aloof silence as he followed her back to Stella's side as if, Roxanne thought sadly, they were a married couple who'd wed for all the wrong reasons and didn't particularly like each other anymore.

'Scoundrel,' she muttered crossly under her breath as she watched him walk away, then she cursed her unwary tongue when Stella slewed in her seat to stare up at her incredulously.

'Charles? What on earth has he said to you to lead you to name him so? I swear he's usually so meticulously polite to single ladies of fortune or expectations that I'd given up all hope for him, but if he's been living up to that ridiculously overblown reputation of his with you, then perhaps there's hope for him, after all,' she said with a familiar glint of mischief in her eyes that almost led Roxanne to shudder, except that would really give her away.

'Banish the very thought from your mind,' she cautioned sternly.

'Why? It would make such an excellent solution for two stubborn conundrums—he'd gain a lively and knowledgeable wife, and you'd get a fine husband with all the qualities he does his very best to disguise or deny.'

'I haven't the least desire to marry Sir Charles,' Roxanne defended herself far too fervently and felt Stella's scrutiny while she pretended to watch her fellow guests as if the idea wasn't worth a moment's consideration.

'Then you must be blind or light in your attic, my dear. Not one woman in a hundred could look at my disreputable cousin and *not* want to be wedded and bedded by him, or at least one of the two if that wasn't possible.'

'A very strange chaperone you're proving to be, encouraging your charge to fall for a rogue who seems to have no intention of marrying anyone, even if he's perfectly happy to bed as many beautiful women as are foolish enough to throw themselves at him without benefit of clergy.'

'Now there I think you're wrong—would you care to lay me odds?'

'Really, Stella, that's going a little far in such polite company,' she reproached her friend mock-seriously, deeply relieved when her next partner presented himself and the whole uncomfortable topic was dropped.

Could Stella possibly be right, though? The very thought of Sir Charles marrying anyone else sat uncomfortably with Roxanne, despite her long-held conviction that, if she let him, he'd break her heart along with all the others already in his vast collection. Lingering infatuation, she dismissed uneasily and smiled incautiously at Joe Longborough before regretting her stupidity for the rest of the evening when he took it for more encouragement than most gentlemen would an open and shameless attempt at seduction.

'Is that cub bothering you?' Sir Charles asked her gruffly as soon as they were fairly launched on the supper waltz, and at least it distracted Roxanne from the inevitable and deeply annoying reaction of her body against his powerful one for a few moments.

'Joe is a mere boy,' she told him, incredulity in her voice that he could doubt it. After all, Joe had proved his immaturity from the moment he had shambled into his parents' hall and set about offending their guests.

'He's more than powerful enough to force his silly wants on a woman, even one who thinks herself invulnerable,' he said stiffly.

'Now why do I seem to sense I'm the deluded female you refer to?' she asked with a weary irony she'd probably learnt from him.

'I haven't seen him paw and growl over any other female here tonight. Whatever can you be thinking of to encourage him, Miss Courland? If it's intended to make me furious with you both, I have to say it's working and you might regret the fact before we're much older.'

'What a very fine opinion of yourself you do have, Captain,' Roxanne informed him coldly, trying her best to hold herself aloof and rigid in his arms when the music relentlessly beat on and bound them closer to each other than any unengaged couple could hope, or fear, to be and keep their reputations. 'I don't share it, and you have no right to interfere in my affairs.'

'You intend to marry the young idiot, then?'

'Of course not. I'd rather marry you, and that's not saying very much for poor Joe's ridiculous pretensions,' she said lightly enough, but she lied and acknowledged it to herself with a sinking heart.

'Be careful, Miss Courland, it's only considered safe to goad a wolf from a much greater distance than the one currently between us,' he informed her rather harshly, then lessened that space imperceptibly to prove how honed and prone to pouncing he was, she assumed crossly.

She did her best to tell herself the racing of her heart was a by-product of the dance and nothing to do with his muttered threat and implied possession of her fullest attention. He might impose his will on hers, if she wasn't a well-connected lady of independent means. So it was quite wrong to wish herself otherwise for one heady night—yes, of course it was!

Roxanne held herself a little more stiffly in his arms and forced herself to remember their respectability and all the watching, calculating eyes following their progress about the room. Nothing could be more wrong than to carelessly grab what she wanted, when he'd be bound to offer his hand to her come the grey light of dawn—if he was fool enough to take her to his bed in the first place. The idea of entering a forced marriage to a reluctant husband should have been enough to kill any feral longing stone dead, so it was utterly wanton to still feel such heat, such a delightful sense of promise and the delicious mysteries tantalisingly close to being solved with that nightmare ringing about her mind.

'You goad yourself, sir. This is all imagination,' she told him scornfully.

'Idiot woman!' he gritted, sounding like a much-tried wolf now, and she should be glad when the heated possession died out of his gaze so it became steely once more.

'Not so, and I can handle Joe's silly infatuation perfectly well, Sir Charles. I've been doing so since he left the schoolroom, after all.'

'Not very successfully since he seems to suffer the delusion he can force you to yield to his absurd wooing if he tries hard enough.'

'He's not usually as bad as this,' she finally admitted.

'I guessed that much, the silly young fool,' he replied, looking slightly self-satisfied that Joe Longborough sensed a potent rival in him.

'He'll grow up one day.'

'Maybe not soon enough,' he warned, and Roxanne shivered at the warning in his voice and wondered if he was right to be concerned.

Bridging that slight gap she'd set between

them with such sterling effort, Sir Charles managed to engulf her in comfort and strength all at the same time. There's nothing to fear from me, he seemed to be suggesting as their bodies resumed an instinctive rhythm. I'm never less than controlled, never fool enough to force what I can't charm and seduce out of you of your free will. He was probably right, she decided sadly, and heard the musicians wind their brisk rhythm down to a dying whisper with what might be relief.

'Be wary, Miss Courland, that's all I ask,' he cautioned as he bowed to her in thanks for their dance.

'Oh, believe me, I shall be,' she promised and saw him smile with a lift of her silly heart as he acknowledged what a double-edged sword he'd just handed her.

Chapter Eight

Sir Charles made sure that when he took Roxanne into supper they formed part of a merry party with Stella and the Squire's eldest daughter and her bluff and uncomplicated husband. There was nothing intimate or threatening about the way he somehow guessed what she wanted to eat or drink before she hardly knew it herself. Then he handed her over to the Squire at the end of the supper interval and watched them dance an energetic measure as if he was an indulgent octogenarian rather than the biggest rake in Kent. She'd never understand men, Roxanne concluded wearily as Sir Charles finally handed her and Stella into the carriage he'd sent for them earlier, then sprang lightly on to his horse to follow it through a mere three miles of moonlit lanes.

Luckily Stella seemed as weary after her exertions on the dance floor as Roxanne felt at the conclusion of an oddly unsatisfactory evening, despite much merriment and the presence of so many good friends. She ran admiring fingers over her silk gown even if she couldn't see colours in the faint light of the moon. It suited her, she thought with a pleased smile not even aching feet could wipe away. Dressed so, she'd shed her insecurities and her inhibitions for a few heady hours and fooled herself she was seventeen again, but this time dressed to perfection and as close to being the belle of the ball one rather castaway gentleman had proclaimed her as she'd ever be.

Fortunately they were home before she'd had time to reach the end of any silly fantasies about Sir Charles finding her irresistible now her hair was almost tame and her dress as smart as any London Incomparable's. He wasn't the romantic hero she'd once dreamt of so single-mindedly. She was certainly no heroine and forced herself to watch carefully in the moonlight and the flare of a flaming torch that her new butler produced rather dramatically to light his ladies safely within Mulberry House for the night.

Unfair of that torchlight to pick up the rich

gold of Sir Charles's wind-ruffled hair then, or of the moonlight to outline his powerful form all the more while it shadowed his expression as he helped her down and held her hand just a moment longer than he needed to, as if almost as conscious as she was that she was holding her breath, waiting for something wonderful or terrible to happen. If Stella hadn't been there, if Simkins wasn't standing waiting with his fiery brand flaring and fussing on the breeze, she thought Sir Charles might have kissed her. Instead, he turned until the light revealed his usual careless smile and bid them both a pleasant goodnight, gave Simkins a friendly wave, then got on his horse and rode away.

'Annoying man!' Stella announced as they turned and walked into the house. 'Always was, always will be.'

'I know, but I hadn't realised you did. I thought you were even quite fond of him,' Roxanne teased to hide her acute sense of anti-climax, as if the night had promised her the moon and the stars, but instead delivered nothing more glamorous than tired feet and a mild headache.

'I am, the great blundering fool,' his exasperated cousin confirmed as they made their weary way upstairs. 'Although I quite often ask myself why.'

'And the answer?' Roxanne couldn't stop herself asking.

'Because he's nothing like he pretends to be,' Stella responded after long moments of careful consideration, 'and because I know very well there's no more loving and selfless man on this earth when he truly gives himself in love or friendship.'

'And does he do that very often?' Oh dear, Roxanne, and where did that betraying, faux-casual question come from? she asked herself with a shake of her head that Stella probably saw, despite the late hour and her apparent tiredness.

'He's a very good friend,' Stella evaded, then seemed to realise that wasn't enough of an answer to a question that had taken on ridiculous importance for her listener. 'He loves some of his family and one or two close friends—Rob Besford and his wife, to name but two—and he was as sure and solid as a rock for me when Mark was killed. If you're asking me how he rates as a lover, I must pass. As his cousin I'd be the last person any of his flirts would confide in on that subject.'

'Have there been so very many of them, then?'

'Very many, as he's an excellent flirt, which you can see well enough for yourself. He's usually funny and gallant and light-hearted, and ladies fall over themselves to be flattered and flustered by him, but if we're talking about anything more serious then I suspect no, not nearly as many as his colourful reputation suggests.'

'Then why is he considered so notorious?'

'Because he chose to be, once upon a time. Initially his dubious reputation annoyed his father and stepmother and most of his stepsisters, mainly because they're a pack of mawkish idiots, which gave him a great deal of satisfaction. I've sensed that since the end of the wars and his retirement from the sea, he's found his bad name more of a millstone about his neck than something to preen himself over, though.'

'I often used to wonder why he seemed nothing like the rogue he's reputed to be,' Roxanne said dreamily, picturing the dashing young man she'd once thought she knew deliberately setting out to blacken his own name in order to annoy his absent family. They must have hurt him so badly to cause him to do that, and for some reason, the pain of that young man hurt her, too.

'It seems to me that you used to wonder about

my wild young cousin a lot more than you ever let on, Roxanne Courland,' her friend accused lightly, and Roxanne shivered as she realised how close she'd come to revealing that past infatuation with Lieutenant Afforde.

'I was young and impressionable,' she managed to say lightly and shrug, as if she'd long ago put off any last wisp of that girlish crush.

'And now you're so very, very old,' Stella teased.

'I'm certainly extremely weary,' she countered with a wide yawn.

'Of course you are.'

'And pining for my bed, which will be cooling by the minute since I told Tabby not to wait up.'

'Then sweet dreams, Roxanne. I wonder what my cousin Charles will be dreaming of tonight as he tosses and turns in that ridiculous bed and echoing barrack of a chamber the master of Hollowhurst is supposed to sleep in of a night?' her so-called friend ended archly and whisked herself into her room with a pert goodnight before Roxanne could think of anything crushing to say in reply to such a ridiculous question.

Puzzled by her own dreams, when she had eventually managed to have them, and somehow out of sorts with her new life once again, the next morning Roxanne donned her most ancient riding habit and ordered a challenging mount brought round, then strode restlessly out to the stables because she couldn't bring herself to stand still and wait.

'He's full of devilment and oats, Miss Roxanne,' Jake, her newly promoted head groom, warned as he struggled to hold the fiery young colt.

'So am I,' she snapped back in a fit of unaccustomed temper she knew she'd be ashamed of later, and so restless that she paced the spotless yard until Jake led out the curvetting horse from the back of the sweetest and fleetest mare he could find. Despite the allure of Juno's presence, the colt was too eager to be off and running to follow even her like a meek farm horse.

'Down, Donnie lad,' Jake grumbled half-heartedly as the young horse reared, then danced with impatience.

'How's my boy?' Roxanne greeted him with obvious delight and Jake watched the young rogue sidle up to her as if he hadn't the faintest idea who'd been kicking the sides out of his stall just now. 'My handsome Adonis, my darling boy,' she murmured in his responsive ear as it twitched to catch every word she said as if he understood every one.

'He's a young devil,' Jake informed them both dourly.

'Nonsense,' she defended her favourite, 'he's just young and full of life and you spoil him even more than I do.'

'Perhaps,' Jake conceded, still looking glum as he contemplated the young chestnut. Sure enough, he watched the pair of them disappear over the horizon ten minutes later and wondered dourly when he might be privileged to see them again and if there was any point continuing. Shrugging as he set lively Juno into an easy canter, he decided even Miss Roxanne was beyond his ken and he wished she'd find a husband to control her starts. He contemplated another thirty or forty years of trying to save her neck and nearly marched up to the castle and asked for his old job back.

Even Roxanne didn't know what was stirring her into such a fidgety state today, but she was damned if she'd ride sedately and disappoint Adonis because a lady was never supposed to be out of sight of her groom or to gallop or allow her horse to take fences when a gate was there to be opened.

'They can all go straight to perdition, can't they, Donnie?' she murmured and his ears flicked back eagerly to catch every word. 'I'm not cut out to be a sedate and proper lady.' If he had been human, his snort might be interpreted as amused and even scornful agreement. 'That's right, they're welcome to their tatting and their delicately refined nerves, aren't they, boy?'

She sounded less certain than she liked, for without a great estate to manage, her dominion over a grand house and her assured place in the world, how could she maintain her rebellion against the role of fine lady and stay sane? There was so little to do when you were a lady of means and no real responsibility. So little that your mind fell to mulling over the alternatives unless you were very careful indeed. She'd been so careful not to do so that she'd hardly slept a wink for what had remained of the night and knew sooner or later her idiocy would catch up with her. Not yet though, for she was still young, still strong and still far too alive to give in to the notions of polite ladylike behaviour and turn about to go tamely home.

'Come on, Donnie, there's the sea!' she cried and let him quicken his pace as the lure of a long gallop across the flat beach caught them both.

Her heartbeat quickened to almost match Adonis's mad pace as they thundered across the sand, until they reached the sea and he amused himself and her by playing with the waves as they would have played with him. All the pins finally fell out of Roxanne's hair with their speed and her neat jockey cap fell away with them to let her midnight locks flare out behind them in a silky banner caught by the speed of their passage. To the devil with being a respectable gentlewoman for a few blessed hours, she decided, and with Sir Charles Afforde with his questions and conundrums. She gave herself up to the sheer exhilaration of feeling her long hair flow free with the speed of their passing, the fire and vigour of her mount and the youthful, singing blood coursing through her lithe body.

From his vantage point above the beach, Sir Charles Afforde checked his own fidgeting mount and watched her headlong progress, trying hard not to admire her reckless bravery. No, it wasn't even that, he concluded, half-exasperated and half-captivated by the sight of her flouting every convention she could with determined abandon. The female centaur down on the sands didn't even *think* of the dangers even a brilliant rider could encounter when she was so caught up in speed. How could she be brave in the face of a danger she didn't possess the sense to recognise? So he did it for her, and the potential terror was like a frozen fist around his heart.

How dare she? How could she, when she must know she was his to her very bones and they'd end up man and wife as sure as today would be followed by tomorrow and this week by the next? In that agile, supple, stubborn female frame there might well beat the heart of a lioness, but their future was at the mercy of her ill-timed, cross-grained struggle to evade him and her destiny. What if she let her concentration slip and took a tumble—would she survive to become his wife at such a reckless, ridiculous pace? Not in one piece and it was fury at her lack of consideration for anyone who cared for her that made his fingers clench on the reins until his own spirited mount began to dance in protest, nothing more painful.

Charles soothed the gelding; for once in his life, he had to watch and wait on the hand of fate rather than shape it himself. When had she become his fate, then? Was it when he made his old friend David Courland a promise neither of them had considered seriously enough at the time or when he saw her across that shadowed room and wanted her with a long, silent and merciless roar of possession? Who knew?

Then there was the shameful germ of need he'd carried with him for much longer, since he first set eyes on her when she was all of fourteen years old and already passionate, stubborn and vital, yet as wild and innocent as an unbroken filly. He'd made himself turn aside from that painfully young Roxanne, reproached by her innocence; he was already the other side of a vast ocean of experience compared to her total lack of it. She'd been completely ignorant of what she was encouraging when she eyed him with unfledged encouragement during that memorable Christmas season so long ago, but would she eye him with half that much enthusiasm now she was old enough for him to return it with compound interest?

Instead, all he got was constant provocation and her cheerful flouting of every rule society put in place to protect single, unprotected females with more daring than sense. He glared at her retreating back and decided he'd given her enough of a start to risk following. He nudged his horse into eager motion and let him run out a fraction of his rider's frustrations. Now Roxanne Courland was four and twenty, and every glimpse he had of her lithe figure as she pelted along the sands roused him to painful consciousness of how much he needed her, yet the contrary female was determined not to admit how profoundly *she* needed him.

She was his lady, his bed-mate, the woman he wanted to seduce until she was near to weeping with longing for his very thorough possession and the one who might one day match his hasty passion as he took her before they both fainted for the wanting of each other. One day, very soon, he promised himself as he rose in the stirrups to crouch on Thor's neck and to give him that small extra advantage he needed to catch up with their fleet-footed rival, as well as distracting his rider from the very physical discomfort that the bare idea of what he'd really like to do to Roxanne Courland inflicted on his disobedient body.

It wasn't until the eager young colt Roxanne was riding began to slow at last that he gained enough ground for her to hear him over the noise of her own passing, and she finally reined in to see who had the audacity to follow her. She might have known, she concluded as she recognised Sir Charles Afforde and a power-fully muscled gelding a couple of years older than her Adonis and therefore not at all easily outrun. Nothing to do but turn and greet the last man she wanted to see this morning with careless politeness, she decided. So why did her heartbeat insist on quickening instead of slow-ing, and why was a wild fantasy of him riding towards her as her lover, her other half and her strength, insisting on playing out in the feral part of her imagination that she dearly wished would give up and go away?

'Sir Charles,' she managed to greet him coolly enough, as she soothed Adonis who scented a challenge on the morning breeze that insisted on playing with her wildly tangled tresses and reminding her she probably couldn't pretend she was in her drawing room greeting an acquain-tance.

'Roxanne,' he acknowledged shortly, looking as if he would prefer her to be brought before him aboard ship for suitable punishment.

'I can't recall making you free of my name,' she said recklessly, given the sharp fury and something even more feral and dangerous that she could see in his eyes now he was too close for comfort.

'Oh, you do that by your conduct this morning, Rox-an-ne,' he replied, drawing out the syllables as if preparing to carry them off to his lair, along with the rest of her, and ravish them away until she couldn't recall if they belonged to her or not.

She hadn't known how much she liked the glint of respect, and that suggestion of wild heat held in temporary abeyance, in his azure eyes whenever they rested on her, until it was banished by the wolfish boldness he turned on her now as he let that heat blaze without control. To punish her. Somehow she'd roused the devil in him by trying her best to exorcise it in herself and wasn't that an irony to conjure with when she had the leisure and safety to do so?

'A true gentleman adheres to his own standards, whatever the imagined provocation of others,' she told him coldly, as if images of their limbs tangled in some wanton, private dance were a million miles from her mind.

'How noble of him,' he informed her huskily, sin and desire informing every word as he leaned forwards and snatched a hard, hot kiss from her lips that told her he'd been restraining himself fiercely at their first truly adult encounter, after all.

Only Adonis's dancing, protesting furiously under her as he reacted like the wild spirit he was to the proximity of the gelding Charles rode, reminded her to be equally angry. Young as he was, Adonis was still a stallion. Maybe it wasn't the quieter beast under her tormentor he was objecting to, after all, she decided darkly, as she glared at the man who rode him. He was shameless and stared at her as if her clothes had blown away along with her hairpins and her cap. At least Adonis's restless reaction to a possible rival gave her the excuse to concentrate on something other than the man who seemed to think he'd bought a right to govern her along with Davy's inheritance.

'Go away!' she ordered hotly, nodding at Adonis as he bared his teeth at the infuriating gelding, who looked as if he'd whistle and cross his legs to prove how ridiculous he found all this, if he were only a human. Adonis roared a challenge and would have given his imagined rival a nip if she hadn't turned his head at the last moment. 'You're annoying my horse.'

'Only your horse? I must be slipping.'

As she controlled Adonis with her knees and her will, she bared her teeth at him in a mock snarl and met his blue gaze with a glare of her own. 'Oh, no, you're being every bit as annoying as even you can contrive today. Congratulations, Captain.'

'I haven't even started yet,' he slapped back, then unfairly took the wind out of her sails by suddenly seeming to find them sitting here trading insults irresistibly amusing.

'Unfair,' she reproached, wondering what a third party would have made of their half-spoken, half-taken-for-granted conversation.

'Don't do it again without me?' Suddenly his voice sounded less supremely arrogant and demanding than driven and even, heavens above, pleading.

'Can he keep up?' she heard herself ask, with a nod at the gelding she knew was unnecessary, but it gave her time to think about how that second kiss might change things between them if she let it.

'Easily,' he drawled, understanding of her evasive tactics easy to read in his eyes.

She would never be a woman of mystery while Sir Charles Afforde knew far too much about her sex for comfort. Roxanne shifted in the saddle as the sharp goad of something too close to pain bit into her at the thought of just how he'd gained all that annoying insight, whatever

Stella's reservations about his reported legion of lovers. If he'd only had even one or two, which she doubted, it was one or two more than she'd had.

'A little too easily,' she muttered and pretended to believe they were talking about horses while she impatiently gathered up her streaming tresses and deftly tied them back with the length of narrow, corded ribbon Tabby always put in her pocket for just such an eventuality. A pity, then, that the possessiveness in his eyes was all too easily read as his gaze lingered on the shiny ebony mass of it and frustrated her attempts to turn their encounter into something more restrained, along with her hair.

'I find it extraordinarily beautiful, whatever you do to it, and so I won't beg you never to cut it lest you immediately decided to do so. Even cropped about your ears it would still be an enchantress's lure, so you can forget that notion a-borning, Miss Courland.'

'Black hair shows a woman's age more surely than any other colour,' she assured him repressively. 'In a few years time you'll see that clearly enough whenever we meet.'

'Rather more than a few, I think, my dear, but I can't see the day ever dawning when I'll find it less than lovely, even if we're both white as snow.'

She felt a quick rush of that fierce heat she was growing so reluctantly accustomed to at the thought of him being there to see her grow old, then a flush of sweetness overlaid it at the idea he'd see beauty in her when youth had abandoned them both. Not that vigour would while they still had breath in their bodies, she decided wryly, as the notion of such a lifetime of intimacy felt even harder to beat than the one of letting him teach her the glories of love in his bed, then watch him walk away. No, that way madness lay!

Chapter Nine

'Flattery is just words when all's said and done, Sir Charles,' she informed him stiffly and tried not to read his opinion of her craven avoidance strategy in his mocking gaze.

'And words can sometimes mean exactly what they say, Roxanne, but you're obviously not ready to hear them today. We'll revisit the topic when you've gained a better grasp on truth and lies, along with your temper.'

'There's nothing wrong with my hold on reality, I assure you, sir,' she snapped, exasperated at his assumption he knew her better than she did herself. 'I'm a respectable lady who has no intention of becoming otherwise, and you're a rake. I won't let you play your games with my heart or my body.'

'Ah, but I'm not playing, Rosie, dear,' he informed her in a husky undertone that seemed to pick out some wicked air on the way to her ears and warm it. It trailed heat and shivers down her spine to earth at that feminine core of heat that she really was going to have to learn to control better in future.

'I don't answer to that absurd nickname any more, or to the presumption you follow it with, so I'll bid you good day, sir.' She would have wheeled Adonis and left Captain Afforde to enjoy a temporary victory, if only he'd let her. Instead he shot out a lean, strong hand and clasped her reins as easily and surely as if they restrained a fluffy puppy instead of seventeen hands of restive young stallion. 'Let go!'

'No, you just agreed not to gallop about like a reckless idiot. I didn't expect a Courland's word to mean so little that you discard it so easily no sooner than it's given,' he drawled, ice hardening his gaze as he held hers.

'I didn't promise anything, and I wouldn't need to go anywhere in a hurry if you'd only leave me in peace.'

'You gave me your consent to behave like the rational being you so hotly claim to be as surely as if it was written in blood. Now kindly act like a sensible adult if you wish to be treated like one.'

'Stop it! One moment you kiss me as if you're

entitled to, then you claim the right to govern my actions, Sir Charles. I won't be treated like a thing, and I'm no man's possession, nor will I ever be so.'

'Yet you'll be mine, Roxanne,' he assured her implacably, arrogantly certain that because he said it would be so and then even the fates couldn't argue, let alone Miss Roxanne Courland. 'Just as surely as I'll be yours.'

'Mine and half the faster matrons' and *demi-monde*,' she scoffed, trying to convince herself that she hated his calm assumption she'd accept him as her lover, or even her husband, just because he wanted her to.

'No, yours alone,' he promised without the least hint of a smile or a crossing of his fingers behind his back.

'Well, I won't be yours,' she managed to inform him with gruff steeliness, so it was a shame she failed to hold his implacable blue gaze while she did so, wasn't it?

'Which shows how much you know, Miss Courland—you're mine as sure as the fact that the sun rises in the morning. All that stands between us and that truth is your inability to admit it.'

'Don't be ridiculous, there's nothing between

us whatsoever. I don't intend to marry and I'll certainly never marry you, Sir Charles.'

'I should wait to be asked if I were you, Miss Courland,' he said, with a return to the infuriating flippancy she'd never expected to greet with such relief.

'I'd really rather not,' she told him stiffly and dug her heels into Adonis's side so that he sprang across the sands in an eager canter and then an all-out gallop that gave the lie to any hope Sir Charles might cherish that her magnificent colt was too tired to race anything.

Yet try as they might, neither she nor Adonis could completely shake off their unwanted companions. Any attempt to outpace or outfox them with Roxanne's superior knowledge of the area were easily outflanked, and the four of them arrived in Hollowhurst's stable-yard before Roxanne even noticed she'd gone there automatically instead of returning to her new home.

'Just look at the state of you, Miss Rosie,' Whistler chided and reminded her of one very good reason she'd sent him back to the castle.

None of Hollowhurst's older servants seemed to have noticed she was four and twenty now and quite capable of running her own life, and, however much she loved them for their care of her, it still irked her that they wouldn't admit she was quite capable of taking care of herself.

'What of it, when you've seen me look so hundreds of times before?' she protested.

'Not in front of a fine gentleman like Sir Charles,' he grumbled and Roxanne was glad Charles was too busy checking his mount over to hear.

'No, but in front of a far greater one,' she told him impatiently and Whistler just shook his head.

'No disrespect meant to the old master, Miss Rosie, but this one's a good 'un, too. You shouldn't go about looking just any old how in front of him.'

'I'll go about dressed like a coalheaver's wife if I take it into my head to do so. Now stand aside and at least pretend to do as you are bid for once in your life, will you? I need to get home and see what's to do in my absence.'

'You haven't got the reins of such a compact household safely in your hands yet then, Miss Courland?' Charles asked her with another of those quizzical smiles he seemed to use to keep the world at bay.

Now where had that uncomfortable insight come from? Just as well not to think too deeply on that for now, she decided and refused to be diverted. 'No, shocking, isn't it?' she asked between her teeth and smiled just as insincerely back at him.

'Deeply,' he drawled and suddenly his humour and his smile became open and boyish and let her in. She decided dazedly that she really didn't wish to be in his deepest confidence, but her emotions insisted on ignoring her. 'While it would be as improper of you to visit my drawing room alone as it would be for me to ask you to, Miss Courland, do you care to take a stroll in the gardens while Whistler rubs your horse down for you and cools him down? It hardly seems fair to plunge even so eager a colt straight back to your normal breakneck speed of travel before he's had a rest.'

He was right, damn him! Never having been one to ignore the welfare of any creature because she was in a turmoil herself, Roxanne accepted Sir Charles's hands about her waist and very soon found herself lifted down from Adonis's sweating back and strolling beside her host towards the gardens she'd been looking out on such a short time ago before she met him again.

'Mereson, have a glass of my best burgundy

sent out for both of us and we'll insult that fine statue of Jupiter in the Winter Garden by using him as a side table,' he told his hovering butler as they passed one of the many doors to his new home.

'Very well, Sir Charles,' Mereson agreed with a look that was probably meant to make them feel like errant schoolchildren and no doubt failed in his new employer's case even as Roxanne felt she'd run away from her lessons.

'He never did approve of Uncle Granger teaching me to judge a fine wine,' Roxanne recalled. 'I believe Mereson thinks proper ladies ought to restrict themselves to lemonade or ratafia when not drinking tea.'

'Not even for you, Miss Courland…' he said and she had to tell herself he didn't mean she was special to him at all; it was just a figure of speech.

'Since I can't stand either, you were quite right to order wine for me, even if Stella might not approve of it, either.'

'She might not indeed, but, as she's not here and we are, I suggest we simply don't tell her.'

Now why did she almost hear a certain feral satisfaction behind that comment, as if getting her alone was just what he'd set out to achieve this morning? Best not to think about that just now, she decided, and concentrated on enjoying being back in her old haunts without the pressure of constantly wondering how much longer she could keep them up as they deserved.

'I suppose it was for the best,' she finally acknowledged absently, rather surprised to find she'd actually said it out loud, when only last week she'd rather have been horsewhipped than admit as much even to herself.

'What was that, Roxanne?' he asked, as if he knew perfectly well what she meant, but could hardly believe his ears.

'That you bought the estate when David never cared for it very much.'

'And you cared too much?'

'Maybe. When I was a child I certainly used to wish I'd been born the boy who could inherit it all one day, but I wasn't the first born whatever my sex and so would have missed out on it anyway.'

'I'm glad you were born a girl, even if you're not,' he told her and his smile was so reminiscent of the earlier, brilliantly hopeful Lieutenant Afforde she'd first met that she laughed delightedly. 'Do that again and I shall take full advantage of the fact that we're standing under a tree full of mistletoe, despite the fact that Mereson might come upon us at any moment,' he warned her, still with that joyful wolfishness in his brilliant gaze, as if he'd shed a decade of care all of a sudden and intended to enjoy whatever delights the day might bring with boyish recklessness.

'It would be a shame to waste it,' she amazed herself by replying and chuckled when he looked more startled, before taking her at her word and pulling her closer so he could kiss her very seriously indeed.

It was the kiss she'd dreamt of for so long, before she put aside such fantasies and got on with her life and he became the disillusioned man she sensed under his armour of rakish indifference to the world. His mouth was firm and teasing on hers and she felt every part of her soften towards him as she reached up and wrapped her hands around his strong neck to pull him even closer. Nobody could accuse him of taking advantage of her when she was very obviously enjoying his mouth on hers, his hard muscled body so close she could feel him breathe and loved the fact that his mighty chest rose and fell faster than usual against hers.

'Mmm,' he murmured against her shamelessly

wanting mouth, as if the very taste of her was driving him distracted and his tongue flickered delight along their softened junction until she opened and welcomed him with a sigh they both understood better than words.

Shivers of unimaginable warmth shook her as he began a sensuous dance of exploration, and sensual curiosity begged her to discover more than she'd dreamt possible in her youthful fantasies. Raising herself further on tiptoe, she insinuated herself even closer to his mighty torso and stretched her curves against his angles, as if testing them for the best fit.

When he settled his hands on the small of her back and it seemed as if he might use them to hold her away, she gave a protesting quiver and so he soothed them over her waist instead and then a little lower and something inside her flamed into wanting life as her old feelings for him burst into maturity without waiting for her mind to catch up. Her enthusiasm for this lovely intimacy must have tried him harder than he'd expected, for Roxanne felt as if some last restraint had snapped when he lifted her off her feet long enough to settle her on one of the exposed roots of the old tree and arrange her willing body against the hoary bark of its broad trunk so she didn't have to reach so high, and he had access to even more of her. She was in such a haze of warmth and need she hadn't even the wits left to spare to feel triumphant when he ceased exploring the sleek muscles of her slender back and busied himself with the tiny buttons of her riding jacket instead.

Frustrated by the fine lawn of her blouse and the even finer silk of the shift underneath, he did his best with what was for now and first encouraged her shamelessly peaked nipples by running a long, strong, questing finger to explore each one under the gossamer stuff. Throbbing fire bloomed at her centre and she gasped, lips damp and lush from kissing, so he spared his gaze from what his hands were learning and settled his mouth back against the sheer temptation of them instead. What hope was there of rational thought triumphing over such open masculine appreciation? she managed to ask herself distractedly, then went back to working on pure sensation when he tweaked those pebbled nipples he'd been appreciating so gratifyingly and revelled in the sweet, hot need that racked her.

How heady to feel the tremor of need that shook through her so delightfully echoed by his reverential hands as he cupped her breasts and seemed to find them so perfect that he relinquished her mouth and settled his lips about her nipples to send her to yet another level of arousal as the soft silk between his mouth and her breast seemed to melt to nothing under his questing tongue. Damp and delightful on her sensitised skin, he then left one breast for the other, as if trying to decide where to feast most satisfyingly, and that clutch of heat and light at the joining of her legs flooded with a welcome she half-wanted to clench her thighs against, and half to open them and glory in whatever he could offer to relieve the heady pressure building there.

She whimpered with the unaccustomed drag and the sweet heaviness of that wanting and saw him raise his head and look down at her with a question in his eyes. Unable to deny how eager she was for his attention, and feeling like a reckless maiden risking all with her eager young lover, she just looked back, helpless with wanting, racked with a desire she didn't even fully understand and silently pleaded for more.

He gazed back at her as if trying to decide if he could let them go further. Impatient with his scruples, she bridged the gap between them and rubbed her sensitised breasts against his heavily muscled torso and thought she heard him gasp with an arousal that shadowed her own, so she shyly reached out her hands to find out more. Rubbing her slender palm under his waistcoat, she felt the fine lawn of his shirt over warm, supple skin, muscle and man, then found her goal and allowed herself a tweak similar to the one he had given her prouder nipples. He caught his breath and moaned, so she did it again and daringly leaned up and placed her mouth over the one it could find under all that masculine camouflage.

His hands tightened on her, cupping her, testing her where the straining of her stretched-up legs met her neat buttocks and Roxanne was sure she'd melted. Her cheekbones flushed with a hot bar of colour and she changed her stance so her hands could explore his tightly clenched stomach muscles under his shirt, as that was as close as she could currently get to his skin, unless she explored his absorbed face with her tensed, tactile fingers. Puzzling over such a dilemma, she almost got distracted from what he was doing to her while she was caught between one sensual banquet for her senses and another.

Those firm, strong and yet so gentle fingers of his hand left off stroking sensuous circles on her bottom to ease a little back, as if he was afraid of crushing her between the tree's ancient bark and his own rigid desire. She was a country woman who'd spent so long helping run her uncle's estates that she knew what went on between a man and a woman in bed must be similar to the mating of the rest of nature, or at least she did in theory. Suddenly theory united with practice and the hot need inside her demanded more than this wickedly torturous spiral of urgency and wanting from him. She shifted against the familiar old tree and Charles's completely aroused body, the evidence of his passion for her as blatant as she knew her own would be if he felt the wet heat at the heart of her beckon him to something she understood on one level and now longed to feel and feel and feel for herself.

'No, hush, love,' he whispered into one pink-tipped ear as she keened her wanting impatience.

Feeling him fighting both of them, she squirmed her slender curves against his rigidly aroused body, all the temptations Eve was capable of knowing by pure instinct riding her headlong urgency to complete what they'd started here and now, and to the devil with his scruples.

'I ache,' she told him reproachfully, 'I ache so

much that I don't know if I'll ever be right again if you don't do whatever it is you're hesitating over.'

'I like that you ache for me, my wild lover, but we can't go any further than this here and now. I might get you with child for one thing, as I'm in no state to restrain myself sufficiently to avert one once I'm inside you.'

'It took even Joanna and Tom two years to beget their first one, and I can't think the delay was from lack of application on their part, can you?' she amazed herself by asking, with a look that should tell him just what she thought of such a timid lover, when his reputation argued the contrary.

'And the Besfords not even a week, if what he told me when he was reproaching himself for putting his wife in such danger while Sophia was busy getting herself born was true, and I doubt he was in a state to lie just then.'

Did that make them lucky or unlucky? Roxanne wondered as she surprised herself by indulging in that exploration of his handsome features with her fingers, after all. It made her think about them properly, without the overlay of cynicism with which he usually faced her and the world. His mouth was too sensitive to belong to a jaded rake, she concluded hazily as he shot her straight back into searing desire again by opening it and nibbling her finger, as if it was so delightful to have her in this state that he couldn't help himself. Heavy-eyed, she looked back at him hopefully, but could tell he was exerting his mighty will over his aroused body and trying to force a little space between them, so his manhood might stop demanding he listen to her with quite so much enthusiasm. She should be blushing and refusing to meet his fathomless blue eyes instead of boldly challenging him to ruin her as fast and as furiously as humanly possible.

'I thought you were supposed to be a rake,' she reproached him crossly, even as her wilful fingers explored his lean cheek and firm jaw, then ran over the surprisingly vulnerable line of his neck and round to enjoy the spot where his curling golden locks were cropped at his nape. She felt his response in a long slow shudder that racked his mighty body and raised those fine hairs under her fingers in an instinctive response to her touch that was echoed by her own at touching him so very intimately.

'Anyone who saw us thus would surely agree, as I very much doubt you make a habit of sporting so dangerously with riff-raff like myself, or I'd surely have heard of it by now and been forced to call someone out for even suggesting the possibility,' he joked, but Roxanne felt a deep, primitive shudder of fear—this time at the very thought of him risking this intriguing, magnificent body of his to a duellist's bullet.

'Don't even think of such a thing,' she reproached him, and she felt like shaking him for being such a damnably honourable rake, after all.

'Ah, there you are, boy!' a loud female voice boomed cheerfully from not much less than ten feet away.

Even as Roxanne wished she could disappear into the friendly bark of the huge tree behind her back rather than be seen by anyone else while thus occupied, she marvelled at their complete absorption in each other. Both of them were too guarded to drop headlong into such oblivion to the wider world that they completely forgot about it in their fascination with each other, or so she'd thought until today. Today, she decided fervently, had taught her a great deal more about herself and Sir Charles Afforde than she was altogether sure she'd wanted to know.

'Grandmama,' he muttered with a sigh that

might be a warning or even a welcome and, newly awake to his vulnerability to emotions she'd never credited him with until today, Roxanne detected love in his exasperated gaze, even as it iced to a warning the elderly lady deflected with a look of bland innocence none of them believed for a moment.

'Charles,' she acknowledged him with a brusque nod, then looked questioningly at Roxanne, who was furtively trying to right her appearance as best she could in the hope they were fully occupied with greeting each other. Which was far too sanguine as it happened, Roxanne, she chided herself, and flushed like a schoolgirl when caught tying her hair into that ridiculous pony's tail for the second time today.

'Miss Roxanne Courland,' he introduced her stiffly once she looked passably respectable at last, thanks to her furtive efforts, and he stepped far enough away from her side to allow Roxanne to make a shaky curtsy. 'And this is my grand-mother, the Dowager Countess of Samphire, Roxanne.'

'Your ladyship,' Roxanne managed huskily, and if the old lady had any doubt what they'd been up to, that hoarse-voiced acknowledgement must have given the game away.

'I knew your great-uncle,' the lady responded, as breezily as if they'd met in Hyde Park. 'He was a fine man, even if he did have some totty-headed notions about bringing up his nieces.'

'He was the finest guardian any girl could wish for,' Roxanne defended him hotly and almost allowed herself to groan at her impulsive tongue, but that would only have made it worse.

Lady Samphire looked as if she'd like nothing better than a good sparring match with a worthy opponent, but Roxanne knew very well she wasn't up to it just now, might never be up to it again if Sir Charles didn't step a little further away from her and let her wits settle into some sort of order.

'He'd not be pleased with you today, then,' the lady replied, looking remarkably cheerful at the notion, 'unless there's something you wish to tell me, my boy?'

'Didn't I say?' Charles drawled carelessly, recovering his usual guarded persona again, much to Roxanne's bitter disappointment. 'Miss Courland has just agreed to become my wife.' He took her hand and squeezed it, as if frightened she'd brusquely deny every syllable and flounce away.

'Doubt it, m'boy,' Lady Samphire argued.

'Why?' he challenged sharply, apparently still too finely strung with tension to recall just who he was talking to, which might even persuade Roxanne the man she'd begun to want beyond all reason was buried under all that outraged ice and his usual armour of indifference, after all.

'Doubt if you got round to asking her anything that rational, if what I just saw of how you are together is aught to go by. I've waited a long time to see you thrown so far off your rake's podium by a girl that you'd fall flat on your handsome face at her feet, my lad, so I'd be lying if I pretended I was looking the other way while you did it.'

'Such rare honesty, Grandmama,' he said tightly, but didn't argue with that fanciful summary of his ardour, much to Roxanne's surprise.

Did he feel this tender novelty, then—this sense of barely comprehended possibilities opening up in front of him as uneasily and incredibly as she did? Could he possibly be as wound up with hope and fear and this raging need she was still trying to extinguish, despite such a sobering intrusion? He certainly seemed to be struggling to put his usual cynical composure in place, but what a heady idea, what a dangerously seductive hope.

'With the honour of Miss Courland's hand openly in mine, how could I do anything but renounce any other?' he said with a gallant bow she liked less than his former shaken honesty.

'You haven't really asked me to marry you and I certainly haven't said yes,' she informed him implacably.

'That's it, girl, you tell him,' his unnatural grandmother urged.

'And however much I love you, I'll ask you to keep your long nose out of business that doesn't concern you.' Charles rounded on his grandmother as if rapidly approaching the end of his tether.

'And I certainly won't wed a man who addresses his grandmama so rudely,' Roxanne stated, with what she thought magnificent scorn, considering she'd very recently been more or less begging him to complete her seduction— wouldn't that have made this scene utterly impossible to endure, rather than just excruciatingly embarrassing?

'It'd be better if you enquire into a man's relationship with his family before rather than after you let him seduce you next time then, m'girl,' her ladyship informed her blandly, and Roxanne gave an involuntary chuckle.

She heard Charles groan and recalled what he'd said about that just before she was swept into uncharted waters and for a moment let her fingers tighten on his as it all became possible again. No, she reminded herself sternly, under the chilly sunlight of a November day, it was impossible to marry just because her reputation was tarnished by her lack of self-control around a certain handsome rake. She loosed her hand from his and brazenly faced the surprisingly unworried Dowager Countess of Samphire, even as she felt surprisingly cold and lonely without the warm haven of his gentle, masculine fingers on hers to secretly revel in.

Chapter Ten

'I can assure you that matters didn't progress that far between us, your ladyship,' Roxanne reassured the Dowager Countess with as much dignity as she could summon in the circumstances, 'and therefore I feel no obligation to wed your grandson, even if you did just witness something happen between us that I'd rather you hadn't seen.'

'I'd deem it a favour if you'd have him all the same, though, for you seem to have a lot more about you than the usual wet gooses he saddles himself with, mainly because he's too tender hearted to make them go back to their husbands and actually work at something for once in their silly lives.'

Roxanne couldn't help herself, she snorted sceptically and wondered if the old lady really thought she was daft enough to swallow such a farrago of nonsense, but Lady Samphire's surprisingly clear blue eyes were steady, and instead Roxanne let herself wonder if Charles was such an easy touch for a bored lady, restive within the arranged marriage she'd probably fought so hard to attain and now found hollow and unsatisfying. She couldn't acquit him of all his sins, for hadn't she witnessed him flirting shamelessly, then leaving a ball with a married woman the one time she actually laid eyes on him during her miserable London Season?

He certainly hadn't looked in the least reluctant to be leaving with the loveliest female present that night and had had no attention to spare then for the gawky débutante who had been watching him so intensely she was surprised it hadn't bored a hole in his immaculately cut evening coat at the time. Then she'd felt as if his perfidy had blown the very foundations of her world apart. By living up, or down, to his reputation, he'd shattered the silly bubble of dreams she'd cocooned herself in for the three years since she had first laid eyes on him so terribly painfully that her seventeen-year-old self had been unable to cope with such bitter disillusionment and had had to be taken home, crying inconsolably, much to her newly-wed sister Maria's open disgust. She'd do well to remember that appalling feeling of betrayal and utter desolation and make sure she never gave him a chance to do it again.

'I feel like a bone caught between two very polite dogs,' he said now, trying to deflate the whole wretched business with his usual easy humour, but even Roxanne could see the attempt was off-key and wasn't surprised when Lady Samphire virtually ignored him.

'You could do a lot worse for yourself, Miss Courland,' she coaxed like a farmer's wife at market, trying to sell off a last dubious-looking cheese so that she could go home and put her feet up with a well-deserved cup of tea.

'No, thank you. If I were foolish enough to agree to such a proposal, I should never know if it was made out of concern for the reputation I've just risked of my own free will or for my own fair sake,' she ended, trying for that wry humour Charles so often hit more perfectly and sounding rather pedantic and silly instead.

It was true, though; she wouldn't wed him under such circumstances, even if half-a-dozen dowagers watched her being even more thoroughly seduced than Sir Charles Afforde had allowed her to be today.

'Your wine, Sir Charles,' Mereson chipped in, as he finally stepped forwards and offered a tray rejoicing in three glasses of glowing burgundy.

'Is anyone else joining us?' Roxanne queried almost hysterically, looking about her as if to discover who else had witnessed her being ridiculously careless of her good name in public with an acknowledged rake.

'Miss Roxanne?' Mereson said blankly with a look of reproach that would do justice to an offended duke.

'I take it nobody else will be joining this slightly odd bacchanal?'

'No, miss,' he replied repressively.

'Good, then pray direct them out here if any more of Sir Charles's friends or relatives decide to visit him unexpectedly,' she ordered a little too brightly. 'Oh, no, I'm not mistress here any more, am I? Then Sir Charles may do as he pleases with any further callers he intends entertaining today, because I'm going home.'

'Very good, Miss Roxanne, I will inform the stables you need your horse brought round,' Mereson said with superb composure and returned to the castle to do so.

'As far as I'm concerned, you *are* home, Roxanne,' Charles gently interrupted, stopping any

more brittle words she could come up with, and
Roxanne felt tears gather at the very idea, the
first she'd allowed since the day of her uncle's
funeral. It was as close to a declaration as she
was going to get today, and even that limited
invitation to share his life made her feel ridiculously off balance, especially when it was so far
from announcing his undying devotion.

'Not any more,' she managed with a wobbly
attempt at rationality, before he gave an exasperated sigh and pulled her back into the haven of
his strong embrace. Self-restraint broke down
at last, and she let herself cry out her bewilder-
ment and grief against his broad chest.

'Bring her over here,' his grandmother ordered with a rather satisfied smile, for which
he frowned at her, as if not quite knowing what
to do with the welter of emotions he'd finally
unleashed in Roxanne now she was crying out
so many pent-up woes in his arms.

Lifting a gentle hand to stroke the ebony curls
nestled so recklessly against his torso, Charles
did his best to pretend the warm, contrary,
sobbing female in his arms meant no more to
him than any other. Meeting Lady Samphire's
sceptical gaze with a mixture of defiance and
sheepishness, he knew very well she saw far

too much of his true feelings, as she always did, and concentrated on finding his large and manly handkerchief before Roxanne reduced his shirt to a sopping wet rag instead. 'Here you are, love,' he murmured into the lovely mass of her ebony hair as the ribbon gave up its work and came undone yet again, cloaking them both in the vibrant, fascinating veil of curls.

How any man could look on her thus and *not* want to run the silken weight of them over his hands as she rested naked and confiding in his arms after being well and truly loved was beyond him. The hand not engaged in soothing her tightened into a fist; he doubted whether one single nuance of the wildly heightened emotions between himself and Roxanne had escaped his eagle-eyed grandmother.

'Why were you proposing to take your wine with Miss Courland in the garden in November in the first place, Charles?' she asked curiously as she sat down on a nearby bench and sipped her glass with a connoisseur's appreciation.

'Propriety,' he replied shortly and felt a hard burn of colour flash across his cheeks under her sceptical gaze. 'A misplaced hope, as it happens,' he conceded.

'Still rather a touching idea, so perhaps there's

hope for you after all, m'boy. All you have to do now is persuade the girl you really do want to marry her, and we can get you both up the aisle as soon as possible, after all.'

'I can get myself there, thank you very much, and you're only making my task harder,' he condemned rather harshly, for he'd felt Roxanne's resistance to the very idea and was surprised to find he didn't want her to leave his arms, even if she was only crying out all the tension and misery he'd caused her by buying the estate and then displacing her into a world far too little for her talents. Loving his wife would prove no hard task in one sense, but falling *in* love with her—now that would be another matter entirely.

'I'm not going to marry anyone just to save my reputation,' she muttered gruffly into his damp shoulder. Why did it cost him such a pang to turn his back on the notion of just gathering her up in his arms and carrying her off to his bedchamber to seduce her ruthlessly until she changed her mind?

'I heard you the first time, Miss Propriety,' he assured her and felt almost godlike as she managed a feeble chuckle and finally pulled away from him to look up at him with reddened eyes that he somehow still found utterly irresistible.

'Even I'm not brazen enough to claim such a title after today, Sir Charles,' she assured him and he wondered why the faint hiccup of a fading sob as she tried to laugh at herself touched him far more than all the tears and tragedies any of his former lovers had acted out.

'Then drink your wine, my dear, and when you're feeling fully restored you can ride home and rest until you're your old self again and fit and eager to fight with me again another day.'

'I'm not your dear,' she informed him with a watery and not even very convincing defiance, and Charles fought not to tell her how very wrong she might well be.

'Whatever you say, ma'am,' he managed to say evenly, when all he really wanted was to carry out that very tempting scenario of whisking her off and slaking this merciless need of her that he should never have put into his own head when he was in such a painful state of rampantly unsated desire. 'If Miss Courland will kindly consent to go home and reassemble her usual fearsome armour, I'll engage to try to rob her of it even more thoroughly tomorrow. Is that better?'

'You know very well it isn't, you devil,' she accused, seeming to forget that she was doing her best to pretend to be a pattern card of propriety, whilst still wrapped securely in his embrace and resting against his broad chest as if she belonged there while she absently shredded his fine lawn handkerchief.

Turning away from the temptation to stare down at her until her eyes were velvet dark and full of that heady, driven passion for him once again, he met his grandmother's shrewd, speculative gaze in the act of inspecting them both and wondered once again exactly why he loved her so much.

'I have a very poor memory these days,' she assured them both virtuously and Charles felt Roxanne stiffen in his arms as she recalled exactly where, and with whom, she was.

'Congratulations, ma'am,' he said ironically. 'I never heard you voluntarily admit to feeling any of the trials of your age before today, so perhaps this will usher in a whole new phase to all our lives.'

'And it could be the end of me behaving like an old fool towards you, you undutiful rogue,' she snapped back with undiminished fervour, and Charles watched her appreciatively down the rest of her glass of one of his finest burgundies with resigned fondness. 'You have a fine palate, my boy,' she told him regally, 'although you should have, I suppose, since I taught you to appreciate a good wine when you ought to have been sitting at your stepmother's knee, learning to be as boring as the rest of my tribe of grand-children.'

'Thank you for saving me from that fate at least,' he said ruefully and reluctantly let Rox-anne go.

'I'm sorry for behaving like a ninny,' his lady said with such a gallant attempt at dignity that he felt like snatching her back into his arms and carrying her off to his highest tower room and locking them both in until the world went away, after all.

'I never met anyone less likely to add to that breed than yourself, Miss Courland,' he assured her and for once hated his own smooth patter as she took his very real admiration for mock-ery and flamed a furious glare at him. 'Truly you belong in a class of your own,' he went on, but saw he'd made bad worse as her ridiculous lack of self-confidence bumped up against his wretched reputation and made her certain he was taunting her.

'As do you, Sir Charles,' she informed him icily and turned regally away to offer Lady

Samphire a stately curtsy and a sincere-enough-sounding adieu, before marching away with a swish of her gathered skirts and a toss of those midnight curls that should have informed him, if he needed confirmation, that it was beneath her dignity to even bid him farewell.

'Always told you that glib tongue of yours would lead you to disaster one day, m'boy,' his grandmother informed him gleefully.

'And just whose side are you on?' he rasped back, preoccupied with the sight of Roxanne's neatly rounded rear view as she stormed off towards the stable-yard.

'That of the angels,' she informed him piously, and even as half of his mind and most of his body was enjoying the view, the other half was not that credulous.

'Yes? Which lot of angels would that be then, sooty or sweet?' he asked as Roxanne finally rounded the corner and ruined a fine landscape for him by no longer completing it in his eyes.

'Know very well I can't abide sweetmeats, but that ain't to say I think heaven's anything like those fools of parsons would have us think; nobody with any sense would want to go there if it was.'

'You must be sure to let me know,' he said

with a direct look that made her chuckle rather than take offence.

'To be sure, I will, for if anyone deserves to be haunted by a curmudgeonly ghost it's you, Charles, and at least nowadays I can feel a bit more confident of getting there before you do.'

'I thought I was bound for the nether regions,' he reminded her, nevertheless touched by the genuine emotion behind her flippant words and very conscious that he'd put her through years of constant anxiety during his naval service, for all she'd deny it with her last breath.

'You are, of course, unless you manage to find redemption,' she told him—was there a hint of seriousness behind her determined banter?

Charles thought perhaps there was and re-called his own unease with his life before he finally made the decision to leave the sea and purchase the Hollowhurst estates, where he rap-idly discovered life could be full of surprises after all. But to call Roxanne his redemption—surely that was going a little too far? Especially considering the very compromising position she'd found them in just now. Most grandpar-ents would be marching them before a priest at this very moment and demanding grovelling apologies all the while. Lady Samphire was a remarkable woman, he conceded with a wry smile, and it paid to watch her even more closely than the proverbial cartload of monkeys.

'The only thing I intend to find today is my land steward and the new housekeeper to inform her of your arrival, but not necessarily in that order,' he informed her lightly and was relieved when she accepted he didn't relish discussing the state of his soul or his frustrated body right now.

'Just as well, for I want to meet the latter and have no interest whatsoever in your land, considering it's in excellent heart. That girl should take more interest in her household and presenting a ladylike appearance to the world and less in things that don't concern her.'

'And how, pray, would the rest be paid for if she'd sat at her embroidery and let the estates go to rack and ruin when her uncle became ill? Davy Courland never had any more interest in the place than he would in a book of ladies' fashion plates,' he defended Roxanne rather hotly, realising his error in flying to his grandmother's lure when she forgot a countess's dignity and actually smirked.

'I suppose you think you're devilishly clever?' was all he could manage to come up with in his own defence, and heard himself sound like a fractious schoolboy with a groan.

'I don't just think it, I know it,' she informed him, superbly unworried that she sounded vain about it, and he did his best not to laugh and encourage her.

With Stella on the inside plotting and now his grandmother using every advantage she wouldn't scruple to employ, he and Roxanne stood little chance of remaining unwed long. Which, of course, suited him very well, it just didn't please him so much that they seemed to think it a love match.

Instead it would be a marriage of passionate friendship and good sense, he assured himself doggedly. He and Roxanne suited each other so neatly it would be foolish to ignore their underlying compatibility, and he wasn't a fool. Luckily he didn't believe her to be one, either, and soon she'd see for herself they could amount to more together than they ever would apart. All it would take was a few more of those incendiary kisses and she'd be as eager for the marriage bed as he was. Or almost as eager, he reminded himself ruefully, as frustrated need ground painfully as he reacted like an idiot to the idea of Roxanne and bed of any sort just at the moment, something he was perfectly certain hadn't escaped his grandmother's eagle-eyed gaze.

'I think she'll do,' Lady Samphire told him majestically, 'if you ever manage to persuade her you'll make her a good husband, of course.'

Feeling the sting of her sharp tongue rather more sharply than she probably intended for once, Charles looked back on his rakish past and regretted at least some of it for making Roxanne so very wary of him. After months at sea it had seemed normal for a healthy young male to find relief from frustration and loneliness in a skilled courtesan's arms. He doubted if anyone who hadn't experienced the highs, lows and the occasional becalmed boredom of a long sea voyage would understand the life a naval captain on duty, constantly aware of every detail of the day-to-day running of his ship to keep it at sea and in a fit state to offer battle when the need arose. Charles recalled the tension of detached command, when he'd borne responsibility for searching out the enemy and doing his best to outwit and defeat them. A successful frigate captain must be sharp enough, skilled enough, to bring the unwary to battle or outrun the unexpected day and night. And then he had to avoid being overfamiliar with his officers and crew, without being deemed indifferent to their well-being and aspirations. In many ways, it had suited him to be nigh as powerful as a king in his own country while at sea, waiting for the latest fat French merchantman to sail into his well-placed trap. However, the isolation of it could eat up a man's soul if he didn't take good care to keep himself sane.

'Roxanne, I'm awed by your stamina, but don't you feel worn out after dancing half the night away and then spending a whole morning in the saddle?' Stella asked mildly as Roxanne failed to reach her bedchamber without being seen. She sincerely hoped her face didn't betray her turmoil and did her best not to flush like a schoolgirl under her friend's speculative gaze.

'It seems ridiculous now, but I quite lost track of time and need to set myself to rights before anyone calls and sees me looking like this,' she replied, with an airy wave at her own person that she hoped would excuse her hurrying off without further ado.

'Indeed you do,' Stella agreed with a smile that robbed her agreement of any sting, but Roxanne shifted uncomfortably under her shrewd gaze all the same.

'Yes, well, the sooner I let Tabby make me fit to be seen again the better, for I'm certainly not presentable at the moment. Whatever would your mama say if she could see me now?'

'Heaven forefend,' Stella replied with heart-felt fervour, and Roxanne only had to think of the furore if Mrs Varleigh Senior had seen her brazenly kissing Sir Charles Afforde to blanch at the very idea.

'I really must change,' she excused herself before she gave herself away completely and dashed into her bedchamber to set the bell ringing frantically for Tabby.

Wincing at the very thought, she nevertheless forced herself to look in the mirror and was horrified by the damage that a wild ride and an even wilder kiss from a rake had wrought on her appearance. A stranger coming across her by chance might be forgiven for thinking her a tramping woman dressed in the cast-offs of some charitably inclined lady.

'Lord, I look a terrible fright,' she muttered at herself, but couldn't tear her gaze away from the wild woman in the mirror.

Fanciful though it sounded, she looked as if

she'd had a flame lit inside her, almost as if her normally workaday dark brown eyes had felt the warmth of some star-drenched southern night and now couldn't quite forget it. Or perhaps, her more prosaic self informed her sternly, she just looked as if she'd come close to being seduced by one of the worst rakes known to the *ton*. He was a danger to her reputation, of course, but not her heart—which was perfectly intact this time and only racing because she'd come so close to being forced to wed that rake and regret it for the rest of her days.

'But would you *really* have regretted it so much, Roxanne?' she demanded brusquely of the houri in the mirror and saw the wretch smirk and then wriggle with delight, like an excited schoolgirl promised a heady treat. 'No, I rather thought not,' she condemned herself roundly, then wondered what anyone hearing her would think of her sanity. That she didn't actually have any, of course, but any lady who let herself be kissed and caressed and almost seduced by Sir Charles Afforde, and who then sneakily yearned for him to do it all over again as soon as possible, couldn't be considered totally rational.

'Just look at the state of you, Miss Roxanne!' Tabby burst out as she hurried into the room to find out why her mistress had sounded her bell as if she thought the house might be afire.

'Yes, I just was,' she replied ungrammatically and once again fought an annoying, self-conscious blush as her maid took in her full disarray.

Curse it—she should have done her best to put Miss Courland, spinster lady of means and very much mistress of herself and no one else, back together without any help. Except she'd considered the task beyond her.

'Well, you'll never do to receive visitors as you are, so you'd best hold still for once while I do the best I can and hope Mrs Lavender manages to keep them busy.'

'Who's called, then?' Roxanne asked with would-be carelessness, wondering with a silly leap of the heart if Sir Charles had already followed her back here to continue the forbidden, and yet so mutually pleasurable, task of completing her seduction.

'Mr Joseph Longborough and that Huntley boy, to name but two,' Tabby replied pertly as she seized Roxanne's hairbrush and began a ruthless attack on her wildly curling mane.

'Ouch!' she protested, the sinking of her heart at the very idea of facing those two callow youths after her encounter with the far deadlier, more handsome and much more wickedly tempting Sir Charles almost diverting her from the pain in her scalp.

'If you will go galloping about the countryside like some wild schoolboy, you can just learn to take the consequences, Miss Rosie,' her maid informed her grimly, but Roxanne knew from that familiar form of address that she was almost forgiven. 'And since you've come home without that ribbon I put in your pocket for the very purpose of preventing this mess, I dare say that handsome buck from the Castle had something to do with it,' she muttered darkly, but Roxanne pretended to be deaf—it was either that or protest too much, and she wasn't prepared to risk doing that with someone who knew her too well.

'Finished?' she enquired sweetly instead.

Tabby snorted disgustedly. 'As if anyone could put this disaster in a fit state to be seen that quickly,' she snapped and resorted to the fine silver comb Roxanne dreaded to tease out a stubborn tangle. 'I don't know why I never thought to ask your sister for a reference. I dare say a lady's maid of my experience and patience could command whatever sum she cared to ask from a lady with the least pretension to caring what she looked like if she had a reference from a respectable countess at her back,' she chided, and Roxanne would have nodded sagely to encourage such a scheme, if only she wasn't firmly anchored by a thick hank of hair.

'You're welcome to try it, of course, but I don't know how long such a lady would put up with being nagged and abused by her own maid.'

Tabby sniffed and, finally satisfied that Roxanne's hair was as smooth as she could make it in the time available, began to pin it into a style she'd obviously spent the morning learning from Stella's maid. Watching it take shape in the mirror, Roxanne thought the softer style became her very well. So well that she couldn't bring herself to order Tabby to dismantle it and put her old, plain coiffeur back together to discourage Joe's callow attentions. This told her two things: one, that his clumsy attempts to annex her and her dowry no longer felt significant, and, two, that looking well in case another, more potent, gentleman called was almost too critical to her sense of well-being for comfort.

'Now sit still while I find a gown that's fit for you to be seen in, Miss Rosie,' her irascible maid chided her, as if she was fourteen again instead of ten years older and wiser.

'It's only a couple of youths who've seen me looking far worse while I was busy round the estate about my uncle's business,' Roxanne protested feebly, but Tabby was too caught up in Stella's campaign to turn Roxanne into a fashion plate to take much notice, particularly when Roxanne was half in thrall to the idea herself.

Chapter Eleven

Ten minutes later, just as Stella was doing her best to come up with yet another polite question to stretch Joe Longborough's banal remarks into a conversation, Roxanne joined her in the drawing room and knew she'd made another mistake. The gown Tabby had chosen, and that she'd half-heartedly protested was too smart for afternoon visits from her neighbours, had looked the height of demure respectability until she put it on. Crimson velvet of so dark a hue that it looked almost black, until the soft stuff caught the light and turned to rich burgundy, was not the sort of colour to allow its wearer to fade into the background. Another error of judgement on her part, Roxanne decided, as a shaft of autumn sunlight slanted into the room and made her a little too noticeable in the rich golden light.

'Miss Courland,' Joe observed with what he probably thought of as dangerous slowness while his greedy eyes did their best to gobble her whole.

'Mr Longborough,' she said shortly and dodged him to nod just as abruptly to his friend and skirt around them both to join Stella on the sofa where neither gentleman, fortunately, possessed the scandalous ill manners to try to join them.

'Tea, Roxanne dear?' Stella asked her, eyebrows raised and the faintest, most unforgivable, hint of a laugh in her voice.

'Of course, that would be most refreshing.'

'After your busy morning.'

Roxanne just nodded, wondering what on earth her friend was up to.

'And here comes my cousin to join our merry band,' Stella remarked with the blandest, most deceiving of smiles. 'I must ring for another cup.'

'Indeed you must,' Roxanne managed, the dizzying prospect of meeting the wretched man so soon after he'd kissed her almost senseless, rejected her demands to be completely seduced by him with insulting ease, then had the bad taste to be discovered doing so by his grandmother before he'd made her cry so spinelessly in his arms nearly made her bolt for her room, whatever anyone thought of such hysterical cowardice. 'We all know just how partial Sir Charles is to an excellent cup of tea.'

'Miss Courland, Stella my loved one,' Sir Charles greeted them with a bow of such elegance that Roxanne could see Joe trying to store it away for future imitation, despite the fact he obviously hated his rival.

'Curse the whole damned lot of them!' Roxanne muttered vengefully under her breath, but saved her best glare for the newcomer. After all, Joe might be a self-opinionated lout, but he hadn't failed to seduce her today, then turned up on her doorstep not an hour later as if it was no more significant than a casual wave across a crowded room between friends.

'Longborough, Huntley,' he added, with a nod that should have made both her other visitors conscious he was the dominant male of the party.

'Afforde,' Joe drawled recklessly and Roxanne expected him to be blistered by a challenging stare from Charles's impenetrably blue eyes any second—and just when had she begun to think of him as Charles and not Sir Charles or even Captain Afforde?

Of course, being ignored in favour of Simkins would make Joe squirm far more effectively, especially as her butler chose that moment to produce that extra cup on a silver salver, along with a glass of rich burgundy, which he handed to Charles as if he were already master of the house.

'Neatly done, Simkins,' Charles observed with a smile of complicity and encouragement for her newly promoted butler, and Roxanne wasn't sure whether to agree with him or march out of the room with her nose in the air.

'Have you acquired tickets for the subscription ball at Tunbridge next week, gentlemen?' Stella asked the two younger gentlemen before war could be openly declared.

'Indeed we have,' Mr Huntley agreed eagerly, looking as if he'd like to tow his friend out of the room before he rashly challenged a man who could outwit and outgun him on any field of battle. 'Looking forward to it. Came to beg the privilege of the first dance, didn't we, Joe?'

'How charming of you, Mr Longborough,' Stella twittered as if she believed every word she was saying. 'I'll be delighted to grant it to you, of course—so flattering to be asked at my age.'

Despite her ire, Roxanne almost ruined everything by laughing out loud as Joe's expression gave his thoughts away. 'Honoured,' he finally managed through gritted teeth, while looking as if he'd prefer strangling Stella to dancing with her.

'Then I hope I can claim the honour of *your* hand, Miss Courland?' Mr Huntley asked with a sheepish look at his friend as he took advantage of his confusion.

'Of course you can, Mr Huntley,' she had to reply, and indeed she'd far rather be stumped about the room by over-enthusiastic Mr Huntley than informed how greatly she'd benefit by marrying a man who'd inherit his father's acres and position in due course by Joe.

She thought it was that information that made her dislike Joe Longborough so heartily nowadays, for she was very fond of the squire, and the spectacle of his uncouth son longing for him to quit his shoes so he could step into them the sooner made her feel distinctly sick.

'I fear I have business in town next week and therefore cannot beg for any dances from either of you,' Sir Charles put in smoothly, and Roxanne wondered why the whole idea of attending the local subscription ball suddenly seemed such a poor one if he wasn't to be there.

'Such a shame,' she muttered darkly and received a mocking smile in return as she marvelled at the sharpness of his hearing.

'But I have every intention of returning in time for the evening party my grandmother has decided I'm to throw in her honour, Miss Courland,' he added with a long, intimate look she very much hoped was camouflaged by Stella and Mr Huntley's gallant attempts at cheerful conversation. 'And as my grandmother is to remain at Hollowhurst while I'm in town, she's instructed me to call, Miss Courland, and ask you to visit and be introduced before I leave, in order that she might "have some civilised company whilst you're gallivanting about the country, boy", I think were her exact words.'

'That sounds like my Great-Aunt Augusta,' Stella said with a sage nod, and Joe just looked as if he'd like to strangle every one of them, including the Dowager, very slowly.

'Until next week then, ladies,' he said by way of farewell, along with one of those ungainly nods of dismissal he'd wasted on Charles up until then.

'I think I'd have had to develop a cold by next week, if not for that rather nice young man he brought with him,' Stella said reflectively once the two younger gentlemen had left.

'I'm fairly certain I'd have joined you, except Joseph Longborough would never let poor Mr Huntley forget I'd cried off from that dance on the flimsiest of pretexts,' Roxanne agreed with a brief grimace for Joe's appalling manners.

'So we'll go then, even if we're to be deprived of your company, Cousin Charles,' Stella informed him with that ironic smile that often made her true thoughts impenetrable to Roxanne.

There was obviously a very strong affection between the cousins, but did that necessarily mean Stella was matchmaking? Probably, Roxanne decided with a sigh and sipped her tea as if she'd nothing to contribute to the conversation Stella and Sir Charles kept up with little apparent effort.

Quite when the perfidious baronet gestured his cousin from the room, Roxanne couldn't have said, since she'd been woolgathering for several minutes when he must have done so, but she roused herself from her reverie to see Stella's lilac skirts belling out behind her with the speed of her going and looked up and met his eyes with a haughty question in her own.

'You didn't think I came here this afternoon for the sole purpose of exchanging veiled insults with your would-be cavalier, I hope? Especially since he's not a very appealing cavalier to waste our time on,' he asked with one eyebrow raised in a world-weary look she imagined Joe probably spent useless hours in front of his dressing mirror trying to imitate.

'No, you also came to tell your cousin that you'll be leaving Hollowhurst for a while and that next week you'll be hosting an evening party with your grandmama, did you not? So you see, Sir Charles, I was listening to the salient points of your conversation, after all.'

'You are becoming quite the social adept, Miss Courland,' he informed her loftily and then chuckled as her right hand fisted without her even thinking about it. 'That's better; if I ever feel the need to converse with female automata I can rely on most of my stepsisters to oblige me. Pray don't ever aspire to such vapid correctness, will you, Miss Courland? It would be a crime against nature.'

'I didn't know you had any stepsisters,' she said and despaired of herself for falling into the trap of being curious about his relatives when she should be concentrating on being furious with him for intruding on her life in far too many ways.

'Apparently complete oblivion to my continuing existence is socially unacceptable to my immediate, if not my close, family, so occasionally I'm summoned to spend a few days being bored to distraction at my father's expense. Since he married their mother and I didn't, I really can't imagine why we all put ourselves through the discomfort of finding out all over again that we have nothing in common.'

'How awful,' she was surprised into saying sincerely when she'd been so determined to keep him at a polite distance.

'I suppose it is really,' he agreed with a sigh, and Roxanne felt he was letting her see a side of himself he usually kept well hidden from the world. 'My mother died when I was born and my father acquired my stepmother and her tribe of daughters some years after I'd been virtually adopted by my grandparents, so it wouldn't be an exaggeration to say we're virtually strangers to each other.'

'You and your father aren't close, then?'

'Not by a country mile, Miss Courland.'

'Poor little boy,' Roxanne said with those treacherous tears heating her eyes again, much to her annoyance when she looked up and saw him watching her as if amazed he could engender such emotions. 'Not that you look as if you suffered unduly from his neglect,' she informed him hardily.

'Oh, I didn't, so pray don't waste your pity on me, Roxanne. My grandparents spoilt me within an inch of becoming unbearable.'

'Only within an inch?'

'Torment, but even if the navy didn't have a way of dealing summarily with toplofty boys with too-high an opinion of themselves, can you imagine my grandmother indulging anyone completely, let alone a scrubby brat?'

'She adores you,' Roxanne told him, remembering the softening of her ladyship's gaze as it dwelt on her handsome grandson when she didn't think he was looking.

'It's mutual, I assure you.'

'Good, but I dare say you didn't come here to discuss your family relations, Sir Charles,' she reminded him and herself.

'No, or only in a roundabout fashion,' he said with a thoughtful look at her that for some reason made her shiver with apprehension. 'I really came to ask you to marry me and *be* my family, Miss Courland.'

'Oh, that's all right, then,' she said faintly, as she felt the earth spin on its axis a little too realistically.

'Good, so you're not dead set against the idea, then?' he said clumsily, sounding as if he'd been knocked off his own superb balance for once.

'Of course I am,' she said crossly. 'I've never felt the least desire to make a marriage of convenience, Sir Charles, and you haven't done or said anything to convert me to the idea so far today, so of course I won't marry you. I already told you that and I might add that I find this scene embarrassing in the extreme and wish you'd spared both of us the trouble.'

'You'll just have to endure being embarrassed then, because I haven't finished,' he told her gruffly, as if she'd hurt him—but how could that be so?

To be hurt, he'd have to feel some deep emotion towards her and she doubted he'd let himself be that vulnerable. No, he didn't love her, and she wasn't sure what she felt for him, either, so that was fair enough. It was his serious contemplation of the idea of actually marrying her because she was well enough born, and not exactly repellent, that turned her stomach.

'I'm not obliged to stay here and listen to this any more than you're forced to waste your breath in such a foolish fashion,' she said regally, but he refused to accept her rebuff.

'Yes, I am. If anyone else saw us nearly make love on the lawn this afternoon then I feel every need to try to persuade you to see sense, before they can spread scandal and ruin your good name.'

'They didn't, and I've no intention of wedding you, Sir Charles, so I suggest you leave now before we risk saying something we'll regret.'

'Why not?'

'Why not what?'

'Why won't you marry me?' he asked as if genuinely puzzled.

'Because, contrary to your inflated opinion of yourself, Sir Charles, you're not irresistible,' she snapped contemptuously.

Again he quirked that annoying eyebrow at her and she felt herself blush hotly as she recalled her fiery response to his kisses and more intimate attentions earlier—wretched, wretched man!

'This morning I wasn't quite myself,' she mumbled, as if that explained everything.

'No, you were mine,' he insisted, a certain look in his eyes telling her he was recalling in too-vivid detail exactly how wanton she'd been in his arms.

'Never! Now if there's nothing else, I'm very tired, sir, and intend to rest before I must meet your cousin at the dinner table as if nothing untoward has occurred today, which it hasn't, of course.'

'Not through any fault of yours,' he told her dourly, looking as if he was torn between wanting to shake her or kiss her breathless all over again.

'I find your company tedious this afternoon, Sir Charles, and would prefer your room to your company, if you please,' she said, in an attempt to appeal to his innate good manners and make sure he did neither.

'I came to make a formal offer for your hand, Roxanne, and intend to do so whether you like it or not.'

'Well, I don't.'

'Nevertheless,' he replied through gritted teeth, 'I insist upon offering you the protection of my hand in marriage, Miss Courland, and beg you will think a little for once before you refuse me. I can offer you the role in life you were born to play as my wife. You will run my household, assist in managing my estates and stand at my side in every way as my equal. Can you put your hand on your heart, Roxanne, and say you're content living at Mulberry House as a lady of independent means with nothing much to do?'

Seeing that she opened her mouth to argue as soon as he gave her a chance, then shut it again as the lie wouldn't form, he shook his head to confirm what they both knew.

'Of course not, for you'd be perjuring yourself. Here you are, politely bored in my cousin's very good company, but you're still bored. At Hollowhurst, I can offer you everything that should have been yours by birthright and a husband who honours you, along with the promise of children of our own into the bargain.'

'No,' was all she could manage in reply and even she knew it was inadequate.

'Why, Roxanne, what else do you want of me, woman? What else could you want?'

'Love,' she finally admitted, acknowledging to herself that foolish young Rosie, who'd mourned his leaving that Christmas long ago as if her young heart had gone with him and she couldn't quite function without it, still couldn't face a marriage of pure sense and sensuality with this man.

That silly child, the one who'd languished and dreamt and been coldly disillusioned on her come out, wasn't dead, after all. No, the little idiot had just been sleeping, and here, at last, Roxanne held the answer to her questions as well as his. She'd never properly stopped loving him, and his arrival at Hollowhurst to usurp her had hurt so much because he'd not wanted to marry her for it first. Which didn't mean she had to accept the half-loaf he was offering, as if he couldn't understand why she wasn't snatching it out of his hand and thanking her lucky stars when she was four and twenty and obviously not destined to be offered such splendours again.

The silence in her once-comfortable drawing room grew until she'd filled it with all the answers to that one last, disastrous demand he might wish to agree to, but wouldn't be cruel enough to speak such a lie. Finally, feeling as if she really was at the end of her composure, she raised her hand in an inarticulate denial that she wanted an answer and turned to leave the room.

'Stop!' he demanded and she halted, but refused to turn, for what was the point when all she would see was horror at her words and perhaps even relief in his eyes that she knew it was impossible? 'If I *could* love anyone, it would be you,' he promised, and his voice was husky and his eyes, when she felt compelled to turn and meet them after all, were ardent with such sincerity she had to stay and listen, despite the fact that part of her was hurt almost unbearably.

'Truth to tell, I don't know if I have it in me to love. I remembered you so often, Rosie, the girl with the ardent eyes and the passionate mouth, despite her tender years and the fact that I already knew far more than you would ever dream of and didn't deserve you. That Christmas I told myself I'd found a girl worth waiting for, that you'd stay safe with your family until I could sweep you off your feet and take you with me the instant you were ready to marry me and sail the seven seas at my side.'

Since it was the dream she'd dreamt herself, she blinked determinedly and reminded herself it hadn't come true. He hadn't bothered to come back to Hollowhurst until the day he appeared out of the dusky gloom as if he was the ghost of all her stupid dreams made manifest, but too late to fulfil her childish fantasies, if not a full decade too late then by at least seven or eight years. 'Then why didn't you come back for me?' she demanded huskily.

'Because I saw too much, knew too much by then to besmirch your ardent young innocence,' he explained and ran his hand through his wildly disarrayed golden hair, as if struggling to find the words that usually sprang so glibly on to his tongue. 'I'm damaged goods, Roxanne. The moment I rode away from here that first time, I began to doubt I was good enough for you, but at the end of another few years at sea I knew very well that I wasn't. Did you think I didn't know you were there that night in London? I saw you and made sure that you had to watch me flirt and rake and gamble the night away and then leave that damned ball with a noble harlot on my arm.'

'Because you didn't care,' she said flatly, only to see him shake his head passionately, as if the emotions he denied being capable of wouldn't let her speak such blasphemy.

'No, because you'd grown up so hopeful, so rich with promise of the extraordinary woman you were about to become, and I couldn't let myself have you and spoil it all.'

'Well, I suppose I was a virgin, after all,' she informed him with such off-balance defensiveness she wasn't really surprised when the whip of her inferred meaning made him frown with disbelief, then look at her as if she was some new and not very pleasant species.

'Marriage or nothing, then and now,' he grated implacably.

'I can't recall being offered that choice when I was silly enough to accept eagerly, or we might have been miserably unhappy together for years by now,' she sniped back and groaned aloud as she realised she'd admitted that she would have accepted him eagerly then in her defensive fury.

'I knew it, I knew I couldn't want you like this unless you wanted me back,' he said clumsily and she wondered fleetingly if they were fated to flounder about trampling all over each other's finer feelings for the whole of this interminable day.

'I do feel something—a strong desire for you to go away and not trouble me with your feeble excuses and false promises ever again, Sir Charles.'

'No, you don't.'

'Allow me to know what I want better than you do, sir,'

'No, for you haven't the experience to know what you're feeling.' He held up his hand when she would have spoken, as if commanding his ship once more by force of will and the smallest gesture, and she shot him a dagger look. 'You ventured a little too deep into the sensual world of lovers for your own good today, Roxanne, but you're too much a lady to let yourself feel how deeply your body and mine worship each other now you're out of my arms. I swear that I never felt such a potent connection to any other woman before, so this is new ground even for me.'

'So apparently you desire me, but you don't love me. And, once upon a time, you would have offered for me if you only had had the courage to do so, but you didn't. Then you expect me to believe that now you've decided you can't live without me after all, and insist that a mere kiss that your grandmother kindly overlooked seeing must bind us together for ever?'

'Well, not quite for ever,' he was foolish enough to quip back.

'Not at all for ever, not even for a little bit of it, sir. I won't marry you, and, if you'd like me to do so, I'm quite prepared to have a notice inserted in the relevant papers to that effect.'

'Of course I wouldn't, don't be ridiculous.'

'Then oblige me by going away.'

'I might just as well, since you're going to argue that black's white any moment now, but I'll ask you again, Miss Roxanne Courland, and again and again until you see sense and say yes.'

'I already have, it's you who insists on being a bull-headed idiot.'

'A failing I've possessed since birth, or at least according to my grandmother,' he agreed, with a return to his usual light indifference that she somehow hated, although she'd been silently wishing he would stop being intense and so worryingly persistent for the last ten minutes.

'Good day, Sir Charles,' she replied repressively and stood back from his quickest path to the door in the hope he'd take it.

'On the whole I'd have to agree, it's been a *very* good one,' he informed her with silky menace as he obliged her by strolling toward the doorway as if he hadn't a care in the world, only to pause in front of her to inspect her with wolfish thoroughness. 'Indeed, the more memorable moments were truly exceptional, my Roxanne,' he added as his head lowered to hers, and the force of his gaze fascinated her, even as his mouth met hers with instant fire, complete desire flaming up between them as if they'd left off that long, sensuous embrace just seconds ago.

Her lips parted even as their eyes stayed open and aware, very aware. His were startlingly blue and wanting as he compelled her with his kiss, binding them into lovers as his mouth teased hers open under his and he plunged his tongue into the shameless welcome waiting for him. Before she could give herself away and let her hands reach up round his neck and pull him closer, even deeper into this undeniable need, he lifted his head and gave her a rather boyish smile that all but disarmed her.

'At least promise you'll remember this while I'm away, Roxanne? I'm not sure I can live without you, and whatever I feel for you now, I promise you I never felt for another woman.'

Her turn to raise an eyebrow in sceptical cynicism, but he looked so pained by what he'd just told her she believed him and doubted she'd forget the thrill and heat while he was gone however much she wanted to.

'I'll remember,' she said carefully, unwilling to say anything he could misinterpret as agreeing to a marriage she couldn't endure on his terms.

'Until next week then, Miss Courland,' he said

by way of farewell and made her an elegant bow before striding off with one last hungry look.

Listening to him joke with Simkins while he collected his hat and cane as if he hadn't a care in the world, Roxanne wondered if she'd dreamt the last minutes. At least it argued he suffered her own restless frustration for him to walk here in the first place, and a large part of her wished she was walking back to the Castle at his side, ready to share his life as his wife. Except he'd always keep part of himself back, and she couldn't bear such a marriage with him of all people.

For now it mightn't matter, could even add to her fascination with him and the delights he showed her when his wicked mouth, inventive hands and hard, very masculine body centred entirely on her pleasure for the breath-stealing moments when it didn't seem to matter if he loved her or even trusted her. One day, though, it would part them as surely as if he were still at sea and a thousand leagues away from her. It troubled her that she must find out his real reason for giving her such a disgust of him all those years ago in London before she dare trust him with her future, and she didn't think he'd ever willingly tell her.

No, it was her very self she must know was safe with him before she could be his wife, and love on one side couldn't sustain a good marriage without complete trust to bind them together. A bad marriage with Charles Afforde would be worse than staying at Mulberry House for the rest of her life. She'd long ago realised that fairy-tales were just that, but if he thought she'd settle for a lukewarm arranged marriage, he was mistaken. She touched her lips, exploring what he'd taught her, and felt tingles of heat shiver through her as she relived the memory of his passionate seduction. They were sensually compatible, but what use was that if he didn't want *her,* the real Roxanne?

Trying not to wonder how she'd endure the rest of her life without such delights, now she knew them and that more could follow, Roxanne left her drawing room with most of her flags flying and launched into a whirlwind inspection of her already immaculate house that set the servants' hall humming like a kettle about to let off a lot of steam.

Chapter Twelve

'You're very poor company tonight, Charles. I might as well have stayed in town, for all it's so deadly dull this time of year,' Lady Samphire told her grandson over dinner at Hollowhurst Castle that night.

'You couldn't bring yourself to stay away an instant longer,' he replied.

'Of course I could, but I admit I do have to amuse myself however I can at my age, especially now you've immured yourself in the country.'

'Admit it, you're a nosy old woman,' Charles said with a grin as he nodded dismissal to Mereson and the hovering footmen; he was never sure what his grandmother might say next and it seemed as well to limit the damage.

'I'm not nosy, I'm perceptive and wise,' she argued.

'And nosy.'

'If being concerned for your happiness makes me nosy then, yes, I'm guilty as charged. More dutiful grandsons would be grateful for the interest of their elders and betters and treat them with proper respect.'

'And you'd cut me out of your life for good if I ever showed the slightest signs of becoming such a spineless want-wit.'

'True, half an hour with that mealy-mouthed gaggle of females your father saddled himself with when he wed Euphemia Crawley always makes me wonder why I ain't been allowed to poison their soup as a service to humanity. Louis should've known better than to make up to a widow with five daughters. Bound to end in trouble,' Lady Samphire said brusquely.

Her notoriously crushing pronouncements were one reason why Mereson and his acolytes were probably listening at the door at this very moment, Charles decided ruefully, hoping they hadn't caught her gruff speech. He'd not been fully accepted as the master of Hollowhurst yet and didn't want them deciding the Afforde family were homicidal maniacs.

'I take it you're out of temper because I promised to attend my stepsister Charis's engagement party before you descended on me without warning?' he asked laconically.

'No fun if I'm expected,' she admitted and surprised him into a smile that reached his eyes for the first time that evening. 'That's better, no need to pretend you're a heartless rake and care for nobody with me, m'boy. You've done your best for that woman *and* those die-away girls while your father hides in his study writing second-rate poetry and drinking cherry brandy. Pretend to be hard-hearted as a stone statue with the rest of the world if you like, but I know you better, m'boy, I brought you up.'

'How could I forget, even if I wanted to?' he asked ruefully.

'Did your best to these last twenty years, you reprobate, but I'm glad you're settled at last, Charles. High time you found something to do with your life other than kill Frenchmen, and that girl suits you. She's got character.'

'That she has, too much to be easily persuaded to marry me.'

'Didn't seem to be fighting you off when I came across you both behaving disgracefully this morning,' she observed with a sidelong glance to see how he might react to such a reminder.

Luckily he'd known her a very long time and managed a bland smile, despite his urge to keep his relations with Roxanne fiercely private, even from his grandmother. 'And if only that were enough to convince her we'd suit,' he muttered, half to himself.

'If all you're worried about is her "suiting", no wonder she ain't convinced. You used to have a surer touch with women.'

'Roxanne Courland isn't just any woman,' he said shortly, unable to keep the words back, even as he knew she'd seize on them with glee.

'No, because she's *the* woman, isn't she?' she obliged happily.

'Certainly she's the woman I wish to make my wife,' he answered carefully, but obviously not carefully enough.

'And you think I'm fool enough to believe that's all there is to it? I wasn't born yesterday or even the day before that. You love her, boy, and it's high time you learnt it won't crack the world in two if you let her see who you really are under that rakehell reputation you've fostered so carefully.'

'I don't love her, I value her. Very highly indeed, but love is for boys.'

'And girls?'

'They wrap up their true need to feel friendship and trust towards the man they marry with soft words and rosy ideals. Luckily, Roxanne is a woman now and will soon realise that what we'll have if she weds me is better than a fleeting passion bound to fly out of the window at the first setback.'

'Had this argument about women and marriage with your friend Rob Besford lately, have you?' she said slyly.

'Hah! He's a traitor to the cause if ever I came across one. He made every error a husband could, before, during and after marrying Caro, and still ended up totally besotted with his wife and she with him.'

'My point exactly,' his grandmother said with satisfaction.

'I'm not about to follow his ridiculous example, so you can take that smug look off your face and set your mind to plotting how I can get Miss Courland to accept my suit some time before we're both old and grey. It's you who's always demanding I supply you with yet more great-grandchildren, after all, and at this rate we'll both be too decrepit to enjoy them.'

'I'm not decrepit,' she replied shortly, 'nor am I fool enough to persuade that girl to accept such a bad bargain as you'll make her if you don't feel more than lust and liking for her.'

'I'm not going to offer her a lie. I think too much of her for that,' he said in a hard voice she rarely heard from him.

She sighed and said seriously, 'I love you, Charles, probably too much for my own good, but there are times when I could cheerfully push you into the nearest lake, you infuriate me so much. No, don't shrug me off, this is far too important for that,' she warned with a militant look. 'Just because your father made a figure of himself with his infatuations and his silly affairs when you were a boy, there's no need to think love's a figment of the imagination. Exact opposite, if you ask me, considering the idiot provides you with an excellent example of what love *isn't*. Must have dropped him on his head when he was a baby,' she ended, looking pained and deeply frustrated as she spoke of her third son.

'I dare say, or maybe he's a changeling,' he joked, hating to see her unhappy as she usually was when discussing his father.

'Then how come he looks so like your grand-father?'

'Speaking of whom, I don't see how you can

insist I make a love match when you didn't your-self,' he pointed out cunningly, then instantly regretted it as her eyes clouded with memories and what he could have sworn was a haze of tears.

'That's exactly why. Samphire may not have made a love match, but I did. Not even for you could I sit by twiddling my thumbs while you put that girl through what I had to bear myself, Charles, it hurt too much for me to do that.'

'I'll be faithful to her until our respective dying days,' he protested half-heartedly.

He recalled the casual affection with which his grandfather had treated his extraordinary wife, as if she were a particularly fine spaniel he'd taught a surprising variety of tricks, but still a favourite pet rather than an equal, and wondered anew at just how much pain his light-hearted grandfather had caused her over the years. She'd stayed at Verebourne Park, managing his house and estates and raising their five sons and then himself, while his grandfather lived more or less as he pleased.

Practical and down to earth as his own father had never been, the last Lord Samphire had been largely insensitive to his wife's feelings and needs and had lived an essentially separate life from her and his boys once he'd done his duty to the succession and sired them. He'd taken his seat in the Lords, done his duty and run his estates and then entertained his friends more like a single man than a husband and father. Although Charles had shared a fond relation-ship with the old reprobate, he'd often thought his grandmother as lonely within marriage as many spinsters were without one.

'I didn't mind his mistresses, I even rather liked that fierce Spanish opera singer he never quite dared leave in case she came after him with a dagger,' Lady Samphire told him with rare seriousness. 'It was the absence of so much of him when we *were* together that hurt so much. I can't find words to say how it felt to be unimportant to the man I loved, Charles; all I can tell you is I wouldn't put a female I liked as instantly as I did that girl of yours through a week, let alone a lifetime, of such a marriage if I could prevent it.'

'But she's not unimportant to me, and I'd never treat her as Grandfather did you, love. Do you think I learnt nothing from you all?'

For once his smile only won him a brooding look and he shifted under it and decided he'd rather face the enemy again than see her unhappy.

'No, I think you learnt too much,' she argued sadly. 'Your father is a selfish lightweight who spent most of your boyhood falling in love with whatever bosomy blonde was his muse that week, while your grandfather found amusements outside marriage. You grew up watching me try not to be a fool over a man who set me on the same level as his favourite hunter, so it's little wonder you decided to hold aloof from such emotions.'

'It's not that,' he said impulsively, unable to bear the sight of her castigating herself for his own lack of romantic illusions.

'Then whatever is it?'

'Private,' he said sternly, for he refused to bare his soul even to her, but she'd given him a great deal to think about and at least a week spent with his father and stepfamily would give him plenty of time to do it in.

He was relieved when his grandmother shrugged, as if she'd done all she could to make him see reason, and put her formidable dowager mask back on before regally informing him she liked port and brandy and had no intention of being banished to the drawing room while he enjoyed his.

Yet had he let his father's and grandfather's poor examples colour his thinking? He frowned into his brandy glass and contemplated the idea of being so influenced with considerable dismay. He'd loved them both once upon a time, but nowadays Louis Afforde resented the son he'd rejected for being wealthy and successful when he was neither, and there was nothing he could do about that even if he wanted to.

He loved Lady Samphire, though; she'd filled the lonely places in his heart and given him the steadfast, but not uncritical, affection he'd needed to enjoy a carefree boyhood once he left his father's so-called care. So she was wrong in thinking he wouldn't love anyone. What he wouldn't do was fall for the myth of romantic love between a man and a woman. It was a comfortable enough illusion, he supposed, so long as said man and woman stayed away from high tragedy, of course. He'd never fancied himself a Romeo and the very thought made him smile sardonically into his fine cognac.

No, he'd an affection for Roxanne Courland that had already lasted far longer than any imaginary romance ever would, and he desired her with an unrelenting passion beyond anything he'd felt in the past for other women, but he refused to call it 'love' when love died and left the object of it alone and dissatisfied. His future with Roxanne was too important for that, and if they were to have a lifetime of affection and commitment with each other, he'd no intention of risking it all for the fancy façade of a gimcrack romance that might please everyone but him, until the gilt wore off.

'That colour suits you wonderfully well, Roxanne,' Stella told her as they let Mereson's acolytes take their warm cloaks and then spent a few moments brushing out the few creases the short journey from Mulberry House had put in their gowns.

'And I like midnight-blue velvet a good deal more than the black one you wanted, even if Lady Samphire will tell you she can't see much difference by candlelight, Stella,' Roxanne said as she controlled the slight shaking of her hand as she fussed with imaginary lint on her amber velvet skirts.

It was ten days since Sir Charles Afforde had proposed to her last and nothing short of wild horses would persuade her to admit that she'd

missed him. Or that she felt ridiculously nervous of meeting him in public now he'd returned
home and was probably still waiting for her to
change her mind.

'Great-Aunt Augusta mourns the unwieldy
panniers and acres of brocade I can just recall
seeing her in when I was in my nursery, or at
least when I should have been. Charles and I
used to creep downstairs while our nurses gossiped by the fire in the day nursery to watch the
grown-ups entertain.'

'I dare say you were an impossible pair,' Roxanne replied, as the very thought of Charles as a
golden-haired scamp with a smile as deceptively
innocent as a fair June morning threatened to
melt her determination to resist his present, very
adult appeal.

'According to her ladyship we were a pair
of hell-born brats, but she still saw we got the
finest titbits from her parties before summarily returning us to our beds whenever we got
caught.'

Roxanne laughed and thought that sounded
very like the formidable old lady who she'd soon
discovered concealed a heart soft as butter under
her gruff and cynical manner.

'I can tell you two haven't been pining for

my company.' Sir Charles's deep voice broke into their conversation, and Roxanne thought he ought to be made to wear hobnailed boots at all times to stop him ghosting about the place, making her jump.

'Of course not,' she allowed herself to tell him with a smug smile.

'Whilst I, of course, have been desolate,' he told her soulfully.

'Mountebank,' she categorised him sternly.

'No, it's true,' he assured her, not seeming at all cast down by her unenthusiastic greeting. 'Anyone would be desolate to be marooned in the exclusive company of my closest family. I've just endured it for over a week and not even Miss Courland's finest swallowing-vinegar face, so often pulled at the very sight of me, I mourn to say, can dull the joy of making my escape without being forced to bring at least one of my female relatives home with me so she can make my life uncomfortable at her leisure.'

'You're planning to disown your grandmother, then?' she asked, carefully ignoring the warm glow in his eyes as they rested on her, giving his light-hearted flirtation the lie by silently conveying the message he had honourable intentions whether she liked them or not.

'No, although she says she'll disown me if I can't persuade you to marry me.'

'Oh, hush, Sir Charles!' she urged as she looked about to see who might be listening and would forever be eyeing her with eager speculation from now on. But had his comment been careless or cunning? She was inclined to believe the latter and glared at him militantly.

'I don't think anyone else heard him,' Stella declared, looking very interested while she pretended she wasn't really listening.

'You could always say "yes", and then we could announce it straight away,' he offered, as if it were a real possibility, though she had no intention of being stampeded into marriage by him or his grandmama.

'And I could also have the good sense to hope you're joking.'

'When I never was more serious in my life?' he quipped, but could that possibly be the faintest hint of hurt in his cerulean gaze? Most unlikely.

'I very much doubt it, sir, and this is neither the time nor the place for a serious discussion, even if you were.'

'No, indeed, but it's high time I put my name down for the supper dance, before your besotted swain tries to mill me down in his desperation to claim it.'

'Tries?' she asked with that useful, ironic raising of her eyebrows she'd learnt from him.

'Oh, yes, I'm not too gentlemanly to resist planting him a facer before either of us are very much older, Miss Courland, but I think we'd both prefer it if I didn't have to do so as his host.' She shuddered at the very thought and silently held out her dance card. 'Very wise,' he teased as he initialled away.

'Only two,' she warned.

'Do you think me a country clodpole as well, my dear?' he murmured as he handed her card back, making very sure their fingers met and she felt the spark of desire run through her at the contact, just as he did if the sudden heat in his eyes was anything to go by.

'I doubt you were that simple even when you were in short-coats,' she replied and tried not to feel pleased with herself when he laughed. The real laugh she loved, the one that lit his eyes with humour and lured her into a world of intimacy she'd not dreamt of in many long years, not since he ignored her at her come-out party, she reminded herself, and removed her hand from his as if he'd stung her.

'Until later, then?' he said, standing back and watching her cautiously, the lovely possibility that flashed between them so briefly suddenly gone.

'Later,' she echoed with a shiver that had nothing to do with the temperature in the blue saloon Lady Samphire had very sensibly decided to use for her party, rather than the loftier great hall that would take whole tree-trunks burning in each of its huge hearths to even take the chill off it now winter was so well on its way.

'And just what was all that about?' Stella demanded as soon as they were comfortably seated on an elegant *chaise longue* that certainly hadn't come with the castle furnishings.

'Nothing,' Roxanne said, fervently wishing it were true.

'Then that's the most interesting piece of nothing I've heard in a very long time,' her friend replied with a resolute look in her grey eyes that she'd probably be horrified to hear made her look very like her great-aunt. 'Ah, Mr Longborough, here we are, hardly sat down and you already want me to get up and dance with you. What a very energetic young gentleman you are, to be sure.'

For once Roxanne blessed Joe as she watched

him reluctantly carry off his chattering partner to join the first set forming at the end of the room, where the carpets had been removed for safekeeping and safe dancing. She didn't want to dance, and she certainly didn't want anyone else to know about that disgraceful episode in the garden that she could now see outlined in the darkness by a bright blaze of candlelight and flambeaux. Sir Charles surely couldn't have set them there for the very purpose of keeping it in the forefront of her mind?

It surprised her to find that what she really wanted at this moment was privacy. She imagined dancing by that golden light among the statues with Charles Afforde and him alone. Maybe just an orchestra shut away in the blue saloon where they couldn't see her and she couldn't see them. And Charles, of course—he could even wear a greatcoat in return for her best evening cloak if he didn't like the chill of the November night biting through that rather fine black evening coat and his immaculate evening breeches. She shivered, but again not from any feeling of coldness, and told herself not to be an idiot.

'Good evening, Mr Huntley,' she greeted her promised dance-partner with such a fine impression of delight that his eyes brightened and she gave an internal groan.

Now look what she'd done; soon she'd have three gentlemen proposing to her at every turn and not a one of them she could accept, unless Sir Charles underwent a complete about-face and decided he might be able to love her, after all.

'Miss Courland, you look so very beautiful tonight,' the young man said with such devastating enthusiasm she had to fight a fit of the giggles.

'Oh, no, I was never considered a beauty even in my younger days, and if you'd witnessed my come out all those years ago, sir, you'd certainly never classify me so,' she said in an effort to dampen his enthusiasm.

'Surely not so many years ago?' he asked archly.

'Seven,' she informed him flatly.

That made him pause, but the Huntleys were evidently made of stern stuff and he rallied. 'Then you must have been a very young débutante, Miss Courland,' he said gallantly, and she almost smiled at his ingenuity, but that would only encourage him and she truly didn't want to bruise his feelings, even if she doubted his heart was engaged.

'I was seventeen, sir, but that's no excuse. I made a spectacularly unsuccessful début and don't have the slightest desire to endure the London Season ever again,' she said, hoping her unsociable leanings would put him off angling for such an unsuitable, and ancient, bride.

Another mistake, it seemed, for he smiled with relief and looked at her as though she'd suddenly gone from acceptable to nigh perfect as a potential wife. 'Neither have I; in fact, I hate doing the pretty,' he assured her earnestly, then looked a little uncertain as he realised that might not be the most tactful thing to say to a woman he was attempting to court. 'Except when I mean it, of course,' he added, trying to rescue himself from a dangerous quagmire.

'Oh, of course. Now hadn't we better join your friend on the dance floor?' she admitted in a reasonable imitation of delighted anticipation.

'Not sure he's my friend any more,' he replied and Roxanne wondered how her life had become so complex, when until recently it'd been so simple.

'Young gentlemen have the habit of falling out, so I'm sure you'll very soon make it up with your friend, Mr Huntley,' she said encouragingly.

Once they both realised she had no intention of marrying either of them, any reason for continuing bitterness between them would fade as rapidly as it had appeared, wouldn't it?

'I don't mind telling you I've seen another side to Joe these last few weeks, Miss Courland,' he said uneasily, and Roxanne wondered exactly what had passed between them to turn this delightful young man from Joe's steadfast friend into such an uneasy rival.

'Well, here we are at the floor, sir, so let's forget our worries in the dance, shall we? I do like a merry country dance, don't you?'

'Of course, nothing can rival it,' he gallantly agreed, despite the fact that its measures ensured he spent very little time in conversation with his partner.

Roxanne spared him the occasional glance as he worked his way down the line of ladies, and her heart lightened to see him greet a good many with a far easier smile than he ever gave her. When he'd grown up a little, Mr Huntley would make some lucky girl a fine husband. What a shame he couldn't see how unsuitable a match they would make of it if she was fool enough to encourage him. Not only was she three years his senior, but she'd never make him a docile little wife, ready to adore him for the rest of their days and defer to his superior judgement. No, what he needed was a pretty girl who was ready, willing and able to fall in love with an uncomplicated gentleman with a kind heart. She'd gone past that before she even made her début, thanks to a certain gentleman she was doing her best to ignore as they wound down the measures of the same set.

'You know,' Sir Charles murmured in her ear as she tried to slip past him without any but the most casual contact, 'I'm not sure if I prefer dancing with you, Roxanne, or watching you move so enchantingly while some other idiot does so.'

'You categorise yourself as an idiot then, Sir Charles? Surely you're being a little harsh on yourself?' she muttered back and whisked away before he could retaliate, but soon there would be that first waltz and doubtless he'd have his revenge.

Chapter Thirteen

'So *are* you going to marry my cousin, Roxanne?' Stella asked her relentlessly, as soon as she'd dispatched Mr Huntley and Joe Longborough to fetch lemonade, never mind that they didn't appear to be speaking to one another and neither she nor Roxanne was particularly thirsty.

'No,' she replied as softly as she could when her instinct was to shout it as loudly as possible, in the hope it would then become an irrefutable truth before she began to wonder at herself for turning him down as well.

'I can't imagine him ever meeting anyone who'd suit him better,' Stella replied mournfully. 'Won't you reconsider, Roxanne?'

'Certainly not.'

'Oh, very well then. I suppose he'll have to take his chance with some silly débutante who lacks the sense to ever be his equal.'

'Yes, he will.'

'Such a waste though, don't you think?' Stella said, using her fan to direct Roxanne's attention toward Sir Charles's superbly male figure by the door where he was gracefully waving aside a latecomer's self-reproaches.

He wasn't in the least overawed or out of place in this huge room, designed to trumpet its owner's wealth and position to all comers from royalty downwards. He'd stand out if he'd contented himself with living in a hovel, Roxanne decided despairingly, and little wonder her younger self had only had to set eyes on such a dominant, masculine warrior to decide he must be hers one day.

Now Roxanne watched him with every bit of the fascination Stella might wish for. He bowed to the gruff wife of a neighbouring squire and endured being slapped on the back by her husband with good-humoured patience, and she thought that, yes, he would make an excellent husband, as long as his wife wasn't in love with him. If she were, and Roxanne feared she might very well be, then he'd make her deeply unhappy, because he didn't seem at all willing to entertain the notion he might love her back. Yet wouldn't it also be agony to see him wed another? A question she'd done her best to avoid considering while he was away and might be meeting a paragon who wouldn't demand he loved her before she considered marriage.

'Not all débutantes are stupid,' she protested weakly, unable to tear her gaze from the tall figure of Charles Afforde, whose starkly elegant evening attire only added to his manly attractions, rather than having the grace to make him look just like any other man present tonight.

'But even the ones who are intelligent still have matchmaking mamas, who'll make very sure their daughters don't refuse a handsome baronet with a handsome property and an even more handsome fortune.'

'Rather a lot of handsomes there, don't you think?'

'No,' Stella insisted ruthlessly. 'Most females would tread on the faces of their friends in their eagerness if he danced with them twice, mamas or no, and you won't even consider marrying him when he begs you to.'

'He always dances with *me* twice,' she pointed out rather childishly.

'Yes, because he actually wants to marry you,' Stella pointed out with merciless patience. 'Charles was never one to raise false hopes.'

'But I've never harboured any,' Roxanne protested.

'What, never?'

Roxanne blushed and recalled the headlong, romantic girl she'd once been. Young though Lieutenant Afforde was at the time, he'd have been a fool *not* to notice her blatant adoration when they first met. She'd made sure he fell over her every time he turned round that Christmas when she'd confidently decided he must be her adult fate. Then she'd made her come out at a ridiculously young age, because he might not wait for her if she didn't badger Uncle Granger into arranging her début as soon as possible. Could any girl's hopes have been wilder or more unrealistic than young Rosie Courland's had proved all those years ago?

'Certainly not from the moment I realised at the tender age of seventeen that your cousin was a rake and hadn't the slightest intention of settling down with a wife, or at least not with one of his own.'

'How scandalous of you to have known such liaisons existed at so young an age.'

'Yes, wasn't it? Now can we talk of something else? I find myself growing weary of endlessly speculating about your cousin's wife.'

'As you just pointed out, dear Roxanne, he doesn't actually have one for us to speculate about.'

'No, and long may that situation last, for I pity the poor girl who takes him on when he does find one.'

'I think he already has,' Stella insisted stubbornly.

'Then you're wrong.'

'So does Great-Aunt Augusta, by the way; I can tell that by the way she keeps nodding and winking at me to hint I should leave you alone in order for my cousin to swoop down and claim you,' Stella said, attempting to rise to her feet as Lady Samphire was indeed indicating she should with almost comical contortions. Comical if they weren't aimed at Roxanne's public embarrassment.

'Then she's wrong, too, and don't you dare,' Roxanne said, holding on to Stella's midnight-blue skirts so that she had to pause halfway between sitting and standing, then plumped back down with a rueful shrug at her formidable aunt.

'So undignified,' she protested virtuously.

'Yes, isn't it?' Roxanne replied candidly, and Stella's eyes fell before the resolve in her own not to be manoeuvred into a *tête-à-tête* with Charles.

Dancing with him would be quite bad enough without being forced into his heady company for goodness knew how long while the company gossiped about them and Lady Samphire spread rumours with joyful abandon.

'I won't be trapped, tricked or persuaded into marriage with Sir Charles, Stella. Indeed, I'd choose scandal and opprobrium rather than let that happen.'

'I'm not trying to trick you, it's just that you're so right for each other,' Stella excused herself apologetically.

'Thank you, but excuse me if I disagree.'

'Why?'

'What do you mean, "why"? Of course it's a silly notion.'

'I don't see why it's such a ludicrous idea.'

'Because Sir Charles and myself are opposites in every way. He's just weary of raking and travelling the world, and I'm a novelty to him because I've never been anywhere much or even had a serious suitor. I also know his house and estates better than he does himself, and could run them for him while he's busy elsewhere, and there you have his reasons for marriage.'

'He's made a fine mess of that, then, hasn't he?' Stella said with what looked oddly like satisfaction from where Roxanne was sitting.

'He did his best to seduce me into it as well,' she admitted with a blush.

'How comforting to know some of his famous sangfroid hasn't deserted him, poor Charles.'

'Poor Charles?' Roxanne demanded. 'Family feeling must count for a lot, I know, but why should he be "poor Charles" when I'm the one being bombarded like some foreign citadel he's been ordered to conquer?'

'Because he'd do anything to avoid admitting to himself that he's head over heels in love with you, of course,' Stella explained, as if explaining the obvious to a very slow three-year-old.

Roxanne just sat there with her mouth open, staring at her companion with such astonishment that her ears buzzed with shock and hid the sound of approaching footsteps, if he had made any sound, of course.

'I believe this is our dance, Miss Courland,' the subject of it all observed urbanely, looking far more innocent than he'd any right to.

'Is it?' she asked him idiotically and blushed ridiculously as he met her eyes with an ironic question in his.

'Well, if you doubt me, I suppose we could always take a look at your dance-card,' he offered, but the prospect of having him come even close enough to do that made her wonder if she might lower herself to faking a fit of the vapours—how on earth was she going to endure a waltz in his arms?

'No, I recall it now,' she mumbled, fixing her eyes on the top button of his immaculate grey-silk waistcoat. Maybe if she refused to look at him, she'd be able to pretend to herself that she was dancing with just any gentleman.

'Whatever has my cousin been saying to you, Roxanne?' he asked as they joined the other couples on the dance floor and waited for the musicians to launch into the latest waltz tune from Vienna.

'Nothing very much,' she replied, just managing to avoid his acute gaze by focusing instead on his shoulder as he relentlessly adopted the position required, and her body reacted as if she'd been shocked by Signor Galvini's electrical machine.

'I thought we knew each other better than this, Roxanne,' he murmured, refusing to be the handsome marionette she would have preferred to dance with while she settled her nerves and examined Stella's outrageous assertion that he loved her for any grains of truth.

'Better than what?' she asked incautiously and cursed her body for twining itself as close to his as the dance and propriety would allow.

'Than avoiding my eyes as if you hate the very sight of me, or pretending we're polite acquaintances enduring a duty dance,' he insisted relentlessly. 'I'd rather you refused to take the floor in my company in the first place than this, Roxanne, for your behaviour informs me you regret our kiss and our intimacy, and that's like finding out the world's flat after all, and don't forget I'm a seaman, will you? That would hold serious implications for a man who might sail off the edge if he ever returned to his old occupation.'

Torn between finding him irresistible for his weak attempt at humour and hating the very idea of him sailing away from her, she flinched. Constant fear for his safety had been hard enough to live with when she was a silly girl infatuated with a handsome face, but now she was a grown woman and truly loved him, it would be close to hell.

'Don't,' she urged tensely.

'Don't what? Don't speak of such ridiculous

things, or don't refuse to pretend all's well and it doesn't matter that you turn your eyes away from mine as if I might turn you to stone if you meet them? I'm sorry, but I can't oblige you, my dear; we've come too far for me to allow it.'

'Allow?' she asked haughtily, meeting his intense blue gaze with queenly dignity and nearly causing a collision by unconsciously halting to recruit all her energies to recover from the effort it had cost her.

'Come, you're clearly in no mood for all this flim-flam,' he informed her in a gruff voice and with a polite apology and a dazzling smile for the lady they'd just nearly caused to trip, he murmured something about the heat and swept her off the floor in the crook of a powerful arm.

'I suppose this must be your best commodore's manner?' she asked, as she obligingly wilted into his embrace to lend colour to his tale.

'Well, someone needs to take control,' he informed her angrily.

'I have an aversion to being controlled.'

'That much is self-evident, Miss Courland. You're so stubborn that you're in danger of cutting off both our noses to spite my face.'

'That doesn't even *sound* right,' she muttered darkly and surprised a bark of laughter out of him that nearly undid their whole story of her being overcome by anything but his presence.

'Slight cough,' he explained to Mrs Longborough in passing as he swept Roxanne towards the sofa where Stella was waiting.

'Lot of it about, young people today lack stamina,' she replied blandly.

'Not stamina, just good sense,' he replied with an openly condemning glance in Roxanne's direction.

'Must be catching,' the Squire's wife said with an abrupt nod at her own son that told them succinctly how few of his faults and foibles she'd missed.

'And therefore probably curable,' Charles said, a rueful smile at last eclipsing his unusually savage temper.

The very fact that she could infuriate him so easily made Roxanne pause and consider again Stella's startling declaration that he loved her. She certainly had it in her power to break through the cynically amused façade he used to fend off the world in general. Quite what that meant she hadn't yet worked out, but it meant something. Whatever that 'something' might be, she refused to embroider his story by drooping elegantly at Stella's side while he went to fetch yet more lemonade to revive her when she didn't need reviving.

'I should vastly prefer a cup of tea,' she informed him truthfully as she sat straight-backed in contravention of his fairy story.

'I'll inform Mereson; no doubt he'll produce it in the midst of an evening party with all the air of an archbishop asked to perform conjuring tricks, but he'll produce it all the same if I tell him it's for you.'

'He's always claimed to like a challenge,' Roxanne replied blandly.

'Don't we all?' he answered inexcusably, then strolled off to bother his butler with his impenetrable, ridiculous statements instead of her.

'Speaking of challenges, how *are* you intending to explain your exit from the dance when you now look as if you never had a day's illness in your entire life, Roxanne?' Stella asked curiously.

'Simple,' she explained grandly, 'I'll take a leaf out of Lady Samphire's book and refuse to justify my actions by pretending they didn't happen.'

'Oh, Lord, will you? The prospect of two of you marching about the neighbourhood manipulating all and sundry for their own good very nearly terrifies me enough to make me return to the Dower House and endure Mama and Great-Aunt Letty's endless moralising.'

'I only said a leaf, not the entire volume with appendix and addenda.'

'There are never any addenda to Great-Aunt Augusta's pronouncements for she simply *never* makes mistakes,' Stella declared solemnly, and Roxanne laughed. 'That's better, you look less likely to eat the next person who asks how you are now,' Stella added—how could she stay angry when her friend, companion and possible future relative was so witty, warm and caring?

Charles's family was not, perhaps, his closest blood kin but rather the family he loved and who loved him—Robert Besford and his unconventional wife; the absent and yet often-spoken-of Will, Lord Wrovillton, and his apparently even less conventional lady; then, closer to home, were Lady Samphire, Stella, and Tom Varleigh and, of course, her own sister Joanna. The people he'd just spent a weary week with should be his family, of course, but Roxanne didn't have to be told that Charles Afforde probably felt closer to his dogs or his horses.

'It's all your fault,' she felt compelled to tell Stella all the same.

'What is?'

'That I nearly tripped up Lady Trickley and caused even more widespread social catastrophe just now, as well as serious injury.'

'Oh, why?'

'You know perfectly well why.'

'I do, indeed—so, are you going to marry him?'

'Probably, but you, Stella Lavender, are even more of a devious schemer than your Aunt Samphire.'

'How appalling,' Stella said happily enough and she sat back to enjoy the spectacle as Charles re-entered the room with Mereson and an attendant footman bearing the tea-things on a series of silver salvers, as if presenting treasure to royalty.

'And shall you be joining us for tea, Charles?' Stella asked innocently.

'I've drunk more of the stuff in the last couple of months than I ever did in the whole of the rest of my life as it is.'

'Confess, it's not as bad a beverage as you thought, now is it?'

'Cat lap,' he condemned as Mereson presented him with another of the glasses of fine burgundy he seemed to think Charles needed supplying with whenever tea was mentioned. 'So,' he murmured in Roxanne's ear as Stella tactfully allowed herself to be distracted by a neighbour, 'has this last week dragged on as tediously for you as it has done for me?'

'On the contrary, I was tolerably well amused,' she claimed.

'Maybe you had more conducive company then, for I certainly was not.'

'Stella and your grandmama would be furious if I said they were other than very good company, Sir Charles, and quite right, too.'

'I suppose so, but I badly missed yours,' he informed her, as if she owed him something for even so much as admitting he could do so.

'Very flattering,' she informed him with a satisfied nod she'd copied from Lady Samphire. If she was to accept him without a declaration of love, she'd no intention of letting him be the only one with secrets.

'Flattering enough for you to accept me?' he asked lightly, but with a brooding intensity in his gaze that warned her not to take it at face value.

'That depends,' she prevaricated, feeling as if her younger self was standing behind her, jumping up and down with furious impatience as older and wiser Roxanne hovered between acceptance and refusal of the man of her dreams.

'On what?' he asked, as if he would dearly love to shake her, but was far too sophisticated a man of the world to be so reckless and unmannerly under the interested gazes of their friends and neighbours.

'On what sort of a husband you intend to make me, of course. If you're offering marriage *à la mode,* then I must refuse, for I couldn't live so, Charles.'

'Of course not. I'll never look at another woman if you marry me,' he declared as sternly as if he were about to go into battle.

She sipped her tea and leaned back in her seat, watching him with what she hoped was impenetrable composure.

'Well,' he conceded at last, 'I might look, but that would be as far as I ever went, and when I did it would only be to confirm I'd be taking the most desirable female of my acquaintance home to warm my bed.'

'And would you expect me to occupy a separate sphere to yours? I don't know that I could endure being immured in the drawing room, embroidering every night, while you con your accounts and discuss racing form with your cronies over the best cognac in our cellars.'

'Then I willingly undertake to include you in any and every dissipation I indulge in from now on, and you're quite welcome to the accounts—anything else?' he enquired rather wearily and Roxanne let the words she really wanted to ask hover on the tip of her tongue, then swallowed them down with another sip of finest China tea.

'Then, if you promise to allow any children we might have to be part of our lives, as well,' she went on gallantly, despite the fiery blush she was sure could be seen across the ballroom, 'I think we could come to terms,' she managed without even mentioning the possibility of a love match.

'They will be at the very centre of it,' he promised her huskily, and trust him to turn her practical attempts at laying down a contract between them into part of her seduction. 'Their begetting will be my finest endeavour yet,' he went on, his gaze ablaze with blue heat as he subjected her to a ruthlessly sensual scrutiny that left her in no doubt as to how much he intended to enjoy it.

'Let's put the cart before the horses, shall we,

Sir Charles?' she asked in a voice she had trouble recognising as her own.

'Three weeks,' he told her implacably.

'Three weeks? That's hardly long enough to have a bridal gown made, let alone invite everyone who thinks they have a right to be at our wedding.'

'Three weeks,' he insisted. 'I'm not made of stone and much longer than that and I'll have to insist we make a start on those brats of ours without benefit of clergy.'

'I might have something to say about that,' she protested in a voice that didn't even convince her.

'I shall make quite certain you do,' he informed her arrogantly. 'You'll say "yes" over and over again,' he said, his voice a murmured promise as his eyes locked on hers with such complete certainty that she should be insulted.

'I haven't even said one very important "yes" yet,' she argued gamely.

'Then stop playing with me, Roxanne, and make me the answer we both need to hear.'

'What if one of us falls in love?' she finally offered, revealing the most important caveat of all.

'There's no such thing, and would you risk the

rare accord we have with each other for such a fleeting mirage, Roxanne? I never could and promise I honour you above any other woman on this earth and always will do. I also want you unmercifully, so if you'd just stop thinking up obstacles and agree that we're perfect for each other, I'd be obliged to you.'

'You'd be obliged to me?' she echoed, torn between the terrible temptation of his offer and those seemingly careless words.

'Stupid of me,' he snapped, impatient with himself instead of her this time. 'I'll be honoured, triumphant and the happiest man in England, let alone Kent, if you'll just say that you'll marry me, Roxanne. I've never lacked the right words with any other woman but you, which is *not* be the best way to persuade you, now I think about it. But with you I can't find the easy phrase or casual kiss that might bend your will to mine—you're too important for that.'

It was as close as she'd probably ever get to a declaration of love from him, and Roxanne let herself consider whether she *could* live the rest of her life without hearing anything more. Considering the alternative, which was to refuse him and either live her life alone or marry another man solely for the pleasure of bearing children, she finally made up her mind that she could.

'Very well, Sir Charles,' she said rather stiffly, 'I will marry you.'

'Thank Heaven for that, then,' he said on a heartfelt sigh and immediately called for champagne and silence. 'It is my undeserved good fortune in introducing Miss Courland as my newly affianced bride,' he announced to all and sundry, before she could change her mind.

Chapter Fourteen

Once upon a time there was a foolish, romantic girl who dreamt her days away, longing for her fairy-tale lover who sailed the seven seas in search of adventure and booty, and she *knew* her wild sea-rover would come home and lay his hand and his heart at her feet one day. Which was why, Roxanne reflected, as she struggled against an odd sense of unreality that fitted fairy tales better than it did a sunny winter day, she was about to become Roxanne, Lady Afforde, and one out of the two would just have to do.

When she stepped over the threshold of Hollowhurst Church today, she would commit herself to being Sir Charles Afforde's lawfully wedded wife until death did them part. The very idea of death spun her back over those anxious years when she'd scanned the newspapers for reports of his dashing exploits and studied the lists of the fallen after battles at sea with heavy dread in her heart, then exultation when she didn't find his name. Someone else's loved one, some other girl's hope of happiness, died that day and not Charles Afforde, so Mrs Roxanne Afforde lived on in her imagination. After she'd grown up and realised it was all a fairy tale, she'd still performed that ritual every time an engagement was reported, but never again had she dreamt her dream, and now it was coming true, after all.

'Have you still got my handkerchief for your something borrowed?' Stella asked anxiously as she scrambled down from the carriage to fuss over the precise arrangement of Roxanne's ivory-velvet skirts.

'Yes, Mama,' Roxanne replied with a grin at her nervous matron of honour as she managed not to fall over her fussing senior bridesmaid, '*and* the fetching blue garter your Great-Aunt Augusta presented me with last night.'

'Trust her,' Stella breathed with a sidelong look at the church as if she thought her formidable great-aunt might be able to hear her through stone walls several feet thick. 'But what about something old?'

'I wondered about wearing those comfortable old riding boots you're always nagging me about,' Roxanne teased, laughing as Stella was unable to resist peering down at her fine kid slippers, 'but I decided they didn't match and contented myself with Charles's locket instead.'

'A good choice, for I never knew him to so much as move without his mama's favourite trinket in his pocket until he gave it to you,' Stella said sagely, then scurried ahead to shoo the gaggle of little bridesmaids into the church porch ahead of them and out of a chilly December breeze.

Pulling her fur-lined cloak closer against it herself, Roxanne followed her more sedately. She'd been surprised and touched by Charles's gift, astonished that he'd part with something so personal, so obviously precious to him, when he'd said not one word of love to her all the time they'd been engaged—not that three weeks was so very long in all conscience.

'I'm expecting too much,' she murmured and recalled Lady Samphire's advice to give Charles time to come to terms with his feelings for her.

'He ain't one to let on he even has a heart, m'dear, let alone wear it on his sleeve. Not that he ain't a sentimental idiot beneath all that devil-may-care insolence, you only have to look at the

way he fusses over me to see that,' she'd concluded gruffly as she'd clung to Roxanne's hand
with surprising warmth and strength. 'He won't
admit he's capable of what I'll call romantic love
for want of a better description, though. Deep
down I think he knows he'll give his heart for
all time when he finally does so and probably
hand over his soul and his honour along with
it, and he's far too guarded to give any of them
up lightly. Are you careful enough to hold them
safe for him when he does, Roxanne?'

'I'm a Courland, and we hold fast to what we
love, my lady,' she'd asserted confidently, ex-
hilarated by the thought that one day she might
have the chance to guard Charles's love and
treasure his honour after all.

Now she wasn't quite so sure, despite her
ladyship's assurances and his promise of fidel-
ity. What if he turned his eyes elsewhere, despite his vow not to? Nobody could regulate
love and passion as he seemed to think he could,
and she closed her eyes against the very idea of
such a shattering betrayal, then blinked determinedly and told herself not to be a pessimist.
He was marrying *her,* wasn't he? He'd had most
of the eligible young ladies of the *ton* and a good
many of their less respectable sisters among the

demi-monde scrambling to snare his hand or heart, and preferably both, over the years, and he hadn't wed any of them. So, she only had to walk up the ancient path ahead of her, past the leaning gravestones and the hoary old yew tree she'd known ever since she could first re-member, and he would be joined to her in an unbreakable bond.

'Am I expecting too much, Tom?' she asked her brother-in-law as he waited patiently at her side, arm crooked to encourage her to launch herself into the true purpose of her wedding day so he could give her to her groom and get out of this biting cold wind.

'You must expect it, dear Rosie. It's your right.'

'I don't see why.'

'Because you love him, and I believe he loves you. Every bride in love with her groom must expect too much of him on their wedding day. It's obligatory and turns him from a boy into a man, irrespective of his age.'

'Lord, when did you become so wise?' she asked with such awe it reminded them both of a much younger Roxanne and a time when he was her big sister's devoted admirer and they both laughed.

'Your sister would tell you it happened the

day she wed me, but I argue it was the moment I married her and finally realised what I was taking on,' he said ruefully.

'Very well then, lead on, Oh Knowledgeable One, and when I rue the day I let you guide me up this path to meet my fate, I'll descend on you all at Varleigh and declare it to be entirely your fault I ever found the courage.'

'No, you won't, for by that time you'll be wed, and every married woman on earth knows that when something goes wrong in her life, it's sure to be the fault of her husband.'

'So be it, then,' she said lightly and met his rather anxious look with a confident smile.

'You couldn't wed a finer man,' he assured her seriously.

'I know, so shall we get on with my wedding? Before he decides we're bored with the idea and have gone to Tunbridge Wells for a little shopping and the waters, rather than meet me in front of the altar and all his friends?'

'Aye, it's devilish cold standing here and I want to be back in that barrack you call a home with a hot toddy and my wife and family for comfort as soon as may be.'

'Come along, then, do,' she encouraged him in her best imitation of her sister Maria, and so they entered the church on a triumphant crescendo played by the village band.

With the braziers having burned all night and so many people crowded into such a small church, it was warm enough inside for most to enjoy the spectacle of Sir Charles Afforde embracing his fate at long last. The sight of him waiting impatiently for her at the altar, the winter sun gilding his dark gold hair to fairness and outlining his broad-shouldered figure in close-fitting dark blue broadcloth that nearly matched his eyes, reminded Roxanne of her first glimpse of him across the snow and the shadows that fateful Christmas night.

Warmth caught at her heart, melted some chilly corner of it that was still sore with the thought that he hadn't known from that Christmas day on, probably by instinct alone, that they were fated to love and wed one day. Her breath stuttered, and she let some of her real feelings show in her eyes as she walked confidently towards him down the aisle. She'd waited so long for this day, and now it was come, it was just as wonderful as she'd always dreamt, even if he might never say he loved her. He felt something deep and powerful for her, it was unmistakable in the welcome and triumph and heat in his compelling eyes as he watched the heavy folds of silk velvet outline her supple figure as she walked, her cloak belling slightly out from her sides with the speed of her arrival, until she finally arrived, glowing and a little breathless, at his side with a radiant smile that, if she did but know it, took his breath away.

Pausing to remind herself there were others present to see them wed, Roxanne looked away from her groom to regard the posy of humble holly, ivy and hot-house camellias in her hand as if she'd never seen it before. Luckily Stella had her cohorts firmly in hand by now, so Joanna and Tom Varleigh's eldest daughter Julia seized Roxanne's bouquet, while Stella carefully turned back the bride's veil and little Roxanne Varleigh, her namesake and goddaughter as well as her niece, tottered only momentarily as she enthusiastically strewed the dried rose-petals from her basket now instead of when the married couple walked down the aisle together later because it seemed a good idea to her, which indeed it was. Consequently, Roxanne and Charles made their vows with the lingering scent of summer all about them and the sun casting golden light over them like a blessing.

'What an auspicious start to our married life,' he whispered, before he took full advantage of the vicar's permission to kiss the bride.

'Mmm,' she responded with her usual lack of words when at the mercy of even his lightest kisses. She really would have to develop some way of coping better with the world with her much-dreamed-of lover in it, when he might come upon her at any time and kiss her now they were married.

'Lady Afforde,' he said with a tender, rueful smile at his new wife, 'we really must put some work in on expanding your vocabulary.'

'Oh, but later, surely, Charles?' she gasped in shock at the very idea of what he might do to achieve that, and her husband gave an involuntary laugh that made her sister Maria's countessy nose twitch with disapproval and everyone else smile indulgently.

'Not too much later if I have anything to do with it,' he murmured in her ear before turning about to face the congregation with an openly satisfied smile on his handsome face.

'And how you expect me to make any sense of

today with a threat like that hanging over me, I'll never know,' she chided as they climbed into the fine new coach he'd brought as one of his marriage gifts to her for the short drive back to the Castle.

'Tom warned me everything would be my fault from this moment on,' he said ruefully as he settled her skirts every bit as attentively as Stella had, but with a wicked smile that told her he was enjoying the chance to linger over the way the soft silky fineness of the best velvet available outlined her figure. With his bride now thoroughly discomposed, he sprang into the coach and sat next to her with a merry wave at the assembled villagers who hadn't managed either to squeeze into the church or be invited to their reception.

'He told me that as well, and he was quite right, too,' Roxanne informed him as she, too, smiled and waved at the many villagers and estate workers who'd turned out in the cold to line their route out of the village.

'In ten years' time, do you think we'll be as happily grumpy with each other as they are?' he asked as he took her hand in his, distracting her from being tearfully touched at the enthusiastic cheers as their coach went past by removing her glove so he could admire the broad gold band now joining the graceful diamond ring on her left hand. Perhaps reassuring himself he'd finally caught her? she wondered wistfully.

'I truly hope so, I'd hate to think we might become like Maria and poor Balsover,' she replied, distracted by his touch again. Now the carriage had picked up speed and the short drive to the castle left them a brief illusion of privacy, he held her hand up to catch the watery sunlight and it shot prisms of rainbow light from the stones in the ring she still couldn't believe was hers, made as it was to look like a trail of flowers that formed the most beautiful eternity ring she could have imagined.

When he was tired of admiring that fine piece of the goldsmith's art and the broad gold band wrought delicately with what she suspected were forget-me-nots, he silenced her altogether by lifting her hand to his lips and kissing her fingers one by one, until he finally went back to her ring finger and took it into his mouth, his blazing blue gaze explicit as he ran his tongue along its fine-boned length until her eyelids went heavy and her lips opened with an invitation that he took with ravenous alacrity.

No matter how many times he kissed her, Roxanne thought with dazed wonder, every time was a delicious novelty. Then his mouth opened on hers and demanded all she had to give in return, so she gave it enthusiastically. She was breathless and hot and shaking with suppressed passion and sweet, heavy-limbed anticipation of their marriage bed when she finally realised the horses had slowed and they were almost at the great doorway of the oldest part of the castle, usually kept firmly shut at this time of year to keep the draughts at bay.

'Why didn't I just abduct you and carry you off across the Border so we wouldn't have to wait for half the county to eat us out of house and home and toast us until they're hoarse with my best champagne before we enjoy our marriage bed, my lovely wife?' he asked her rather unsteadily, and she was exultant that his hand shook nigh as badly as her own when he leapt down from the coach and held it out to receive hers, as if every move they made today was significant in some way the rest of the world couldn't dream of.

'I don't know, why didn't you?' she asked, clinging to the support of his strong arm as they mounted the steps like a king and queen taking possession of their palace, made even more of a royal progress by the fact that the castle staff were lined up there to bid them a ceremonial welcome.

'Because they would never have forgiven me,' he whispered in her ear when they finally reached the doorway and she looked back at her old friends and a few new ones Charles had brought to Hollowhurst with him and smiled at them in rather a misty attempt at thanking them for helping to make her wedding day so special.

'Nor me,' she acknowledged unsteadily and blessed Charles's sure touch as he shook Mereson's hand while the butler wished them both very happy on behalf of all the castle staff, inside and out.

'Now let's all get in out of the cold and get on with making merry, shall we?' Charles asked as he shocked and delighted Roxanne by lifting her into his arms and carrying her over the threshold to the cheers of the staff, and the guests beginning to arrive from the church in their wake.

'Put me down, Charles,' she urged him, not quite sure her legs had the strength to carry her as he did so very slowly when they reached the great hall, and he gave her a decidedly wolfish smile. 'You're a very bad man,' she chided.

'Believe me, sweetheart, I could be a whole lot

worse,' he replied with a wicked grin that dissipated some of her awe at the solemnity of what they'd just done and made her long to laugh out loud with sheer joy, after all.

'But not just yet, perhaps?' she replied with a siren smile.

'Not unless we want to be lynched by our staff and our guests, but later I'll have my revenge for every wickedly alluring glance and taunting smile, Lady Afforde,' he promised, and there was no mistaking the seriousness of his intent, despite the easy smile he turned on Maria and Henry Balsover as her sister insisted on entering the room first in deference to her rank.

'Happy?' Tom Varleigh asked when he stepped forwards to offer formal congratulations on a marriage he evidently approved of.

'Deeply,' she agreed, unable to care if Charles heard her admit it.

She *was* happy, after all, ecstatically so at the thought of what was to come tonight, although it was a little diluted by apprehension at the unknown. She knew with bone-deep certainty she'd never have been half as happy with any other man, however much he might have loved her. So, yes, she could admit to being happy, but luckily nobody had the temerity to come out and ask her if she also loved.

If they had, she must either lie and deny it, or tell the truth and cause Charles's eyes to cloud and his smile to waver as he faced the inequality at the heart of their marriage. Blinking tears away, she reminded herself how much she wanted this marriage and did it so well that by the time Charles removed her third glass of champagne from her hand with a shake of his head and a quizzical look she would have argued, if he hadn't whispered he wanted her in possession of all her senses later, so he could drive her out of them with something better than champagne!

After the wedding breakfast there was dancing and the Great Hall rang with music and laughter for the first time in years. Roxanne remembered a long-ago ball held here, when all she could do was observe from the minstrel's gallery as her bridegroom spun girl after girl about the ancient floor with laughing abandon. How she'd hated every one of them, including her sisters, that night. Yet now Charles Afforde was her husband, just as she'd sworn to herself he would be one day, when she was grown up and beautiful and he was loaded with honours and more handsome than ever.

'Our waltz, my lovely,' her handsome captain murmured in her ear with such intimate heat in his eyes while he watched for her blush that she wondered fleetingly if she might want to slap him if she didn't love him so much. 'And maybe we can escape this brouhaha once they're all fairly launched into the dancing,' he added, and was it any wonder she hadn't breath enough left to say yea or nay? He laughed at her confounded state and wrapped his arm about her as he urged her on to the dance floor. 'And pray don't leave me with a floundering bride in my arms as you did the night you finally agreed to all this,' he urged with a lordly wave of his arm at the assembled company, eagerly watching as the bride and her groom took the floor for their dance, their confirmation that this was their day, the start of their joint future.

'You can be very infuriating indeed, Sir Charles,' she informed him sternly. He nodded. 'And very high-handed.' Again that nod of wicked acknowledgement, but very little repentance. 'And as of today you are also *very* married,' she finished ominously, her dark eyes promising retribution.

'I *know*,' he replied with every appearance of triumph and how could she not be flattered and flustered as he held her even closer and their steps matched in a most disgracefully intimate dance the patronesses at Almack's would surely not have approved when they finally gave in and permitted the waltz to be performed in their hallowed halls.

Respect for their guests made them stay far longer than they wanted to, accepting increasingly sentimental or raucous congratulations and dancing duty dances with the one or two who believed precedence triumphed over the sheer joy of a wedding. The early darkness of December had fallen long since, and the huge tree trunks burning in the vast fireplaces at each end of the hall had overcome the chill of the vast room. Even their indefatigable guests were succumbing to heat, champagne and happy exhaustion, when Charles seized his bride from a quiet coze with her eldest sister and Stella and whispered for her ear alone, 'I don't feel married enough yet, my lady, and it's time we did something about it.'

Heart racing, speechless with curiosity and desire, and a nagging jag of apprehension, Roxanne licked her lips nervously as she nestled into his embrace and watched his fascinated gaze linger on that action as if it was driving him demented, so naturally she did it again. He groaned and she felt the triumph of a woman who knew she was wanted above all others by a man she desired exclusively in return; thinking any deeper was banned tonight, and perhaps tomorrow and the next day as well.

'If you don't stop provoking me, I'll probably publicly embarrass you,' he grated out in a husky voice she hadn't heard before.

'How?' she asked interestedly, and he growled.

He really, really just growled at her like a hungry wolf, and she eyed him warily as she wondered, with a skitter of her heart that wasn't altogether fearful, if she really had provoked him beyond safe limits.

'Come,' he demanded savagely, but she excused him that when she saw what looked very like desperation in his eyes, and she let him draw her inexorably towards the door and the more shadowed part of the house, because she'd be a fool to do otherwise when she was finally at the end of an even longer thread of waiting and hoping than he was.

They heard a hue and cry behind them as the rowdier elements spotted their escape, but

Charles's compelling arm about her waist urged her on and they sped along the corridor and darted through the door leading to the servants' stairs, just as the young men tore into the hall and demanded of Mereson where his master and mistress had gone.

'I really have no idea, gentlemen,' he insisted blandly, and Roxanne stifled a chuckle as she allowed Charles to tow her up the narrow stairs and out into the corridor that led to the master suite and safety.

'Remind me to double his wages,' Charles muttered as he scurried her along the splendidly carpeted hallway and, much to her astonishment, Roxanne found time to admire the many improvements he'd put in place since buying the castle.

'Hurry, my lady,' Tabby urged from the open door of her lady's bedchamber, and Roxanne finally felt the weight of her new position as she surveyed the comfort and elegance Charles had created within.

'It's so beautiful!' she gasped, awed by the transformation from dark and rather dingy chamber into a delightfully feminine bower.

'You can thank me later,' Charles said with a return of impudence and eloquence as he sent her a wicked smile and went to engage the locks of his chamber as well as hers, before anyone could run them to earth. Putting his head round the communicating door, he grinned at her, and she felt herself beginning to melt from the inside outwards all over again. 'Not much later, though,' he promised and left her to Tabby's starry-eyed ministrations.

Chapter Fifteen

Speechless for once, Roxanne sat and let Tabby remove her finery with relief, despite the fact she loved every stitch of it and would cherish her wedding dress until her dying day. The rhythmic stroke of the brush as her hair was released to cascade about her shoulders almost calmed her, but then she licked her lips and met her own eyes in the mirror and knew it was just an illusion.

She looked different, did young Lady Afforde. Like a woman awaiting something very significant and special indeed and not sure if she ought to embrace it. Yes, she told herself fiercely, this is what I always wanted, and she squashed the little voice that argued 'not quite', even as Charles strode into the room with a splendid dressing robe open to reveal he'd shed his coat and waistcoat and neckcloth and looked incredibly handsome in his ivory breeches and stockings and shirtsleeves. Tabby finished hastily and scampered out of the room with a cheeky grin that Roxanne promised herself revenge for, tomorrow.

'I've had enough,' her husband ground out concisely, tugging Roxanne into his powerful arms at last, as if he'd found the day as trying, and at the same time as joyful, as she had.

'Enough what, Sir Charles?' she asked with a provocative look into his stormy blue eyes.

'Fine clothes, champagne, relatives and friends, and most especially enough of your teasing, Lady Afforde,' he informed her in a driven voice as he lowered his head in a kiss that allowed nothing for maidenly modesty, but a great deal for the raw, undisguised passion that flamed into immediate life between them.

Luckily Roxanne was as impatient as he was and met his hot kiss with unguarded enthusiasm. Open mouthed, they clashed, took and drove each other mutually crazy. Best not to think that on her side she was crazy with love as well as desire, but Roxanne let her hands explore his strongly muscled shoulders and neck without the annoying restrictions of fashion and convention and ignored the inequality.

This, she decided as she breathed in the scent and sensation of bare, heated, satin-and-steel masculine skin, this was what she'd longed for all those long, frustrated, barren years while he'd been away. His tongue plunged into her mouth and she felt surrounded by heat and need, his and hers, and tipped her head further back to give him even more encouragement.

Unnecessary encouragement, as it happened, for his hands ran heat down her scantily clad back and neat *derrière,* as if he could hardly bear even the gossamer silk of her nightgown coming between the sheer luxury of skin on skin. It seemed that he already knew how badly she wanted him, she remembered, with a very small regret that she'd held nothing back that day when he taught her the breadth and depth and peril of truly adult passion in the castle gardens below their bedchamber windows.

And he'd taught her very well, she reminded herself as she carried out an exploration of her own and felt his tactile muscles tense and shift under her flexing, stroking, approving fingers. And it was mighty, the steely strength under his satin supple skin. He was a mature, dominant male, and how would her younger self ever have coped with so potent a lover? She would have improvised, Roxanne decided with a cat-like smile against the base of his throat. Now, how had her mouth got there? she wondered as she appreciated his unique charms with it, now it was somewhere so intimate, now this place was to be forbidden all other women. Fair enough, she decided, with hazy logic when his hands were wandering ever lower and driving her out of her senses with this dragging sensual curiosity and an almost painful need for the intimacy of his body where she suddenly knew she wanted him mercilessly, for she could never want another man after this.

'Don't wait,' she ordered between lips that felt stiff and swollen with needs beyond any words she had left.

'You're not ready for me yet,' he cautioned in a gravelly voice that made her feel even more urgent for whatever was to come.

'Damn it, Charles, if I were any more ready I'd burst into flames!'

'I like the sound of that,' he teased with some of his old familiar lazy appreciation, belied as it was by the fierce burn of colour across his high cheekbones and the feral glitter in his burning blue gaze as he parted her now unbuttoned night-gown and pushed it down over her shoulders.

'How *risqué*,' he managed a little unsteadily as he paused to undo the beribboned bows among the frothy lace at each of her wrists; finally the insubstantial thing fell about her feet.

'I thought you'd like it,' she parried, resisting the urge to bring her hands up to protect her most feminine places from his very male gaze and watching it rove over her with lazy, unmistakable appreciation instead.

'I do, sweetheart, I most definitely do,' he replied and surprised her by stripping himself as openly as he had done her.

All the time he went about the task with fingers she thought enviably steady, he seemed to encourage her to feast her eyes on him just as he was feasting on her. It was so sensual, so open, so unexpectedly equal that her eyes grew heavy lidded and her tongue came out to lick suddenly dry lips and, instead of shying away with fear as she finally took in how powerfully aroused he actually was, she hoped she was making it as difficult to resist her allure as he was his emphatic masculinity. His manhood rose from his strongly muscled thighs in explicit demand and she found it oddly beautiful, the realisation coming over her in a moment of intense appreciation and arousal.

Maybe the gleam of feminine appreciation was obvious in her dark eyes, for he gave her a quick grin that reminded her of arrogant Captain Afforde, before his searingly hot blue eyes set that rake apart from her new husband. There was nothing carelessly guarded about this Charles Afforde, nothing deliberately held back and cynical, and she couldn't help but hold out her hands and smooth the satin-smooth skin, roughened by curls of dark gold hair on his powerfully muscled chest, with wonder.

'Charles,' she murmured as she stroked over his warm, very human skin with hands that wandered lower and yet lower, down over the hard packed muscles of his lean abdomen and even lower, until she held her breath and marvelled as he let her smooth the velvet hardness of his now even more awesomely aroused shaft, and she found it as wondrous under her questing fingers as she had under her voracious eyes.

'Roxanne,' he replied huskily, the rigid control he was forcing on himself beginning to show in the tension of iron-hard muscles as she let her other hand rove to explore his neat masculine buttocks and the mighty tension in his back, forcing himself to let her explore when she suspected he wanted to be inside her, possibly even more than she wanted him there. Only she didn't actually know the force and feel of a man inside her—no, not just any man, this man and only this man—yet could his need be any greater than hers? Probably not, but fairness made her acknowledge how awesome his control was, and how very far it outstripped her own.

'Yes,' she answered his demand with a whisper that seemed to fill the hushed room, blotting out the faint bubble of spitting sap burning from the fireplace as the seasoned applewood let out its steady heat, the whisper of a December wind outside the heavily curtained and shuttered windows and any noise the revellers might make below that was not held at bay by the mighty oak door of my lady's chamber.

'My Roxanne,' he asserted rather unsteadily, the very hint of a question in his gruff voice robbing it of the arrogance that once infuriated her so much.

'Yes,' she repeated unoriginally, but with a flush of fiery colour on her cheeks now and a challenge in her velvet-dark eyes that should inform him she wasn't going to suddenly shriek and run away in terror. 'Yes, yours; yes, your wife as of today; yes, I'm ready, and yes, I'll possibly expire of too much waiting if you don't hurry.'

Which seemed to do the trick, she decided in dazed appreciation as he launched himself at her, but even then he touched her heart by testing her earlier words and feeling for himself the moist, shameless heat between her legs, rendering them quite useless for their primary purpose of keeping her upright in the process. If she'd thought she was hot for his touch before, suddenly a raging need was roaring there, and she moaned and shifted to tell him even the intimate teasing of his long, strong fingers on her most secret feminine heart was not enough to slake this driving compulsion for more.

'Hurry!' she panted as she resisted his moves to walk her backwards to the bed and a more conventional coupling. 'No, I can't wait for that,' she ordered impatiently as she fought his restraining hands, prepared to climb up his heaving torso and drive them both demented with her inexperience rather than wait a second longer.

'It'll be too rough for a virgin,' he argued distractedly, but he must have been at the end of his self-control, too, for he shifted her so she came down on to his manhood, and at last she felt the smooth, hard heat of him enter her and gave a great purring moan of satisfaction.

'Oh, oh, Charles, oooh!' she praised and triumphed all at the same time as she felt his mighty body tense and change to accommodate itself to her and to discipline himself enough so he could cradle her striving buttocks and restrain her as she felt her maidenhead beat against this hasty coupling.

Unwilling to wait while he played the perfect, gentlemanly lover, she confounded him by letting her legs fall just enough to breach that last, annoying barrier between them. Swallowing a cry at the sharp discomfort that was the end of her long wait for this night, she grinned into his eyes and experimentally flexed a set of muscles she hadn't known she had. Yes, she felt mightily stretched and just a little sore, but the hurt was fading already and it was all part of this glorious night, and there was no way she was going to let him treat her like spun glass just because he'd been annoyingly chivalrous and insisted they wait until their wedding night to do this at last.

'Oh, ooh, Roxanne!' he echoed, smiling impudently in reply as he thrust mightily within her to show her he was only allowing her to dictate anything about their first loving because he was a gentleman.

Her heart seeming to quiver in echo of her body as fire caught mercilessly once more. She leaned her forehead down to rest against his and watched his pupils flare and contract as she moved demandingly once more, suggestively wriggling her hips as if to remind him he was supposed to be the experienced one here. So he asserted himself by walking to the bed and manoeuvring her on to the high mattress under the splendid silk bedcover without yielding an iota of their intimate joining.

'Lie back,' he ordered, unclasping her clinging arms from about his neck and spreading her very willing body against the velvet bedcover until she was lying with her arms over her head and her feminine core at the mercy of his full and dominant penetration, waiting on the explicit fire in his heated gaze.

Not that he showed her much mercy, she decided in a haze of sensual pleasure as he rubbed his palms appreciatively up her slenderly curved torso and spread them over her high and suddenly full and very aroused breasts and flexed them until she screamed with pleasure.

So next he bent to take one of her tightly

budded nipples in his mouth, and the feel of it, the absolute pleasure of him inside her as he did so made her head thrash from side to side and soft little gasps urged him to rock that mighty body so they could climb even higher up this astonishing ascent to something, something beckoning and wonderful beyond words, she suddenly realised, as he abandoned her breast and took her begging, pouting mouth in an explicit, raw kiss and increased the pace of their striving bodies. Suddenly it didn't matter that she was splayed out under him, begging frantically in whatever ways she could for his absolute possession like a harem slave, this was all there was in life that really mattered, and whatever it was leading to, they were going there together. Abandoning any hint of subjection, she raised her knees and wrapped her long, limber legs about his waist, drawing him deeper, closer and faster into the now frantic rhythm driving them.

'Please, oh, please, Charles, I want everything now!' She wrenched her mouth from his to gasp a plea for him to tip her into this unknown glory that was suddenly so close she felt as if she could almost touch it. To end and yet never end this hot, stormy madness inside her as she strove with his driving, fabulous, oh-so-masculine body centred on hers toward a mystery she was desperate to solve.

'Soon, lover, very soon,' he promised before he took her mouth back to silence her, and his kiss was fire and a relentless, heavy beat of even deeper arousal as he thrust faster and deeper and she bucked under him, sensing that something glorious was coming, coming so close she could taste it. For a moment he rode her frantically, and she wondered if she'd ever achieve this beckoning wonder she'd somehow been promised, felt him convulse and hated him for not taking her with him, then at last there it was.

Or there she wasn't, rather. She was elsewhere, with him. She was him and he was her and they were more than themselves, outside here and now and at the very beat of life itself all at the same time. Great convulsions of glory and unutterable joy spasmed through her as he gasped and bowed and thrust into her, into them, again and again, and she felt his hot release even as her inner muscles worked round his shaft as if to hold them within this golden moment for ever, and him with it. Panting with exertion and feeling like singing or shouting with delight, she felt his weight rest full on her outstretched torso for glorious moments, and her arms came up in a loving reflex to hold on to the ecstasy they'd just given each other, even as he raised himself on his elbows and smiled down at her while he shook his head regretfully.

'I'm too heavy, my rosy Roxanne,' he murmured teasingly, even as his index finger outlined her chin and then her brow and down her nose to outline her lips, as if he couldn't get enough of her, the sight of her, or her scent or the touch of her soft skin under his questing finger.

She confounded him by opening her mouth and nibbling on that provoking digit, eyes watchful and ardent as she challenged him and shifted to show him she was quite happy between the softness of the mattress and the hardness of his fit, honed body.

'You didn't marry a properly shrinking young lady, I fear, Charles,' she teased huskily and hoped her half-lowered eyelids and invitingly pouted lips were enough to let him know she was very ready to do *that* again as soon as it might be possible.

'Well, that's good news, then,' he said conversationally and infuriated her by prising himself away from his bride, to stir the dying fire into new life and add a couple more logs to it before carefully replacing the fireguard.

'Not so far as I can see,' she complained and tensed for some hasty action as she refused to admit to herself that he looked like a fire-lit Greek god come down to earth from Olympus.

How could he be less eager to repeat that delightful seduction of each other's reeling senses and eager bodies than she was? Less caught up in the wondrous world he'd just created for them as lovers, then walked away from to attend to the everyday, even if it was to keep them both warm? She felt the burden of her love and his refusal to acknowledge he felt anything but desire and affection in return; after such exquisite pleasure, such transforming joy, she suddenly felt so lonely with her love for him.

Jumping out of bed and donning all her clothes before riding off into the night on wild young Adonis seemed a good idea all of a sudden, so she could put some distance between them as well and ride off the fury and ache of knowing that, yes, he wanted her as his bride and his lover, but not with the driven, helpless need she felt for him.

Yet she had to watch helplessly, because she couldn't trust her disobedient legs to even hold her up after that wondrously tender introduction to the joys of the marriage bed, and her new husband was striding about the room as easily as if he bedded formerly virgin wives every day of the week. Irrational anger and unwilling, merciless arousal at the very sight of him, so magnificent yet so separate, ground deep in her belly, even as she knew she was being unreasonable. Maybe he understood her better than she knew, for his expression was rueful as he eyed her warily, as if she might explode like an unpredictable firework any moment and he was judging which way to jump to get out of the way.

'I'd hate for us to argue so soon after you became my wife in *every* sense,' he asserted lazily as he strolled back to the bed and stood surveying her restless body and stormy eyes cockily, his manly grin as slow and appreciative and infuriating as he surely meant it to be. 'But, after that performance, I'll certainly never regret taking a dutiful little miss to my bed.'

'I'm *not* a dutiful little miss!' she almost shouted at him as she bounced up off the mattress and faced him on splayed knees with a militant frown and, she hastily realised, nothing else to dignify her protest with. She wanted him to be as shaken by that amazing consummation as she was, yet still his iron composure held and he shielded his most private thoughts from her.

'We certainly made very sure you're not a miss in any sense of the word just now, my Roxanne,' he drawled and let his impudent gaze appreciate the effect her restless bouncing about had on her naked breasts, even as they betrayed her by visibly tightening and thrusting themselves at him in shameful argument with her brain, or most of it anyway, the part that wasn't as deeply in thrall to him as her wretched, disobedient body.

'And luckily I'd far rather have my wayward, headstrong wife than a pattern card of all the virtues any day,' he added, his eyes devouring her naked curves as she drew deep breaths to try to calm her temper and wondered whether to be furious or deeply complimented.

Whatever he needed to do to revive his passion for her had clearly been done, for there was no hiding his aroused state any more than she could conceal hers when neither of them had a stitch of clothing between them.

'Yes, you're quite right,' he observed as he took in her wide-eyed survey of his manly assets, and not even her simmering temper and this muddle of love and resentment and frustration fighting for supremacy inside her could overcome her appreciation. 'I'm clearly unable to keep my hands, or anything else of mine, off you for five minutes together, wife.'

'And fortunately for you it's mutual, or we'd have a reckoning for your insults right now instead of later,' she informed him as crossly as she could manage with a flush of excited anticipation burning on her cheeks and a gleam of wonder in her eyes as they roved over his body with admiration and avarice and a possession that he looked right back at her with interest. 'I believe the night is yet young, husband,' she murmured in what she hoped was a seductive husk that would remind him this was their wedding night, and therefore to be savoured and looked back on with joint and distinctly smug nostalgia during all the years they might have together.

And definitely not filed away among all the other nights he'd spent in other women's arms, she decided militantly, as she discovered much of her irrational fury was made up of jealousy. She reminded herself she had an advantage none of the others possessed: she was his wife and he'd promised to be faithful. All she had to do now was make sure he forgot the rest and stayed happy within that rash promise for the rest of their lives.

'I do believe you're right, your ladyship,' he drawled with a flattering intensity in his caressing gaze and stopped striding about the room displaying his manly attributes for her delectation and seduction, only to stand next to the bed and stare down at her instead.

Close to her, he was suddenly dangerous again, powerful and untamed and potent, and she swallowed a little nervously in deference to the maiden she'd been until such a short time ago. Then she recalled the wife and lover she now was and reached for the glorious reality of him and shamelessly plastered as much of her receptive body against his as she could physically manage.

'I'm always right,' she managed to assert, despite her tightening nipples and a shudder of pure delight he must be able to feel.

'So I'm content to let you believe, for now,' he murmured and surprised her by kneeling in front of her and pulling her across him so he would penetrate her only as her body adjusted itself to his rampant and eager shaft within her. It was gently compelling, urgently wanting on both their parts, but above all it felt deeply sensuous and caring as he fitted himself to her. 'Take it slowly, my darling, there's no hurry, and if we're to do this every night we must be gentle now, since it's all so new to you.'

'I don't care how it is, just so long as it is,' she admitted distractedly and felt his chuckle vibrate through her so intimately she wondered if it was possible for a woman to melt of pure desire and love.

'Well, I do,' he informed her with not altogether assumed sternness.

'Teach me then,' she responded crossly as he used his superior strength to gentle her frustrated striving and settle her into a dreamy, leisurely rhythm that none the less threatened to drive her slowly insane with passion and her absolute desire for more and more and yet more.

'Very well,' he murmured at last in reply to her demand. 'We've tried fast and furious, let's see how you like slow and sensuous and sweet.'

It was very slow and infinitely sweet as he showed her how the finest, most gentle of movements could drive a pair of lovers to the edge of insanity and then over it, into a satisfying and lengthy climax beyond even her wildest fantasies, now reality had so far exceeded any pale imitation of the truth she'd dreamt of before her wedding night.

And after that extravagant intimacy, that protracted loving introduction into the joys of the marriage bed, he watched her drift off into a sated, contented sleep and sighed regretfully before pulling the covers up round her and sliding out of her bed to resume his heavy silk robe and take one last, memorising, protracted look at his bride before he took himself off to his own chamber for the night.

Chapter Sixteen

A week later Roxanne wasn't quite so new to the delights of her husband's lovemaking, although he'd taught her more every night as promised, and she often wondered how any woman could ever be expected to actually sleep when there were such fiery glories to be experienced. All the same, she yawned over her luncheon, knowing full well that Stella and Lady Samphire, who'd driven over from Mulberry House where they were staying for now, were exchanging amused, indulgent looks across her weary head. Yet somehow she was struggling to feel as happy and content as such a well-pleasured new bride ought to. The urge to confide and even seek the counsel of more experienced ladies was strong, but she nobly resisted it.

Charles was an attentive husband, even during the day when there was little chance of anything more intimate between them than a lingering kiss, or a stolen embrace. He consulted her about estate matters and even took her advice when it didn't clash with his own views, and when it did they had a vigorous and enjoyable argument, and sometimes the day went her way and sometimes his. After simmering over his solution to a dilemma being favoured over her own this very morning, she'd stormed about the garden for at least half an hour before she forced herself to acknowledge he was right. Infuriating and inconsiderate of him though it might be, she couldn't hold it against him and would tell him so when he returned from the Home Farm.

Yes, Charles was a very good husband in so many ways, so why did she find it so disturbing, so distancing, that he'd never once spent the entire night with her? He always left her bed when she was asleep, so exhausted by his passionate lovemaking and her equally passionate reception of it that she couldn't stay awake to watch him go, however hard she tried. She'd done her best to tire him so much with her demands for the exquisite pleasure his body could give hers that he'd let go his defences and sleep in her arms for once, make himself as vulnerable to her as she seemed fated to be to him every single night. Yet fulfilment and weariness always defeated her and she'd never managed it.

No matter how many times they made love, no matter how many new ways he showed her for a man and a woman to couple and give each other glorious, heady pleasure doing so, he'd not slept with her. Not once. She sighed and regarded the beautifully cooked chicken and the warm, crusty bread roll spread with golden butter from Hollowhurst's own farm as if she despaired of them and not her guarded husband.

'Perhaps a rest would do you good this afternoon, Roxanne, my dear,' Lady Samphire suggested indulgently.

'Yes, indeed,' Stella said with a mischievous, knowing look that Roxanne shouldn't find irritating, but did so all the same. 'It'll never do if you fall asleep in your soup on your first bride visit tonight. There would be far too many ribald jokes over the port and brandy once the gentlemen were alone if you did that; poor Charles would be mortified.'

'Poor Charles, indeed! He'd be slapped on the back and congratulated on his startling vigour until he preened like a turkey-cock,' she replied irritably.

'Then I wonder at you for putting yourself up to make a fairground diversion of yourself, girl, when a few minutes of being sensible and actually sleeping when you seek your bed for once will prevent it,' Lady Samphire told her far less indulgently, and Roxanne thought ruefully that, if Charles ever lacked a defender in his besotted wife, he'd have one until she breathed her last breath in his grandmother.

'Quite right,' she conceded as she decided she'd probably be impatient with her herself as well today, if she didn't inhabit her own skin, so she smiled at the peppery old lady. 'I'll take myself off on that worthy errand as soon as you've told me what you're both intending to wear tonight, for I can't seem to relish my food today, however much Cook tries to tempt me.'

'Very well, then,' Lady Samphire observed with a sharp nod and bent a look on Stella that forbade her to comment on that curious fact.

'It's far too early to tell,' she warned her niece as soon as they were alone in the well-sprung carriage on their way back to Mulberry House.

'Of course it is, and I certainly had no intention of implying the dear girl could possibly be *enceinte* yet, they've only been married a week, after all,' Stella replied indignantly.

'The way they've be stealing off to their bed early every night to mate like a pair of lusty rabbits in the springtime, it'll be a miracle if she isn't before very long and you'd be a fool if you didn't suspect it. All the same, she don't need us watching her like hawks every time she pecks at her food or lies abed a little later than usual in the mornings. This is Charles we're talking about, after all, and anyone can see he's intent on seducing her whenever and wherever he gets the least chance to do so. Little wonder if the girl's at risk of becoming exhausted from his incessant attentions.'

'Lucky thing,' Stella said with a rueful look that admitted to her aunt she very much missed the joys of the marriage bed herself.

'Aye,' that lady agreed with a sigh, then shot her startled niece a militant glare. 'I may be old, Stella Lavender, but I ain't dead yet, even if I do have to rely on my memory to tell me Charles's grandfather at least had the good taste to lust after his wife when he recalled he had one.'

'If he'd had better taste, he'd never have left you alone long enough to risk another man noticing you were a neglected wife.'

'He knew I loved him too much to take comfort elsewhere, the rogue. I only pray Charles don't follow him in that as well as impudence and arrogance.'

Seeing a very genuine concern on her aunt's face, Stella considered such a notion for a moment and dismissed it with a decided shake of her head. 'Not he, Charles is more like you in character. He'll love once and always, and I think he's already done so, whether he admits it or not.'

'I truly hope you're right, but there's something holding him back from admitting it to himself or Roxanne, and it vexes me to know what. Anyone can see that girl's head over ears in love with the damn fool.'

Stella shrugged and was looking almost as troubled as her aunt when the subject of their anxiety breezed into their temporary sitting room before they'd hardly settled down for tea and a good worry, and he told them they looked like a couple of professional mourners at a wake.

'Cheek, my lad, that's all I ever hear from you,' his grandmama accused him stalwartly.

'Considering you'd very likely throw something at me if I informed you that you're the light of my life, Grandmama, cheek is my only option.'

'Don't waste your breath bothering me with such an untruth, when there's someone not so far off you should waste your cozening words on rather than me,' she said with enough seriousness in her brusque tone to make him frown.

'I'll not cozen my wife any more than I would you.'

'You're an idiot, boy,' the Dowager informed him wearily as she sighed deeply and looked her age for once, 'and likely to lose everything you hold most dear if you don't look into your heart and let someone else know what's rattling about in there for once.'

'Handing out advice, Grandmother?' he asked satirically. 'How very unusual of you.'

'No need to mock my natural wish to help those I love not to make a complete mess of their lives. I mean it, Charles, you risk far too much if you persist in refusing to do as I recommend.'

'So it's your wise counsel you're offering me and not royal commands for once, is it? That's a notable first, I must say.'

'I'm sorry I just told Stella you're a better man than your grandfather, because it's plain to me now you're as impervious to the finer feelings of those about you as he was. Well, go to the devil in your own way, then, and I wash my hands of the consequences, but disturb that poor girl of yours when she's finally getting some rest this afternoon instead of more of your rakish attentions, and I swear I'll swing for you.'

Saying which her ladyship swept from the room in a swirl of silk petticoats and indignation and marched off to pace her chamber out of sight and sound of the rest of her household.

'I'm not sure whether to follow her or stay and sympathise,' Stella said with a wry smile.

'Oh, stay, Stella mine. It seems I'm to avoid my lady's chamber when I get home *and* be at odds with my formidable grande dame, so stay and tell me I'm not quite as bad as I'm painted, before I sink any lower in my esteem and everyone else's.'

'You're well enough, but I wouldn't want you for a husband,' she told him bluntly.

'Just as well I never had the least inclination to stand in a better man's shoes then,' he observed a little more seriously.

'Even if we weren't related, I wouldn't wed you, Charles. I value my serenity far too much.'

'Yet my wife seems happy enough,' he challenged, oddly stung by her implied criticism.

'Yes, but I made a love match, Cousin, so "happy enough" wouldn't offer the least temptation for me to risk my heart and peace of mind, even if either of us wanted me to.'

'Well, it does very well for me,' he defended himself dourly and strode out of the room without any of his usual meticulous courtesies and, instead of speeding home to his bride as he'd intended, rode off to inspect a faulty roof he'd meant to put off seeing until Roxanne was with him.

He was quite capable of running an even larger estate than this alone, after commanding a man of war for the last three years of his naval career, then his own squadron. And if Roxanne wasn't happy with their bargain she should tell him so, instead of leaving Stella and his grandmother to decide there was something amiss.

Charles brooded over his wife and his acres all the way to Deevers Farm and had to force himself to examine the gables and hips in the minute detail Deever insisted on when he was there.

It wasn't as if he was a domestic tyrant or careless of his wife's happiness, he assured himself as he finally made the journey home through the fading daylight of the December afternoon. He was a considerate husband who applied himself enthusiastically to satisfying her every desire, and he'd even ceded her some of his responsibilities. That was more of a concession than she knew, when he'd commanded a ship's company for more years than he cared to remember. Perhaps that was the problem, he decided with a sigh. He was used to command, and it was a solitary business. No matter how fine his lieutenants and warrant officers, a naval captain was isolated by the respect he must command if his ship was to be an effective weapon of war.

Yet he was at peace now and intent on building a new life, so *had* he set Roxanne at too great a distance? And if he went on doing so, might it prove dangerous or even disastrous? 'Yes' and 'perhaps' seemed to be the correct answers to those uncomfortable questions, but she wasn't the one complaining, so perhaps he'd not been wrong to give her room to live a life of her own, after all. They'd only been wed a week, every night of which he'd spent in her bed, proving to both of them she meant more to him than any other woman he'd ever encountered, in bed or out of it.

Even so, Roxanne had spent most of her adult

life at Hollowhurst as companion and lieutenant to her great-uncle, then had taken Davy Courland's place while he evaded his responsibilities. She probably didn't know she was more crucial to him than any other female could be. She was four and twenty, but did that mean she was up to snuff any more than some little débutante, pitchforked from schoolroom to ballroom between one day and the next?

One Season in London when she was far too young to fit her exotic looks or passionate temperament had done nothing to tell her what power she might have over a man's imagination and ardour. His fists clenched at the thought of her discovering she could enthral other men with enchantress's eyes and a responsive, tactile body, when it had been formed for their mutual delight. But could any woman be so ignorant of her own charms and remain completely safe in mixed company?

Probably not, and then there were the wolves. More unscrupulous rakes than he'd ever been, waiting, hoping that he'd get her with child before the honeymoon was hardly over, so they could pounce while he complacently turned his back on his wife and preened himself on his own potency. His frown became a glower as he tried to get a vision of Roxanne being seduced by one of the scum who preyed on young society wives out of his mind. He'd kill the carrion who dared, then put a watch on his wife every waking hour of the day, while he kept her so occupied at night that she'd lack the energy to stray, even if he left her any will for it.

His expression was still formidable when he returned home with bare minutes to get bathed and dressed for a night of mild dissipation at the Longboroughs. Even so, he was ready to offer Roxanne his arm as they met at the top of the stairs like models for a marriage portrait. She was in her beautiful ivory-velvet bridal gown, as she was to be the guest of honour tonight as befitted any new bride in her first month of marriage, and he was tricked out like a dandy in his dark blue coat, gold-embroidered ivory-silk waistcoat and a cravat so exquisitely tied that young Longborough would probably long to plunge a knife in his back even more ardently than ever.

'Good,' his grandmother pronounced when she greeted them on entering the Longboroughs' drawing room, 'I despise this shabby-genteel fashion of gentlemen dining out in their riding breeches, or even worse, those new-fangled trousers instead of decent knee-breeches and silk stockings. I'd not put up with having the stables or barracks brought into my house, so why should any other respectable woman endure such cavalier treatment?'

'And it does show off a finely turned, gentlemanly leg so beautifully, don't you think?' Stella added with apparent innocence.

Charles was relieved to see a wicked smile crack through Roxanne's too-correct façade and reveal the woman he liked. Yes, the woman he liked so much. He raised one eyebrow at her in question, doing what Charles Afforde never did and seeking reassurance that perhaps he wasn't so hard to look upon, after all. She'd changed him, his passionate, headstrong bride, and he'd been more than ready to change after all, hadn't he?

'Yet one wonders what the gentlemen would think if we ladies went about flaunting our nether limbs as blatantly as they do?' Roxanne speculated mischievously, apparently not needing any more answer than the green glint he was sure must now be visible in his eyes.

How very satisfying that she only had to suggest such a fashion to have Charles looking as if he'd rather lock her in a cupboard than let any other man see her thus, Roxanne decided with a rather feline smile. The idea of another man seeing her dressed so made her shudder, but that was neither here nor there. Charles was jealous at the idea of other men leering at her legs and anything else on display in such a scandalous form of dress, and that was more than good enough for her.

There was no reason for him to know it, she decided vengefully, for in general he was altogether too sure of her fascination with him. He might own her body and soul in the eyes of the law, but there had to be some compensation for that state of wifely slavery, or there'd be no more wives willing to tumble into matrimony at the drop of the right man's handkerchief. No, she was his wife, and that counted. She raised her chin and met his eyes with pride and just a hint of desire in her own. If she ever managed to look on him with anything less, it would mean she was either very ill indeed, or more probably dead, but he didn't have to know that.

'Come and meet my sister and her husband, my dear Lady Afforde, if your husband can spare you, of course?' Mrs Longborough interrupted with an indulgent smile for what she imagined were a pair of true lovers.

'Oh, I'm quite sure he can,' Roxanne muttered darkly and went off to pretend to be delighted to meet Mr and Mrs Risborne, when she really wanted to have a furious, purging argument with her husband, largely because he was as handsomely self-sufficient as ever.

It went on in the same way for yet another week, this half-happy, half-terrifying state where Roxanne felt suspended between joy and the threat of something dangerous underneath the fragile surface of their marriage. Meanwhile, Christmas was almost on them, and she'd never felt less full of joyful anticipation of Christ's birth. Guilty at her lack of appropriate feeling for a season she'd always loved, she refused the carriage when Mereson offered it upon seeing her bundled up in a warm cloak, thick gloves and her stoutest boots against the gloomy cold of a day that threatened anything the elements might think up in their worst moods.

'No, a walk will do me good, and I only intend to visit Mrs Lavender and her ladyship, Mereson. I dare say I'll be back before anyone misses me.'

'Sir Charles won't like it, Miss Roxanne; it looks as if it might snow.'

'I'm quite capable of walking little more than a mile, even if it were blowing a gale and snowing a blizzard, Mereson, and I'll thank you and my husband to remember it,' she snapped, giving up on getting in the mood for the season as she swept out of the house and strode toward Mulberry House as if her life depended on getting there at top speed.

'I'm so glad to see you, Roxanne,' Stella said gamely when her stormy-looking visitor strode into the room and dared her to comment on her flushed cheeks and generally ruffled state.

'I thought I might as well come and see what her ladyship wanted to discuss so urgently.'

'I don't think it was urgent, which is just as well considering Great-Aunt Augusta's dashed off to Westmeade to see Caro Besford. Caro and Rob finally have a son at last, Roxanne, isn't it wonderful?'

'Yes, indeed,' Roxanne agreed, but it didn't need her friend's over-cheerful smile and too bright eyes to tell her that accompanying her great-aunt would have been painful for Stella, now that she would never be a mother after losing the husband she obviously still loved very deeply. 'I'm so very glad.'

'So am I, truly, Roxanne, so please don't think I envy them. I do, of course, but not enough to begrudge them a moment of their joy. Apparently Caro sailed through her labour this time, and Rob's having trouble persuading her to rest, so I'll go tomorrow and spread our visits out.'

'I'll go the next day if it'll help, and Charles can escort me. If he's to be the child's godfather, he might as well start as he means to go on.'

'Famous, although if Great-Aunt Augusta doesn't set out early this afternoon she'll be staying there, for Simkins informs me it's sure to snow by nightfall.'

'So Mereson insists as well, and I suppose two butlers can't be wrong,' Roxanne answered, eyeing the heavy clouds.

'Anyway, I'm glad to be spared a walk to the Castle with your letter.'

'Oh, what letter's that?'

'Now where did I put it? Sorry, Roxanne, but my mother sent me one of her epistles this morning and I forget where I put the rest now.'

'Never mind,' Roxanne murmured, trying not to look as impatient as she felt, for nothing about her current state of unrest was Stella's fault.

'Ah, here it is. It looks as if it had quite a journey to get this far and I can only suppose it got lost somehow between here and the Castle since Simkins found it in with a box of ornaments in the lumber room nobody thought to unpack until today. I dare say it was slipped in there as you all left the Castle and someone forgot all about it in the excitement, for one or two of the maids are silly enough to forget their own names at times. Anyway, I thought you'd want to have it as soon as possible now it's finally found.'

'Thank you,' Roxanne managed as she recognised her brother's impatient scrawl on its best behaviour long enough to inscribe her former direction. 'It's from my brother and I'd dearly like to read it.'

'Considering he's your only brother and thousands of miles away, I'd be surprised if you didn't. Hurry home first, though, before this fabled snow can make it hard work for you, or Charles comes looking for you.'

'You're a good friend, Stella,' Roxanne told her sincerely, giving her a fierce hug before she turned face about and marched out again.

Chapter Seventeen

There was no chance of waiting until she was home to read Davy's much-delayed letter, and it wasn't even raining yet, let alone snowing, so perhaps the combined wisdom of Mereson and Simkins would be proved wrong for once. Undoing the seal with only just enough patience to make sure she didn't tear the paper, Roxanne hungrily read her brother's letter as she walked. It began with news that wasn't really news any more. He was married and delighted with his bride, who seemed to combine such beauty, charm and wit as to make her an almost impossible paragon, except Davy was obviously fathoms deep in love with his Philomena.

Luckily Roxanne allowed for that and was glad her brother had found such happiness. At the time she'd been hurt he'd sell Hollowhurst without consulting her, but it had brought Charles back into her life, so how could she wish it any other way? Except to have Davy and his wife living in the next county instead of half a world away, of course. Her steps slowed as she read her brother's account of the sale of his estates and his marriage.

It sounded as if Charles had been in New England much longer than she'd thought. Long enough for lawyers and bankers to exchange all that was needed to be exchanged, in fact. Six whole months, and he'd never told her much about even a week of it. Fool that she was, she hadn't taken in the fact that the sale of such a large estate must be a long and complex business, even between friends. Her heartbeat stalled, then raced as something about that sale struck her as out of kilter, a warning that came not a moment too soon when she deciphered the next few lines.

Now she halted at the side of the road and stared at Davy's letter as he told a truth that leeched away her every last hope of happiness. 'Don't hate me for selling my birthright, Roxie,' her brother pleaded as she read his words again and wished fervently her eyes had deceived her the first time.

'There's no man on earth I'd sell Hollowhurst

to other than Charles Afforde. You ought to be heiress to everything in England that only held me back, yet I couldn't sign it over to you. Joanna and Maria would have been hurt and furious, and you *are* a woman, after all. Charles will be a better master there than I could ever be, but that wasn't the reason I relented and sold it to him.'

Roxanne gasped and turned ferocious eyes to the leaden skies, blinking furiously as she refused to cry but was tempted to scream and curse and rend her clothes because there was such pain raging inside her, desperate for an outlet. Instead, she forced herself to read on.

'I sold Hollowhurst to Charles Afforde because I knew you wanted him more than any other man on earth. You're four and twenty now, Roxie, so please consider his offer sensibly and don't dismiss it out of hand. I made it a condition of sale that he propose marriage to you within three months of taking possession, so I know he'll do it soon. Don't spurn the chance of a happy marriage with him just because we arranged it between us. When he comes to know you, he'll love you, my dear sister, and it need be no more complicated than that.

'Forgive me, little sister, and wish me happy?

Charles is the only man you ever showed any interest in marrying, so please do so, love, or I'll be haunted by regret for the rest of our lives.'

Forgive him—her wretched, conniving, managing, wrong-headed fool of a brother? How could she ever forgive him? Or Charles Afforde—her snakelike, worm of a husband, the man who'd promised to love and cherish her for the rest of his days, probably with his fingers firmly crossed behind his back? Oh, no, she'd never forgive either of them!

Charles finally appeared an hour later, looking so cold and weary that a concerned wife would have offered him hot punch and waited until he'd warmed himself with a bath in front of his dressing-room fire before she confronted him with his sins. Except that now nothing was as it had been just this morning. Her whole marriage was a fiction, so she'd no intention of playing the part he and Davy had scripted for her any longer. Seeing that she made no move to offer comfort or accept the kiss he might have placed on her wifely cheek with the least encouragement, he stood back and eyed her with that look of satirical interrogation she'd so recently found irresistible.

Refusing to look at him directly, Roxanne silently handed him her brother's letter and watched him register just what it revealed. Pain should be doubling her up, desolation robbing the colour out of her life, but just now she was too numb to hurt, too dazed to see anything as he bent his head but the dark gold hair that curled despite everything he could do to stop it, the sailor's lines about eyes more used to watching vast horizons than one perfectly discernible woman. Letting herself see him again, but feeling as if there was an invisible wall between them that might never be breached, she noted that the startling blue of his eyes looked as unique as ever, and she knew perfectly well that under his neatly masculine tailoring there was a magnificently masculine body.

Yes, Charles Afforde looked much the same as he always did, so why was her whole life tumbling round her as all she knew became untrue? Not a wild fiction, not even that. Just a small lie he'd allowed her to believe, probably out of kindness. A small but so important a lie, the one that had allowed her hopes and dreams instead of arrangements. The one that made a distortion of everything she'd ever wanted from this man.

'It's not what you think,' he told her gruffly,

as if, just because he said so, Davy's words were unimportant.

'It's exactly what I think,' she assured him coldly, and that chill seemed to bite into her very bones now. 'At least David has enough honour left to tell me the truth.'

'You doubt my honour, madam?' he demanded as if she'd accused him of the most heinous crime in the calendar.

'Oh, no, for it led you to cozen a superannuated old maid into thinking you wed her for the joy of it, didn't it? How could I doubt the *honour* behind such a noble action, Sir Charles?'

'Be damned to that,' he swore, running the hand not holding her brother's letter like a scroll of that precious honour through his hair and wreaking even more havoc with his fashionable Brutus haircut. 'Do you think I make love to you night after night because it's my *duty,* woman? You must be out of your wits if you think I've made it my pleasure and yours to seduce you in and out of our marriage bed, just because we're wed and making do with one another.'

'I suppose finding you can enjoy rather than endure bedding me must have been a pleasant surprise when you wed me to order.'

'Then you suppose wrongly.'

'Ah, you found it unpleasant, then? What a fine actor the London stage lost in you when you were born in a lady's chamber and not an actress's.'

'If I wanted to wed for convenience, there were heiresses enough, and land and fine houses to go with them. There was no need for me to wed a sharp-tongued virago to gain what I could buy easily enough.'

'Then why the devil *did* you marry me?' she burst out with the question she'd managed to keep inside for so long.

'Because I wanted to, because I wanted *you,*' he rasped, as if it cost him dearly to admit even that much.

Not because he secretly loves you then, Roxanne, she acknowledged with a wince of pain he seemed to see, for he held out a hand as if appealing to her not to probe this wound any deeper.

'Because of my childish infatuation with you?' she asked relentlessly.

'No, not that, it was never about that. I wanted you from the moment I set eyes on you again, and you certainly weren't suffering from hero worship then. In fact, I began to wonder if I'd ever persuade you to marry me. But make no mistake, Roxanne, I wanted you mercilessly the instant you appeared out of the shadows that dusky night and, God help me, I still do.'

'My turn to be flattered,' she returned, cold to her very toes with the conviction that all she'd ever been to him was a warm body in his bed, wife or no.

'There's clearly no reasoning with you now; we'll discuss this once you're rational again.'

'No, we won't!' she shouted furiously as he refused to even take this terrible misery tearing at her seriously. 'I won't be soothed and petted into resuming the role of besotted wife and mistress to you, Sir Charles. Take yourself back to London where your dubious talents will be appreciated, and while you're at it, please take a woman into your keeping who *knows* she's only there to serve your more animal needs, for I want no more of them.'

At that, she turned to march out of the room and slam the door behind her, but he was too quick for her. Before she could head for the door, he grabbed her by the waist and spun her round to face him. Never before had she seen him so furious, his eyes hard and merciless as they bored down into hers, as if he could see into her soul and didn't like anything there.

'Do you not, Roxanne?' he snarled as if he'd been well beyond the end of his civilised tether even before she provoked him to dangerous fury. 'Now I beg to differ, Lady Afforde. I'd wager Hollowhurst Castle and all its lands and demesnes that you adore fulfilling my needs, especially the "more animal" ones. In fact, you'll cry out for them until you're hoarse before you leave this room.'

'I'd rather die.'

'No doubt,' he grated and seemed to find that silly little lie the last goad to lose hold on whatever restraint had held him back every other time they'd made love.

No, not love, she reminded herself sadly, even as his mouth ground down on hers in a savage demand and his powerful body pinned her against the oak-panelled wall with little consideration for her slighter frame and relative inexperience. They'd never made love and they weren't about to now, but lust, oh, yes, now *that* they were good at.

His hands were everywhere and she wondered ludicrously if he'd suddenly grown an extra pair, then she took in the way her ridiculous, disobedient body was writhing against the smooth old oak to assist his plundering and might have despaired if she wasn't beyond it. She heard the fine wool of her morning gown rip like rotten gauze under his impatience, listened to a curse that should have made her blush to her very ears when he encountered the petticoats she wore against the winter chill. If only she'd donned a sensible spencer instead of the voluminous shawl that was to have kept her warm, she might have had time to come to her right senses while he tore through that, but the fine Kashmir wool just slipped away and he reached his first target before she had time to even shiver at the loss of its warmth.

His large hands cupped her breasts emphatically, nothing coaxing or worshipping about his touch today. There was just lust, stark and searing hot in his examining eyes as he observed them rising high and rounded in his kneading, assessing hands. They shamed her by peaking and thrusting towards the rough seduction he'd threatened to strip her of her dignity with, or did they? Perhaps not, because by responding to him so eagerly, so blindly, wasn't she seducing herself and reducing his threats to humiliate her?

Perhaps, she answered herself, then decided she didn't care, as he concluded that part of her had been seared by whatever white-hot passion drove him long enough. Holding her against the now body-warmed panelling by her hips, he knelt at her feet, eyes lancing into hers with a terse demand she stay where she was. He positioned her carefully, as if watching her in thrall to this wild seduction pleased him nearly as much as the prospect of taking everything she had to offer, and perhaps a little more.

He used his thumbs to urge her legs apart, to reveal the heat and scent of a thoroughly roused woman with exploring hands as he drew them mercilessly upwards. Then, shockingly, he bent his head and licked and suckled and thrust his tongue into her most intimate centre until she forgot herself enough to let out a small, gasping scream that she muffled behind a hand that shook, but for the life of her she couldn't find the strength to reach down and push him away. He looked up with triumph and possession and need openly revealed in his wolfish smile and went back to demolishing every barrier, even a few she hadn't known she had.

He used a wicked, exploring finger to test her arousal once more, then followed it with too much knowledge of exactly where she needed pressure and where tantalising would do better.

His mouth on her once more, he must have felt her shiver on the very edge of losing control. Again he lifted his head away and this time had the effrontery to raise one eyebrow at her as if they were engaged in trivial small talk.

It took a mighty effort, but she bit her lip and refused to plead as he'd promised she would. He grinned as if happy to push her even further and this time his tongue was less persuasive and more demanding and she no longer shivered lightly, but began to shake with racking shudders as she held back from the agonisingly wondrous edge of bliss with such an effort she wondered she was still conscious. Then one last butt of his golden head against the dark curls at the very centre of her and she screamed, she actually screamed with the power of her climax and a small part of her heard the pleas he'd promised she'd cry out leave her lips and despaired, even as the rest of her was racked with such pleasure that she couldn't have cared less about those betraying demands if she tried.

Maybe afterwards she'd have felt humiliated and terribly lonely, if he hadn't surged to his feet and joined with her as if driven by a lot more than revenge, just as a last powerful spasm of pleasure nearly rocked her off her feet. He forgot himself, just as she'd done, and took his wife in a heated, driven rush of need against the wall of her boudoir, in broad daylight. He forgot he was a gentleman, forgot he was anything but a man driven half-mad with wanting her any way he could get her. Amazingly, wild shudders of completion rocked through her irresistibly again, just as he gave a great wrenching cry and drove into her with deep, powerful surges of extreme pleasure, and his thrusts took them both to the peak of satisfaction and beyond.

For a long, precious moment all was quiet in the room, as if the labour of their breathing and lingering shivers of an ecstasy neither could resist feeling would keep everything else at bay. Her breath sobbed between lips that felt as if they might never speak sense again. Maybe in a moment she'd have to think, but now she put her energy into just breathing as she revelled in the undeniable. She'd done just as he said she would and begged, but he'd proven he couldn't keep himself separate and cynical from her while she did so. Yes, maybe he'd won on a technicality, but it wasn't outright victory, and hope was running strong in her. Such a glorious, unarguable tide of it that she had trouble concealing it from the stubborn, infuriating wretch.

'I beg your pardon,' he said stiffly when he finally seemed to notice he was still pinning her against the wall, the weight of his body still hard against and inside her softer one, and she wondered for a ridiculous moment if she bore the imprint of finely carved linen-fold panelling on her bottom.

'Don't,' she protested as he began to ease away from her, hating the chill of reality that was threatening now all the heat and sensual clamour were fading, along with some of her certainty that he felt far more for her than he ever could for a convenient wife.

'That was unforgivable,' he muttered as he pushed himself away and looked as if he was the one who'd just lost their sensual battle instead of her. 'I threw myself at you like a rutting bull, and I dare say I've hurt you.'

'No, you didn't hurt me,' she comforted him, even while her mind reeled at what they'd done. She felt as if she'd just become his lover or his mistress as well as his wife, but, in that case, why did it seem so wonderful? 'Nothing you did caused me pain.'

'But I've caused you more than enough anguish since I came here, haven't I, Roxanne?' he asked bitterly, setting himself to rights as best he could while he eyed her state of dishabille as if he dared not come near enough to help her attempts at tidying herself in case they seduced each other all over again.

It really was quite flattering to be considered irresistible by a man who'd flirted outrageously with some of the most beautiful women in Europe and beyond. He'd flirted and perhaps more with them, but, she reminded herself rather smugly, he'd wed her and then he'd made love to her as if driven to seduce her into thrall to him. Not that there was any need, when she was about as resistant to his charms as most of her sex not otherwise enchanted.

'My life has certainly changed since you came to Hollowhurst,' she admitted warily, 'but who's to say change is a bad thing.'

'I walked into your life, took your home and your occupation from you, and then manipulated your situation to suit my own convenience.'

'Oh, dear, so you did,' she agreed, without feeling in the least bit sorry that he'd done just that all of a sudden. 'Now whatever can I do to devise sufficient punishment for your perfidy, Sir Charles?'

'The dungeons, d'you think?' he mused, catching her lighter mood as if he couldn't resist it, despite the fierce argument that sparked their stormy loving, and his and Davy's diabolical plot.

'Not nearly severe enough, considering they're now the wine cellars, and you'd probably enjoy yourself far too much down there. No, instead of so light a punishment, you're tasked to ride out to the very spot where we had our encounter on the beach that day and not to come back until you've sat out there in the cold and seriously considered the subject of marriages of convenience and how you truly feel about your wife.'

'Now that really is severe,' he joked, but she could see in his eyes that he knew how serious a quest she'd set him.

'I need you to carry it out, though, Charles, and not to come back until you've fought your demons,' she said lightly enough, but she let her eyes speak for her and hoped they were as steady as her conviction that love ran like a fierce undertow under their every word and action together since their wedding day and perhaps before. 'As I waited so very long for you, the least you can do for me now is to give me honesty.'

'I gave you that when I asked you to marry me,' he told her flatly, but this time she did what she'd just hoped he would and searched his gaze for a deeper truth.

Yes, it was there: a spark of doubt, a hint of uncertainty and the slightest suspicion of what looked like dread. For the latter she might well flay him with her sharp tongue now and again for the rest of their lives, but for the rest she made herself turn to look out of the window in case she weakened and just assured him her love would be enough for both of them.

'It'll be black dark by five,' she warned as if he hadn't spoken.

'I hate a nagging woman,' he muttered, but he impatiently ran his hands through his disordered hair and restored it to something close to normality for a man who'd just weathered a hurricane and stalked to the door, turning back to say, 'I'll probably be out later than five, so don't send half the neighbourhood to find me and see what a fool marriage has made of me, will you, wife?'

'Not if you wouldn't like it, dear,' she said in such a meek and mousy voice that he simply glared at her and frowned all the harder.

'Vixen,' he bit out and marched through the door before slamming it behind him, as if he needed that small release of frustration.

'Idiot,' she said fondly and set about the task of making herself fit to be seen again without letting her household guess what their master and mistress had been about.

She'd have to hide her ruined gown and smuggle it to the ragman herself next time he came. Time to worry about that when the time came, for now she'd have enough trouble convincing Tabby it was quite normal to change her attire halfway through the day, from the skin up, without the help of her maid, and she must bathe as best she could, too. Tabby might suspect what they'd been about for the last however long, but Roxanne refused to announce her enthralment to her husband if Charles was bull-headed enough to carry on insisting they shared a marriage of pure convenience.

Only half an hour ago she'd have turned on anyone who suggested her hope of a happy and fulfilled life at her husband's side were recoverable and snarled out a bitter denial. Yet her husband had just taken her as if she were an equally wild lover he'd dreamt of for many long months at sea, and now they had all those accumulated weeks of desperate ardour to slake on each other's desperate bodies. He'd just treated her like his whore instead of his wife, and contrarily his uncontrolled need of her had given her back hope. If the risk paid off, these half-wonderful, half-terrible weeks since their marriage would end and their real marriage begin. Of course if it didn't, she'd be far worse off than before, and truly trapped inside an arranged marriage.

Chapter Eighteen

Charles cursed all women and his wife in particular for at least the first mile of his solitary gallop to the beach. Then he added the other half of humanity to the mix when he thought of Davy Courland's ridiculous letter, and that occupied another two or three miles. At this rate he'd be in Rye or even Brighton by nightfall, and certainly not back at Hollowhurst where he wanted to be, but he checked Thor when they finally reached the shore, and he could spread a rug over the gelding's sweating sides and brood over dull, cloud-mirroring, grey-brown waves all the way to the horizon.

She'd been quite right to send him here to contemplate his sins, he decided grimly at last, not yet ready to forgive Roxanne for being Roxanne and not letting him hide behind the conventions and cowardly evasions any longer. The English

Channel was as familiar and yet as resistant to any human influence as it always had been. Ever changing and at the same time unchangeable, and as much beyond the orders and purposes of a mere captain or even a commodore as ever. And I'm still standing here, busily avoiding the conundrum my wife has set me, he decided with a wry grin at the unresponsive waves.

Of course he could just turn about and go home, admit he loved her without telling her the rest and perhaps save his marriage, because he knew very well now that he did love her. He'd discovered it when he read that damning, infernally interfering letter of Davy's and thought it made an end to everything. The end of their marriage, of seducing Roxanne to their mutual pleasure night after night for the rest of their lives. Of the family they might have…Oh, just of everything that suddenly mattered to him so vitally. So why not just admit it and nothing more and hope their lives would go back to normal, to the very pleasant everyday they'd established between them these last three weeks of marriage?

Because she deserved more, he concluded with a heavy sigh and wondered if telling his story would produce the same result if he went back to Hollowhurst and told her he didn't love her after all and probably never would. Ah well, that would be a huge lie now he'd found out he needed her with him to make every breath he took worth taking, so if the truth produced the same result as an untruth, why not hand her that lie and watch all her hopes and dreams vanish into nothing? Because she'd see through it, he decided grimly, categorising himself as a coward for knowing that if he thought he could get away with it, he would indeed lie to his lady, his lover, in the hope a falsehood might wriggle him off the hook he richly deserved to hang himself on.

And how the *devil* had he been idiot enough to let himself fall in love with her? He'd promised himself he'd never do such a stupid thing after watching his friend Rob fall into the trap of loving a wife he'd sworn never to love or bed. Then, even with that stark example of husbandly lunacy in front of him, *he'd* wed Roxanne Courland and been ass enough to think he could emerge heart-whole from *his* marriage bed, even with her in it. Was any fool on earth as great a want-wit as Charles Afforde proved to be by thinking he could marry a woman like Roxanne and keep himself aloof?

Probably not, and so now he'd have to pay for his folly by confessing exactly what, and who, he really was. Little point putting it off, he thought gloomily. Testing his fate would be bad enough if he did it before all the reasons not to occurred to him; leave himself room to think, and he would probably ride off to one of the Cinque Ports after all and drink himself into a stupor just in case he could get away with being a coward again. Who'd have thought Charles Afforde, rake and cynic, would contemplate drinking himself into oblivion to escape telling his own wife what lay behind his bravado?

'Come on then, old fellow,' he murmured to his fidgeting horse as he turned his back on the rapidly calming sea at last. 'Let's get you back to your stable and arrange some comfort for you at least tonight.'

By the time he guided the weary beast back into the stable-yard it was pitch dark, and Charles could taste snow on the dying wind. As he rode, the whole of nature had seemed to fall silent around them in either awe or dread of what was to come. Now he thought about it, there had been a curiously yellow tinge to the leaden sky as it faded into dusk over the sea, but he'd been too occupied with his own thoughts at the time to notice, when getting home safely to Roxanne was suddenly more important than anything else in the world. She would see to fetching in firewood and distributing food to the needy before it was too late, and Charles thanked his stars for the wonderful wife he'd gained undeservingly. If he got this right, he'd have a wife at his back any man must envy him for the rest of their lives: a wife of rare beauty combined with her extraordinary strength of character and a unique mind.

Not that he ought to leave out her incredible body, he decided, as he contemplated all the other benefits of having married Roxanne with a wolfish grin while he saw to his horse himself and sent the stable-lads back to their wood chopping and water carrying. No, the endless exhilaration of wanting his wife and being wanted passionately back for the rest of their joint lives couldn't be underestimated, and he promised himself that from now on he never would fail to thank God for her every day.

Roxanne was upstairs, doing her best to reassure the housekeeper that the Castle could now withstand a siege from the weather as stalwartly as it repelled enemies hundreds of years ago. Even so, she couldn't resist looking out of the window so she could peer helplessly into the snow-blinding darkness outside and worry about her husband. He'd survived battles and terrible storms at sea, for goodness' sake, so why was she struggling with this sudden terror that he'd take a tumble from his horse and lie unconscious and in acute danger under a suffocating blanket of falling snow until morning? Common sense informed her he was perfectly safe, but that didn't stop her being furious with herself for sending him out into the early darkness of a December afternoon to consider his true feelings in the first place.

'And then there's all the pensioners, your ladyship,' the housekeeper carried on fretting as Roxanne listened with only half an ear. 'There wasn't time to fetch them all in from the more outlying cottages.'

'Then we'll have to rely on their families and neighbours to take care of them,' she pointed out firmly, as if all her attention was on the subject. 'It's just as well Sir Charles insisted on removing Mrs Bletter from her tumbledown old shack to one of the almshouses, is it not? She lived miles from anyone and would certainly be cold and comfortless if she'd stayed where she was.'

'I hope nobody expects thanks for that mercy, my lady. A more cross-grained, awkward old biddy than Dame Bletter you'd go a long way to discover, if you were silly enough to want to in the first place.'

'Yes, I dare say Sir Charles exerted all his famous charm to get her to move, but at least he put it to good use and we're spared worrying about her.'

'Roxanne! Roxanne, where the devil are you?' the masculine voice she'd been waiting so anxiously to hear again bellowed from somewhere close by and she felt a silly snap of annoyance at him that might disguise her huge relief from the suddenly amused housekeeper.

'As if you'd be doing anything other than setting the household in order at a time like this, Miss Roxanne,' Mrs Linstock said with an indulgent smile for the follies of gentlemen and her new employer in particular, who clearly hadn't been restricting his fabled charm to Dame Bletter.

'Here!' she went to the door and called before he roused the household, who were much better occupied with the tasks she'd set them.

'Thank heaven—I thought I'd never find you.'

'Then you didn't look very hard,' she told him repressively and went back into the housekeeper's room to ask if there was anything else left for them to worry about before asking Cook and her minions to prepare dinner.

'Nothing at all, my lady, so I'll go down to the kitchens and ask her to do so now, shall I, your ladyship?' Mrs Linstock replied rather disobligingly, for Roxanne was suddenly very nervous indeed about what Charles had decided on what must have been a freezing cold beach and an unpleasant ride through the gathering gloom and the start of a snowstorm.

'Yes, indeed,' she just had time to agree before her husband's patience ran out and he grabbed her hand to tow her gently towards his personal sitting room, so at least it wasn't the scene of her most recent demonstration that she found him irresistible.

'Hadn't you better change and get warm, Charles?' she said hopefully.

'No, I've more important things on my mind, although thank you for the fire in my rooms,' he observed as he finally tugged her in through the door and eyed the cosy intimacy of it. 'It's just the place for a weary man to warm himself after a strenuous afternoon.'

'I had a strenuous time of it as well, you know.'

'I could see that, but I don't think you sent me off into the teeth of a blizzard to think about organising logs and bread for our pensioners.'

'That's true,' she managed meekly, wondering if she'd known what she was doing when she suggested he go and think about their lives together. He seemed to have concluded he needed to be a benevolent dictator and she didn't relish feeling like a rating under Commodore Afforde's command.

'Come and enjoy it with me, Rosie,' he demanded, using their still-joined hands to tug her down on to the thick Persian rug in front of the fire and she plumped down beside him as if her legs had suddenly become boneless.

For a long, precious moment he just held her, one strong arm hugging her close as warmth seeped into them both from the mesmerising flames, and some of the strung tension drained out of her.

'I want to tell you a story,' he began, and she wriggled restlessly. 'Don't you want to hear it?' he asked rather severely.

'That depends on the ending.'

'You'll have to judge what that is for your-self,' he returned, and she could have sworn he sounded nervous, but since when had mighty Captain Afforde succumbed to nerves in any form?

'Very well, you may continue.'

'Thank you, my dear, gracious of you.'

'Whatever you say,' she replied, stealing a look at his rather stern profile and fighting a strong desire to distract him by running an exploring finger over it and luring him into warming them both up very rapidly indeed. 'Just get on with it, will you though, husband, for I want my dinner.'

'Been busy, have you then, my Roxanne?' he said, the sultry memory of their vigorous loving in his half-closed eyelids and slow, sensuous smile.

'Yes, someone had to prepare your household to be snowbound for Christmas.'

'Our household,' he chided with a frown.

'Yours, ours, whichever. Now, are you going to tell me this tale or not?'

'Aye, I'd best before I lose my nerve for it,' he said with a suddenly very serious sigh and she nestled herself closer into his powerful shoulder and wriggled pleasurably.

'Just tell me,' she encouraged with a contented

smile that should tell the great idiot she'd never flinch away from a man she loved so deeply as she did him, whatever he had to say.

'It all began one snowy Christmas,' he said very seriously and she had to control the leaping of her pulse and the ridiculous arousal of all her senses, for she knew perfectly well he meant that first Christmas they'd met, when she'd fallen headlong in love with him at first sight.

'For me, too,' she breathed and risked a look at his face, both mellowed and shadowed in the firelight.

'Perhaps, but this isn't half as pleasant a tale as yours, love.'

She'd have forgiven him everything and just contented herself with that one significant word if left to herself, but evidently he'd resolved to tell all and she must hear it, now she'd forced him to confront it, whatever 'it' might be.

'Anyway, I met a girl, not much more than a child really, and knew one day I'd come back and marry her. For all she thought herself grown up and insisted on staring at me with her heart in her stormy dark eyes, I decided she must be at least three years older before I didn't have to be an arrant rogue for marrying her and carrying her off to sea with me. I confess I didn't leave Hollowhurst in love with you, Roxanne, or think I'd even let myself love you when the time was ripe and I could wed you. I was four and twenty and knew with all the supreme arrogance of youth and privilege, that by the time I was three years older I'd be a captain and considerably richer. Life's always lonely as captain of a great ship, however sociable he might be, and heaven forbid I be confined to a mere sloop. *I* would command a frigate, then a man o' war.'

'Fair enough,' she interrupted, 'that's exactly what you did.'

'By good luck more than any outstanding talent.'

'That's not what I heard.'

'But you couldn't have listened with unbiased ears if someone paid you to, now could you, my passionate, partisan wife?'

'Never about you, but it wasn't only me who thought you a hero and a superb commander of men, Charles. The news-sheets were full of your dashing exploits and quite determined you were to be the new Nelson.'

'More fool them then. I knew enough of him before he was killed, for even a callow youth such as I was, to sense I was in the presence of genius. And I haven't the heart for battles not fought in a war, Roxanne, whatever small talents I might have. Once Boney was beat, all my famous fierceness and daredevilry went flying off my quarterdeck.'

'Which is perfectly acceptable, considering you had a castle to buy and a new life to live with me,' she said with a smile and a happy wriggle as she slipped off her shoes and flexed her toes so they could feel the fire's warmth properly and leant back against him.

'Fool that I was, I thought that when I reached New England on my discontented wanderings about the globe and met Davy there, that his dilemma solved mine and there was nothing more for either of us to worry about. He wished he could sell his birthright and I wished I could buy it. Simple enough, we both thought, as he trusted me to love and look after it as he somehow could not. Then he suggested I set his mind at ease about our whole bargain and wed his sister, and suddenly I could have my cake and eat it. So I promised to marry Miss Courland, if I could persuade her to have me, and that made our deal all the sweeter.'

'Very convenient,' she said in a cool, non-committal voice.

'It would have been, too, if I hadn't arrived here one dusky night and wanted you more urgently than any female I'd ever laid eyes, or hands, on.'

'It was more than hands you laid on me that night.'

'One almost-chaste kiss, and I dared not risk coming any closer, or I'd have done my best to seduce you right there and then.'

'Funny,' she murmured with a reminiscent smile, 'I don't remember it being so very chaste.'

'Wanton,' he accused, and his other arm came up to hold her closer, as if he revelled in their closeness nigh as much as she did. 'Now, where was I?'

'Seducing me in the twilight.'

'Ah, yes. It came as a terrible shock that you'd grown into a stubborn, capable and independent woman while I was away, as well as one of the most beautiful females I ever laid eyes on.'

'Come, Charles, we must deal honestly with each other now,' she scoffed and sat a little more upright in his embrace.

'Roxanne, I found your complete innocence of your own powerful allure exasperating and dangerous even before I got you up the aisle.

Don't make me regret you weren't born with a squint or a wooden leg.'

'Nobody could be born with a wooden leg.'

'I dare say not, but you know very well what I mean.'

'I don't.'

'Then you should; you have the finest of finely made features, the most lusciously curved feminine body I was ever privileged enough to lust over and I could lose myself for hours in appreciating your hair, my dearest love. I love the look of it and the heavy silk feel of it between my fingers, under my hand, and I dare say the male half of the local population would feel the same, if they ever saw it down about your naked shoulders in a witchy web as I have. Of course, if any of them ever do, I'll have to kill them, then lock you up in the tower for the rest of our lives.'

'Harsh,' she murmured in what sounded even to her like a sensual purr rather than an indignant protest.

'But interesting.'

'Hmm? Well, maybe, but I believe you didn't sit me down all undignified and unladylike in this fashion to flatter me beyond reason, sir?'

'I can see I have a lot of enjoyable work ahead

of me, convincing you that I speak only the truth, but for now let's get back to our sheep.'

'If you must, but if you truly love me I need nothing more,' she said, turning enough to watch him with her feelings in her eyes.

'No, I need to tell you now, even if you've turned cat in pan.'

'Go on then,' she told him huffily as she swung back round to stare into the fire again.

In retaliation, he settled his chin on the top of her head and drew her back into his arms, so she settled into his embrace and finally let the tension drain from her muscles. There seemed no point fighting her compulsion to snuggle as close to him as possible, when he liked having her there nearly as much as she did being held as if she mattered.

Chapter Nineteen

'It was after that joyous, carefree Christmas I spent with your family, which somehow makes the memory of it seem so much more shocking.'

Charles began his tale with his eyes fixed on the fire, but she could feel the tension in the tightly packed muscles of his torso and almost wished she'd never demanded he purge whatever horror haunted him and for so long had stopped him admitting he loved her just as surely as she did him. He needed to tell her and she needed to hear him out, however terrible his tale might be, so they could face it and defeat it, together.

'I rejoined my ship and found everyone fit to sail scrambling to get us to sea. As many ships as were even half-ready to embark were under orders to sail to Spain and pick up as many of Sir John Moore's expeditionary force as we could save from falling into Bonaparte's clutches.'

'I remember wondering if you'd got back in time to sail with your ship.'

'I'm not sure to this day I wouldn't rather have missed it. Anyway, we reached Vigo at last and discovered we were in the wrong place, and most of the army were waiting at Corunna while the French got closer with every hour that passed. We sailed off to find them in the teeth of a gale that seemed as if it would never give over, until at last we reached harbour and began to embark as many as we could carry. We took on men until it seemed as if one more might sink us, but I begged the captain to let me take one of the transports and collect any poor souls the French would capture if we left them behind and eventually he let me go.

'It was like a scene from hell, Roxanne, the beach covered in the corpses of their horses, the town with all its windows blown out from our army exploding its remaining powder. The people did their best to defend their town from the advancing French, and even the women braved the French fire to wave farewell at us from the rocks, but it was hopeless and we'd just taken off what few men we could and were preparing to return with them when a French battery opened fire. There was a great panic and some cut their cables without bracing their yards, so their transports ran aground and those poor souls aboard were either wrecked or drowned.

'Hardened to battle as I thought I was, it horrified me to choose between the wretched souls we already had aboard and those at risk of drowning or capture on shore. Still, the second lieutenant I had with me pointed out we must save what we had, so we were halfway back to our ship when we came upon a most pitiful spectacle of all. Apparently one of the men on another boat had smuggled his woman on board with him, disguised as a soldier of the 38th, although not particularly well, it must be said.

'On hearing the French shelling, she screamed and scrambled upright in her terror, so the master of the vessel took out his pistol and shot her, then calmly ordered her body thrown overboard. We saw it all from afar and were powerless to do anything, Roxanne, but I was bitterly ashamed to be part of the same navy that day. We found her floating in the water, but there was nothing we could do for her, she was dead as the poor horses on the shore. She looked to be Spanish or Portuguese rather than English, for masses of black hair floated about her and she looked almost peaceful, if you discounted the bullet hole through her heart. She was also heavy with child, which makes me wonder even more what sort of a wicked fool failed to note he had a pregnant woman on board and then shoot her as casually as I might a rabbit.'

'Oh, Charles, how appalling. No wonder if you were deeply shocked, and you were still so very young to see such a desperate sight.'

'I saw men blown to pieces in battle from the age of thirteen when I became a midshipman, my love, so I really can't tell you why this one affected me so. We never managed to track down the man who did it, and, even if we had, the Admiralty wouldn't have disciplined him. We had orders not to take camp followers, although many ignored them and pretended they hadn't seen the women among so many men, and most of them were a pitiful sight, grey-faced, starved and sexless after that terrible retreat. One dead Spanish girl shouldn't have meant much when we were carrying so many starved and hungry soldiers from a chaos of regiments, yet from that day on she haunted me as if I'd put that damned bullet in her breast myself.'

Roxanne slewed round in his arms and hugged him close, feeling him tremble at the memory of that day and cursing the callous, black-hearted rogue who'd shot a helpless girl for no real reason other than that he could.

'It wasn't your fault,' she informed him fiercely, kissing his lean cheek and horrified to feel the wetness of tears under her lips. 'You would have saved her if you could, and you'd never kill a woman, Charles, or a child.'

'Maybe not, although it's astonishing what men will do in battle. The wisp of a man who you expect to climb down among the ballast and cower there, despite the stink and the danger, will fight like a lion until he's hacked to pieces by the enemy or carries the day, and some great hulking bully of a sailor might just as easily break down and scream like a baby at the first sound of cannon-fire. I may never have been tested enough to know what I'd do in the grip of panic and the certainty I could die if I didn't strike out.'

'Don't be a fool, Charles, you've been in acute danger more times than I care to think about, and I would have heard if you went about screaming and striking out at the first vulnerable creature to get in your way,' she told him sternly. 'The public likes nothing better than knocking down this week a hero they made last week, so if you'd a cowardly bone in your body we'd both know it by now.'

'Not if you went about organising my defence, we wouldn't,' he told her with a wry smile she saw in the fading firelight as he disengaged himself long enough to add a couple more logs to the fire and watch them catch. Then he sank back on to the rug at her side and took her into his arms again, as if he needed her in them to be able to confess more. 'Shortly afterwards I began to have nightmares about her—she'd lie there in the water as she had that day and suddenly open her eyes accusingly. Funnily enough, she didn't seem any less dead as she watched me with hate in her eyes, as if I'd fired that shot and ended her and her baby's lives, but the worst part of it was she watched me with *your* eyes, Roxanne, and it was *your* wildly curling ebony hair that floated about her at the mercy of the current. Then sometimes she'd raise her hand and point at me with hate in her eyes and a curse on her pale lips.'

He paused, watching the flames lick over the new applewood with sombre eyes. 'I knew then that I wouldn't come back to Hollowhurst and claim you after all. I'd never risk taking you to lose your life at some stranger's whim on a foreign sea, maybe with my brat in your belly to rob me twice over of all that mattered in my useless life.'

'Oh, Charles, my love, I'd never think my life useless if I spent it at your side, however long or short it might be. Never think that, never!'

'I might dare to now, love, but I didn't then. I was a coward and all the more so when I woke one night and found I was wrestling with Rushmore, my personal servant, in my sleep, because he'd heard me cry out and come to see what was wrong and I thought I'd finally got my hands on that murdering bastard and could end my torment by avenging her.'

'No wonder he treats you with quite a ridiculous amount of respect then,' she said, quite unimpressed by another reason he'd found not to be happy with her and not to come back and marry her, which seemed even more important, considering she'd spent nearly ten years being denied her wildest dreams.

'Just say I'm a coward, why don't you, my love?'

'No, for I never met a braver man, but you *are*

a fool, husband. Do you still have these nightmares now, after ten years?'

'For the first few months after it happened I did, but in the last eight or nine years only the once, after that first night we met again. I roused Rob and Caro's household with my shouting in the process, and if Rushmore hadn't been there to cope with my ridiculous starts, heaven alone knows what I'd have done.'

'Did you try to attack him again, then?' she asked.

'No, he developed the knack of talking me out of my terrors after that first time, no doubt out of respect for his own skin if he didn't,' he joked weakly and she blinked back a tear.

'And apart from that time, you never had a repeat of your nightmare?'

'Not so far as I know, but d'you see why I dared not sleep beside you, Roxanne? Much though I'd like to sleep with you in my arms all night long and wake to you and everything you do to me every morning, so we can do something about it for once. I can't put you in danger.'

'Nonsense, do you think me incapable of doing what your manservant has learnt to and talk you out of it and back to sleep? Waking or sleeping, or even in the grip of your darkest nightmare, you could never hurt me, Charles, so if you dare to sleep anywhere but in my bed from now on I'll track you down to where you *are* sleeping and make your nights hell without any help from a long-dead spectre who never had any grudge against you in the first place. Is that understood, husband?' she ended briskly, believing common sense a far better antidote to his fear than the tears and sympathy she longed to pour out over him after his long thrall to a tragically dead girl he'd done nothing to harm and would have risked his life to save if he could.

'It is, wife, and how can I argue when all I seem to have done for the last few weeks is long to have you in my arms all night and at my side every waking moment of our days?' he responded with a boyish grin that made her heart wobble for a brief moment, then skip with joy, it was so like the one he'd entranced her with that first snowy night she had set eyes on him.

'And maybe we can do something about your primitive morning urges as well, husband,' she promised with a wicked smile. 'But one thing I can assure you of, Charles Afforde, is that if you don't share my bed from now on, I'll very likely come in one night and murder you myself. And I'll be awake while I do it, what's more.'

'In that case, I'd best keep you so content you'll only want to kiss me all night instead,' he jested feebly, but she knew instinctively he'd have no more nightmares of drowned women while she slept content and fulfilled at his side.

'Is the memory of that poor woman really the reason you made sure I took a violent disgust of you the one time I laid eyes on you during my come-out Season?' she asked as she sat up in his arms and glared at him accusingly.

'Of course. I knew there was no point trying to reason with you when your eyes were full of hero worship and your smile was warm as the sun rising over the Mediterranean on a July morning.'

'Horrible man.' She thumped a balled fist into his chest and heard the 'Oof!' of his protest with some satisfaction. 'You broke my heart, or at least I thought so at the time. I was seventeen and thought I loved you more than any woman ever loved a man.'

'But it mended.'

'I patched the poor battered thing up as best I could and went home to Uncle Granger and a life of single blessedness.'

'So did I,' he said virtuously and she thumped him again, a little harder.

'You raked and caroused your way round the world,' she accused and thought of those lonely years when the only news she had of him was Maria's satisfied letters, informing her that Captain Afforde was still busy flirting with all the most beautiful women in England whenever he was home on leave.

'I certainly appeared to, but I doubt if any man could satisfy as many conquests as rumour credited me with, or not without killing himself from the effort at least. I've led a far more blameless life than you'd credit, love. It's far easier to give a dog a bad name and hang him for it than it is to actually find out he's not as much of a dog as he appears. I made myself useful by helping on some deserted ladies' campaigns to make their husbands and lovers jealous and a lot more attentive as a consequence.'

'So you're entirely innocent of all the sins ascribed to you and have lived the existence of a monk for the last decade? Just how gullible do you think I am, Sir Charles?'

'Certainly not that gullible, my lovely, but whilst there have been a few women I liked and even lusted after and bedded to our mutual satisfaction during that time, I never even came close to loving one.'

'Well, you can stop looking so smug about it, you didn't think you loved me, either, until I made you stop and decide you might, after all, manage to do so, if you worked at it hard enough.'

'Oh, that wasn't anything like work, love, more of a poor, stupid, ignorant male's realisation he'd finally met his fate and stood no chance of escaping it this time.'

'How lovely to be a "fate", as if you can think of nothing more terrible than meeting me some dark night,' she said crossly.

'I forgot to add that I don't want to escape you this time, that being without you now would be an arctic waste of a life—in fact, no life at all.'

'Really?' Sitting upright enough so she could face him and look deep into his eyes, Roxanne closely examined his handsome features and most particularly his dark blue eyes for any sign of insincerity.

'I hope my countenance has the wit to tell you the truth of what's in my heart, Roxanne, for I love you to my very soul, and I'm afraid I always will.'

'Afraid?' she asked, mock-horrified even as brilliant joy sang in her own heart and probably shone betrayingly in her own eyes, as there was so much delight inside her fighting to express itself. 'You're afraid, husband?'

'Aye, wife, for a rake who's fallen so deep in love with his wife is such a bad example to all damn-your-eyes rogues who look to me as a model. They'll surely disown me now and drum me out of town.'

'Damn examples, Sir Charles, the ex-rake. Come here and kiss me.'

'Willingly, my sweet vixen, willingly,' he murmured, and suddenly speech was not only useless but deeply undesirable as he succumbed to the lures of true love in his wife's arms and seemed to find the experience of proving how fervently he returned her lusty passion for him matchless.

Epilogue

'So tell me again exactly why we're standing out here in the freezing cold, up to our ankles in slushy snow, Roxanne?' Mrs Thomas Varleigh quizzed her youngest sister.

'Because we're both ridiculously in love with our husbands,' Roxanne said, trying not to let her teeth chatter out loud and give Joanna an excuse to drag her inside to the comfort of a blazing fire and Mereson's delicious hot punch while they got warm again.

'True, although I'm still not quite sure my devotion to Tom extends to standing about in depths of the holly grove at midnight while my feet become strangers to the rest of me.'

'It did once,' Roxanne told her abruptly, trying hard not to recall she was four and twenty now, not a silly, over-romantic schoolgirl about to fall in love with the handsome outward image of a man, when the real, faulty, human one beneath all his flash and glamour and animal magnetism was so worth loving. Not that his very masculine, very superior good looks exactly repelled her, but they were a bonus, a wonderful addition to the man she adored, just as he adored her.

'I do remember that night as well, you know,' Joanna answered as if she thought Roxanne had claimed the monopoly on folly and needed to be told it was a family failing. 'Standing here with such hope and this odd, inexplicable ache at the heart of me I couldn't understand. All I knew then was that Tom was the only man who made me feel that ache and I couldn't imagine ever feeling it for anyone else. Come to that, I still can't,' she added ruefully. 'Even after nine years of marriage and three and a half children.'

'Three and a *half?*' Roxanne squeaked and even to her the sound rang loud on the still night air.

'Did I not tell you about that?'

'No, you didn't or I'd never have included you in this mad idea in the first place.'

'Just as well I didn't then, for I believe number four is perfectly comfortable where he or she is, and that I won't break just because I'm going to have another baby. Anyway, why should you two have all the fun?'

'It sounds to me as if you've been having some of your own.'

'You're just jealous, which is outrageous considering how late you and your captain rise of a morning nowadays, even when you have guests in the house to entertain at Christmas.'

'Guests who haven't been spotted at breakfast ever since they arrived, although I suppose you have some excuse if you're *enceinte*.'

'Thank you, but I'm past that stage now.'

'Goodness, when's it due, then?' Roxanne asked, rather alarmed she was so in love with Charles she hadn't even noticed Joanna's baby bump.

'May or June, so don't panic, I'm not about to drop it here and now.'

'But perhaps you'd better wait for Tom inside?'

'No, I've had three babes without suffering more than a couple of weeks of morning sickness; now I've finally managed to persuade Tom I don't need wrapping in cotton wool all the time, I'm not having my little sister take over where he left off. I'm very well and quite safe. If my feet were only a little warmer, I might even consider myself comfortable.'

'All right then, I'll stop worrying, but do you think it's really enchanted?' Roxanne asked with a sigh, so reassured about her sister's continuing well-being she went off at a tangent in pursuit of her own dreams.

'Is what enchanted? I don't want to give birth to a changeling.'

'Idiot, I mean this holly grove. Remember all the wild tales in the villages that it's the haunt of witches and their familiars?'

'Who's the idiot now? If you believe one word of that hoary old tale, then I'm calling a halt to this nonsense right now.'

'Of course I don't—well, not the bit about witches and their covens anyway. It just seems a little strange that all three of us stood here that night wishing for exactly what we've finally got, that's all.'

'That sort of enchantment I'm more willing to countenance then, although I'm not sure poor Balsover altogether deserves his fate at Maria's hands. Our illustrious brother-in-law would far sooner be at Balsover Magna among his acres and his horses than in London while she conquers the social world.'

'He loves Maria in his way,' Roxanne defended her sister's illustrious marriage, although she preferred piratical sea-rover baronets to earls herself.

'No doubt, but sometimes I wonder if she loves his title more than she does him.'

'Well, if I were Henry, I wouldn't risk playing host to any mysterious strangers who might be long-lost heirs.' Roxanne laughed joyfully and, since both of them seemed to have decided there was no point pretending they weren't here, Joanna joined in and they were both giggling like schoolgirls at the thought of their solemn and dignified sister being usurped by a rival countess when just then the jingle of harness finally reached their dark hideaway.

'Here they are at last—do you think they've been partaking a little too much of the Vicar's sherry?' Joanna asked as she strained her ears and her eyes through the now rather worn snow.

'No, he'll have hurried off to his vicarage to sleep. I believe he's expecting a busy day tomorrow.'

'Indeed, who'd have thought it, what with it being a Christmas morning and all?'

'Christmas morning, ten years on,' Roxanne managed with an infatuated sigh as Thor's rider became visible through the gloom at last.

'And this year at least I know you're happy as well.'

'Oh, I am, Joanna, I am indeed.'

'Wife!' a powerful bass rumble boomed out of the darkness and Joanna fluttered a quietening hand and hushed frantically.

'You'll wake the children,' she protested, stumbling out of her prickly hiding place and into her lover's arms.

'The nursery is on the other side of the castle and it'd take a cannon firing outside their bedroom windows to do that, so tired and over-excited as they are about tomorrow,' Tom assured his wife as he picked her up, kissed her soundly and threw her up into his saddle to carry her off.

'And what about you, wife? Have you gazed on your handsome husband from the gloom long enough, or would you like me to fetch a lantern so I can show you my best profile?' Charles said as he stood holding Thor and smiling as easily as the laughing young man of a decade ago had done.

'No, Charles, I'd like you to come in here and kiss me. Then you can take me inside so I can study your faults in peace and comfort.'

'D'you hear her, Thor? What a nagging wife I've wed,' he confided in his fell mount, although this one was far better tempered than the demon he rode in on a decade ago. He slapped the patient animal on his rump and Thor obediently trotted off to his stables and the oats Whistler had waiting for him.

'Are you never going to kiss me, Charles?' Roxanne said impatiently, for a cold wind had suddenly blown up, and it was dark, and she could feel a branch of holly dancing threateningly close to her face and she wanted it to look as perfect as possible for the best Christmas she'd ever had.

'I'm letting you savour the moment, love, so you can relive the full glory of my first sparkling appearance in your dull life.'

'Popinjay,' she scorned.

'Not a bit of it. My wife thinks I'm a hero, I'll have you know. Ever since I found that out, I knew we were made for each other.'

'Stop it,' she demanded, swatting him with the ancient muff she'd found in the attic for tonight's expedition.

'I will in a minute,' he promised, batting away that intrusive branch and standing very close to her. 'What a fine view you had of us that night; I dare say Tom and I would have felt self-conscious, while secretly preening ourselves like turkey-cocks, if we'd only known you were here.'

'It *was* a fine view, I'm glad I saw it.'

'Still, after all I've put you through these last ten years, love?'

'Always,' she promised with such heart-felt fervency that he kissed her.

And Sir Charles Afforde kissed his wife of just over three weeks with all the passion and sincerity fourteen-year-old Roxanne could have dreamt of, and an added undercurrent of sexual, sensual desire lay under his enthusiasm she certainly couldn't have conjured up then, all innocent and headlong in love with a handsome face as she'd been at that tender age.

'I'm glad you did, too,' he said, suddenly serious. 'Imagine how terribly empty my life would have been if I'd never laid eyes on you and married some poor echo of my fierce, brave love.'

'Although I'll try to if you absolutely insist, Charles, I really don't want to just now if you don't mind,' she said as she stood on tiptoe and kissed him in her turn, slowly, passionately and with deliberate, slow-burning invitation.

'No, to the devil with all my other possible wives, I love only this one,' he said huskily.

'Just as well.… Now, about that hot punch and nice warm fire Mereson has arranged for us…'

'If he's half the butler I think him, our punch and that fire will be in our suite and Joanna and Tom's will be in theirs.'

'D'you know, I think he *is* the very perfect example of his kind and that you're quite right?'

'Of course I am, Roxanne, it's my mission in life.'

'When it took you ten years to come back and marry me? I rather think not,' she scoffed even as he decided to risk no more nonsense and lifted her into his arms for the short trip back to their castle, their home.

'I came back though, didn't I? *And* I managed to persuade your brother to sell me this millstone because you loved it so much.'

'Bah! You bought the castle and had to accept me as the millstone,' she argued gruffly, and there was still a trace of hurt in her voice, just a sliver of pain in her velvety dark eyes as he walked close to the lantern set burning above their door to guide benighted travellers toward a warm welcome, this night of all nights.

'If I had to choose between you and a pile of hoary old stones, my Roxanne, it would be you every time,' he assured her and kissed her under that lantern, perhaps because even Mereson allowed himself the occasional waggish moment and had caused a sprig of mistletoe to be suspended from the bottom of it, or perhaps he just kissed her because he wanted to, something he did rather a lot nowadays.

'And you for me, Charles, so you really didn't need to buy me a castle.'

'Damn, d'you suppose your brother will take it back?'

'No, I think you're stuck with Hollowhurst as well as your nagging wife.'

'Never was such a burden shouldered so joyfully, my love,' he told her and carried her over the threshold to find their household virtuously, even ostentatiously, in their beds, preparing for the most joyful Christmas Hollowhurst could remember in ten long years.

Not that the master and mistress of the house would have taken much notice if they'd all been up and dancing a jig, but as Charles insisted on carrying her up the stairs, protest how she might, Roxanne looked back to the great doorway of Hollowhurst and for a fleeting moment thought she caught a glimpse of a tall and still-straight figure much like Uncle Granger's standing beside it looking very pleased with himself about something.

'I love this wonderful old house you bought me so selflessly, and I love you, Charles Afforde,' she whispered in her lover's ear, then kissed him soundly when he would have put her down at the door of her chamber and reached down with the hand that wasn't feeling the suggestion of golden stubble on his lean cheek and undid the door handle for him.

'That's good to hear,' he managed, before walking into their fire-lit bedchamber and reaching behind his wife's temptingly curved back to shut the door on any interested spectres who might be listening or, heaven forbid, even watching Charles Afforde seduce his final lady love.

* * * * *

HISTORICAL

Large Print

GLORY AND THE RAKE
Deborah Simmons

As if the continual vandalism of the spa she's renovating weren't enough for Glory Sutton, she also has to deal with the enigmatic Duke of Westfield! As they get drawn into the mystery, they must reveal their own secrets in order to uncover the truth…

LADY DRUSILLA'S ROAD TO RUIN
Christine Merrill

When her flighty sister elopes, Lady Drusilla Rudney knows she has to stop her! She employs the help of ex-army captain John Hendricks. Drusilla's unconventional ways make him want to forget his gentlemanly conduct…and create a scandal of their own!

TO MARRY A MATCHMAKER
Michelle Styles

Lady Henrietta Thorndike hides her lonely heart behind playing Cupid—but Robert Montemorcy knows it has to stop! He bets Henri that she won't be able to resist meddling…only to lose his own heart into the bargain!

THE MERCENARY'S BRIDE
Terri Brisbin

Awarded the title and lands of Thaxted, Brice Fitzwilliam waits to claim his promised bride, but Gillian of Thaxted will *not* submit to the conquering knight! Will Brice risk exposing the chink in his armour by succumbing to the charms of his new wife?

MILLS & BOON

HISTORICAL

Large Print

RAVISHED BY THE RAKE
Louise Allen

The dashing man Lady Perdita Brooke once knew is now a hardened rake, who does *not* remember their passionate night together… though Dita's determined to remind him! She's holding all the cards—until Alistair reveals the ace up his sleeve!

THE RAKE OF HOLLOWHURST CASTLE
Elizabeth Beacon

Sir Charles Afforde has purchased Hollowhurst Castle; all that's left to possess is its determined and beautiful chatelaine. Roxanne Courland would rather stay a spinster than enter a loveless marriage… But Charles' sensual onslaught is hard to resist!

BOUGHT FOR THE HAREM
Anne Herries

After her capture by corsairs, Lady Harriet Sefton-Jones thinks help has arrived in the form of Lord Kasim. But he has come to purchase Harriet for his master the Caliph! Must Harriet face a life of enslavement, or does Kasim have a plan of his own?

SLAVE PRINCESS
Juliet Landon

For ex-cavalry officer Quintus Tiberius duty *always* comes first. His task to escort the Roman emperor's latest captive should be easy. But one look at Princess Brighid and Quintus wants to put his own desires before everything else…

HISTORICAL

Large Print

SEDUCED BY THE SCOUNDREL
Louise Allen

Rescued from a shipwreck by the mysterious Captain Luc d'Aunay, Averil Heydon is introduced to passion in his arms. Now she must return to Society and convention—except Luc has a shockingly tempting proposition for her…

UNMASKING THE DUKE'S MISTRESS
Margaret McPhee

At Mrs Silver's House of Pleasures, Dominic Furneaux is stunned to see Arabella, the woman who shattered his heart, reduced to donning the mask of Miss Noir. He offers her a way out—by making her his mistress!

TO CATCH A HUSBAND…
Sarah Mallory

Impoverished Kitty Wythenshawe knows she must marry a wealthy gentleman to save her mother from a life of drudgery. Landowner Daniel Blackwood knows Kitty cares only for his fortune—but her kisses are irresistible …

THE HIGHLANDER'S REDEMPTION
Marguerite Kaye

Calumn Munro doesn't know why he agreed to take Madeleine Lafayette under his protection, but finds that her innocence and bravery soothe his tortured soul—he might be her reluctant saviour, but he'll be her willing seducer…

MILLS & BOON

HISTORICAL

Large Print

MARRIED TO A STRANGER
Louise Allen

When Sophia Langley learns of her estranged fiancé's death, the last thing she expects is a shock proposal from his twin brother! A marriage of convenience it may be, but Sophie cannot fight the desire she feels for her reluctant husband…

A DARK AND BROODING GENTLEMAN
Margaret McPhee

Sebastian Hunter's nights, once spent carousing, are now spent in the shadows of Blackloch Hall—that is until Phoebe Allardyce interrupts his brooding. After catching her thieving, Sebastian resolves to keep an eye on this provocative little temptress!

SEDUCING MISS LOCKWOOD
Helen Dickson

Against all advice, Juliet Lockwood begins working for the notorious Lord Dominic Lansdowne. Juliet's addition to his staff is pure temptation for Dominic, but honour binds him from seduction…*unless, of course, he makes her his wife!*

THE HIGHLANDER'S RETURN
Marguerite Kaye

Alasdhair Ross was banished for courting the laird's daughter, Ailsa. Six years later, toils and troubles have shaped him into a man set on returning to claim what's rightfully his. When Ailsa sees him, she knows a reckoning is irresistibly inevitable…

MILLS & BOON